SOUTH BY SOUTH BRONX

SOUTH BY SOUTH BRONX

ABRAHAM RODRIGUEZ

AKASHIC BOOKS
NEW YORK

This is a work of fiction. All names, characters, places, and incidents are the product of the author's imagination. Any resemblance to real events or persons, living or dead, is entirely coincidental.

Published by Akashic Books
©2008 Abraham Rodriguez

ISBN-13: 978-1-933354-56-9
Library of Congress Control Number: 2007939594

First printing

Grateful acknowledgment is given to Scherl/Süddeutsche Zeitung Photo, for permission to reprint the photograph of Leni Riefenstahl and Adolf Hitler on page 102. The photograph of Marlene Dietrich on page 107 by Scotty Welbourne from the 1941 film *Manpower* was provided by Deutsche Kinemathek, Marlene Dietrich Collection Berlin.

Akashic Books
PO Box 1456
New York, NY 10009
info@akashicbooks.com
www.akashicbooks.com

MECHANICS-MERCANTILE LIBRARY

This book is dedicated to US

PART ONE

All of the true things I am about to tell you are shameless lies.
—Kurt Vonnegut, *Cat's Cradle*

1.

That night, she ran. Rain-splattered, cars honking. Headlights blurred wetly. She crept along tenement brick, back alleys. Side streets. Avoiding cop cars.

A bodega man stepped out for a smoke. Offered her a cigarette as they stood under bodega awning. The rain dropped in mad, thin streams. He lit her with a long, thin flame. She sucked in that first nicotine hit. His eyes, looking at her. She couldn't blink them off.

"There's blood on your cheek," he said.

She wiped at it with the palm of her cigarette hand. It was blood, it was her blood. She hoped it was her blood.

The cigarette taste flattened everything. She kept busy sucking in that smoke, contemplating that glowing tip like it was good company. The words the *bodeguero* spoke, drowned out by rain patter.

She left before the cigarette ran out. If it did, she would have had to ask for another and that much involvement she didn't want.

There was no point in walking wet streets, rain slapping her up like that. She wouldn't get anywhere in this town knocking on doors. There were those cop cars, flashing silent, like fireflies.

The way off the street, was to climb.

The building was a big gray job. It towered over this block of small shuttered stores. The fire escapes were easy to reach from the stoop after a hop and a pull. On that 4 a.m. street there was nobody to wonder about the crazy white girl climbing the access ladder. Barefoot, in a clingy wet minidress. A second skin, flowered print. Up there, respite from rain. Not blinking from wet, better to breathe. To think a moment and see the down below.

She slid past half-open windows, so close she could hear the calm slow sleep breath. Some radio chatter. The buzzy hum of an air conditioner.

(Climb, climb)

Through the open window on the third floor she spotted a couple, dancing. Luis Vargas playing soft on the stereo. The one candle flickered unreliably. The woman was in a red dress, fringe splashing her thighs like water. The guy was bare-chested. Black dress pants, like a matador. She watched them dance slow and close. Took a moment before she realized the guy was wearing an eye patch.

The candle went out. The rain pattered a drum beat against fire escape steel. Creak of springs like child giggles.

She kept climbing. To the very top.

The window she chose was wide open, as if the person living there wanted no impediments for whoever arrived. She sat on the edge of the window. The room slowly took shape, a charcoal sketch coming to life under a gray moon.

It was a corner room. The windows along the far wall showed sky and moon like paintings. There were no curtains, no clutter, no mass of things. No bureau or dresser, no big mirror. (It must not be a woman who lives here.) A cluster of milk crates. A chair with some clothes on it.

The bed was placed right in the center of the room. There was no headboard, no frame, no connection to the walls. It floated in the middle of the room like an island.

The man looked like he had fallen. Facedown on the bed.

Legs and arms splayed as if he had taken a couple of shells in the back. The sheets did not hide his body from her.

She sat there by the window a long time, shivering from wet, from the pinpricks Alan had given her to make her tell the truth. The skies brightened. The rain stopped. The first hit of light added color with slow brush strokes. A blue room. Bare walls. A bottle of something lying on the bed, as if it had slipped from his hand and rolled a little.

She invaded slowly. Inhaled the room. Liquor, sweat, and sleep breath. Varnish, old socks, cigarettes. A bare foot protruding from the side of the bed. It was the softest foot she had ever seen on a man. No calluses no hard ridges or bumps. She almost touched it.

Peeled off, the wet sticky minidress. She was soaked, down to bra and G-string. It all came off, made a bundle on the slick floor. The guy must have worked on it himself to make it look so waxy fresh. A museum floor.

She rubbed herself dry with a shirt that was on the chair.

The slow, steady. Rise and fall of his breath.

On the very edge of the bed. She sat, slowly in. Set off no ripples of movement from him. She lay down in one quick move.

Waited. Nothing. No break in the rhythm.

She slipped under the sheet.

The trembling, deep shudders. Flashing lights. She was running down a long hallway. He murmured, he turned, he put his arm around her. So snagged, hitched, she waited for words but he slept on. The trembling would not stop. He was good to strain against, to hold onto. Clutching, arms and legs. Wasted into tiredness. The sense of falling down a dark shaft.

Those seagulls flew by with cries that couldn't wake anybody.

2.

Waking from dream. Or still dreaming.

Or not. Barely memory of dream, just black after drinking. Sharp jumpcut from then to now. No sense of sleep. He could have been dreaming if not for that pasty sick taste in his mouth. The need to piss, bad. That was what woke him.

The woman in his bed did not wake him.

He had been snuggled into her, forked and spooned. His knees into the back of her knees. Secure around like a seat belt, almost as if it had always been like this. Bodies linked, instinctive. Like it happened without him.

He breathed into her back. Blond hair, streaked reddish. Warmly damp from rain. White skin speckled with freckles. It made him think of cherry vanilla. His dick stirred against her ass.

He tried to get a better look at her face. Her curly hair blocked the view. It wasn't long, but thick, waved and coily like a '30s cut. Covering her closed eyes. The straight nose and pouty lips could have come from an old silent movie. He pressed into her closer, or she pressed into him with a murmur. Into his hard dick.

He quickly scrolled through last night's scenes with Robert. The party had lasted until 2:00. Then, a bar on Second Avenue. Lights, noise, two women in spandex taking a break from performing their lesbian circus act. A colored prism of images faces and drinks but no sign of this woman in any of the footage. She wasn't sitting at the bar. She wasn't at a table where a candle danced in red glass like a stripper in a cage. Not outside as they rushed into cabs to escape the sudden downpour. A storm of rain that clouded all the windows. There was a ride up to 113th Street with Robert. There was a Puerto Rican woman named Lourdes and a black woman named Sharon.

After that, blank. A bottle, a cab going somewhere. A woman's legs in a shaft of streetlight flashing the rear window like a strobe. (Seamed stockings always made it hard to tell real from dream.) The solid curves of that tall slim vodka bottle.

Slowly, he tried to free his hand from hers.

It was Benny who first told him about blackouts. Horror stories about people who woke up with a bloody knife in hand and all their loved ones, gutted. Benny had done time at virtually every organization in the books devoted to helping people kick whatever obsessive compulsion there is. His rap was peppered with beneficent altruisms and cautionary parables gleaned from Alcoholics Anonymous, Pot Smokers Anonymous, Cigarette Smokers Anonymous. There was even a Sexaholics Anonymous that Benny insisted he should look into, reasoning that women and liquor were his two biggest obsessions—but he wasn't like Benny. Blackouts didn't scare him. Those deep cuts in the narrative kept things swift and curt. He found himself in a subway station in Brooklyn. He came to in the stairwell of some strange building. He woke up in bed with a strange woman. These things happened and he was starting to believe it wasn't just because of the drinking the drinking always the drinking. Blackouts came at certain times, with certain combinations. They were a safety valve. He was somehow making them happen without being conscious. He wanted to be conscious. He spent some time reconstructing, refitting parts. Sometimes he did this with Monk, who believed blackouts were a kind of time travel. Some things come back. Others, maybe you invent them.

It made perfect sense to forget, to rid the mind of all that clutter.

(She held him, even in sleep, not letting go.)

It was a process, waking up in strange terrain. Fragments of memory dribbling over the rim. Piece by piece to make the puzzle fit: this time, to wake up in his own house, but no clues. No snapshot of her talking, laughing, wiping hair from her face. No sense of him stepping out of a cab with her, rain slapping. Her glittery stockinged foot losing its high heel. Laughing, and he fell. The hard sidewalk and how she slipped and fell too. Still laughing as her eyes . . . her eyes. What color? No sense of looking into them.

"Did I kiss you?"

She didn't say.

"Did we fuck?"

It never happened that he had forgotten a fuck. This was generally a field of great clarity. She stirred, turning toward him. He freed his hand, moved his legs. The sheet slid down. Her breasts soft feathery, no memory of touching them kissing them sucking them. His hand floated over her naked tummy. Close, but not quite feel. Rising and falling with her every breath, the way a seagull hovers over a wave. Fingertips have memories. Skin talks to skin. That was how he knew that this was as close as his hand had ever been to that tummy, that white skin, that clustered galaxy of pinpoint freckles that led around her hip.

Slowly. Rose from the bed. His moves did not wake her.

In the bathroom. Relief drained from limbs and loins. He flushed the toilet, splashed sleep from his face, rinsed the metallic taste from his mouth. There was only one thing for that buzz of irritation, that sick trembly feel. He searched the kitchen cabinets, but there were only empties. That bottle he took to bed had been the last. (Had he taken it to bed?) No splash of eye-opening clarity. Nothing but empties.

Back in the bedroom, he saw her gathering up a pillow to snuggle into. He put on a pair of running pants, stepped into his old loafers that doubled as *chancletas*. He grabbed a T-shirt, and saw her eyes open. She did not look surprised to see him, not startled nor uncertain. She stared expectantly, a vague glimmer of shyness.

"Hey," she said.

(Green eyes.)

"Hey," he said back.

She stretched her legs a little. The sheet slid further down. Followed the curve from her tummy to the triangle of pussy bush. Her bulby tits rubbed together as she burrowed into the pillow. She gathered up sheet slow.

"So where you going?" she said, her eyes slitted from sunlight, from sleep.

Her voice did not register a memory. It was new, a little raspy with morning.

"There's no drinking stuff," he said.

"Mmmm."

The slow movements of her hands over her breasts and tummy seemed caused by dreams. She would burrow deeper into bed, into the pillow, out of sight. A woman who loves her sleep. Her large eyes staring at him from behind a rim of sheet.

"Will it take long?"

The words muffled by sheet.

"No," he said.

Her eyes fluttered shut. Curled around his pillow, she sleep-grinned like she would soon dream of him.

3.

The sunlight was a real slap. The wood floor glimmered like a lake face. It was hard to stop squinting.

The first place she went was to the window.

The streets looked bare. A milk truck pulled up to a bodega. A woman with a heart-shaped purse waited at the bus stop. A young guy with an Afro pushed up a clattery riot gate. The big-ass donut shop looked drowsy with its foggy windows. No people sitting at its long winding counter. The round empty stools, the clunky window booths. It was an Edward Hopper postcard from a shop on West 4th Street, but Edward Hopper never came to this small town. The postcard views did not prepare her. She couldn't read the calm South Bronx street.

She wasn't from here.

To wander those streets—the thought depressed her. This room. It was sanctuary. Her breath, fogged the window. Helped hide her.

Inside was safe.

The street was the danger.

To hide was divine.

The apartment was like a museum. Blue walls, empty space. The few objects stood like exhibits. A pair of tatamis, a TV, an old armchair. No curtains on the windows. The group of plastic crates contained a minimal amount of stuff. Either something had been taken away or there had never been anything there. The masses of empty bottles in the kitchen. The two closets full of shoe boxes.

She checked the view through each and every window. Got a feel for the shape of the place. Played with the locks to see how they worked. (A rhythm for the locks can be crucial in a moment of mad-dash escape.) Another look out the bedroom window—an assurance that nothing had changed.

She took her things into the bathroom. Shut the door in case he came back. There were no shower curtains. The meager spray made enough noise to hopefully get him to knock first—"Ma'am, are you okay?"—the words of the bus driver, his oblong black face melting in the rearview mirror. Shooting her glances.

The bus had been a sudden inspiration. There were only three other passengers. They stared as she mounted, barefoot and wet, clutching her strapless Blahniks. She had to RUN to CATCH THE BUS, get it?

"I just need 149th Street," she said. Did she hear him say this wasn't the right bus?

"Stay on until the last stop," he said. The rain poured dark streets blacker. She sat in the back, more leg room. To wipe her bloody ankles, to put her shoes back on. Ever run down a fire escape, barefoot? She tried to stop trembling. It had just started to rain and she'd caught the first mad outburst all the way to the bus. It poured down sheets. Bus engine sound muffled under the patter blasts. She was trying to breathe, but images came in sharp flashes. It seemed outside every bodega sat a cop car, lights glimmering hello. A line of cars followed the bus as it crawled along under the el. Heart throb heart quake. She couldn't stay on the bus. Not to the last stop. (She could see his face in the rearview mirror.) The driver would call the cops.

"Stop the bus," she said, banging on the back doors. "I wanna get off!"

The bus stopped.

She was under another big elevated train station, at the spot where Longwood intersects with Prospect. There were small shops, an electronics store—everything riot-gate shut except for superettes and those candy stores that sold nothing but potato chips, Lemonheads, and beer. A train roared by above, flashing light against tenement windows. 149th Street? The guy she asked gave her a funny look. Couldn't talk, but he pointed. Must not be so normal on South Bronx streets to see a wet white woman in a minidress, clacking along fast in those stiletto sandals—she calls them her *Jackie O*'s—there was no way she wanted to wander those South Bronx streets in that dress again. She could still wring water from it. The back was ripped, maybe snagged on a fire escape ladder. Was that blood, there amidst the loopy colored flowers? She walked it over to the small bathroom window that glowed bright with sun. She thought she could smell blood. There was some kind of smell on her.

She scrubbed the dress under the warm shower water, then hung it to dry on the curtain rod. Same for the bra, the G-string panties. She was in a strange bathroom doing her laundry. It made her laugh, not laugh, some sort of spasm. Like choking. She squeezed her burning eyes shut. The wave of nausea almost keeled her over. She heard shattering glass, the thud of bullets. Bent over the toilet, the sick coming out of her in throbbing blasts. She flushed. She flushed. She flushed and the water would not move. The tank was filling slow. The handle made a hollow clank sound. She fought off the images that hit her like electric shocks.

She stepped into the shower. The water fell weakly into her mouth, lukewarm on her face. (There was a smell.) The water felt prickly like a cat's tongue. She rinsed her bloody ankles, cuts and scrapes that stung. She held the moist bulb of soap to her nose, the scent cleansing her of stink, some stink. It was inside of her. No way to scrub that out. In her nose, her pores. She rubbed soap everywhere, desperately. Still, a smell. She soaped her hair, rinsed fast.

She turned the shower off, listened for steps. A steady drip faded to nothing. She dried off with the only towel hanging there, then emptied out her purse. It was long and brown with a detachable strap. She spilled its contents on the blurry furry foot mat.

The shoes came out first, the thin clattery Jackie O's looking no worse for wear. She would place them by the bed as if they had been there all along.

The lipsticks, compact, other makeup items. Checkbook, passport. A CD slipcase. Daffy Duck plushy. All into a pile.

The cellular phone. She put aside.

The cassette tape. She put aside.

The Smith & Wesson .22 pistol with spare clip. She put aside.

The yellow envelope had writing on it. A signature, some numbers: an address. David had always said she had a real head for numbers, the way she could remember them just by hearing them once or quickly scanning them off a page. "You have a head like a master spy," he said. Forget ever playing memory games with her. Could recite whole sheets of figures, pages of random prose after a glance. Whole Anne Sexton poems committed to memory like scripture. Names dates facts—she never needed a phone book. The perfect world of numbers fascinated her. Random integers battling it out to absolute conclusions. Irrefutable, perfectly provable. How he relied on her logical mind. A bitter sting a bad taste, those flashes of last moments. She shut her eyes, cleared the slate.

Inside the envelope was a card, a letter, and a key.

The card was proof she had permission.

The letter was permission.

The small silver key. She rubbed it with her fingers. Shiny, metallic, real. Logic and mathematical precision had plenty to say about the key. It was nothing she wanted to hear.

There was no way to give it back.
There was no way to pass it on.
There was no way to get rid of it.

A sound. A rush, a whoosh of air. A door banging against the wall. The running steps, coming closer. She had pushed and pulled him. They threw words at each other frantic, each one believing it was the other's turn to listen.

"David, please! We have to run."

"No," he said. "I'll talk to them."

"David, he's not coming to talk!"

"Just promise me you won't let him get it."

(A sound. A rush, a whoosh of air.)

She opened the bathroom door. Gun drawn. Listening. Still alone.

The cassette, cellular phone. The lipsticks, compact, house keys, checkbook, passport, other makeup items, CD slipcase. Daffy Duck. Scooped back into purse.

The key she hid in a place that was always with her.

The six-shot clip went into a zippered pocket of her purse. The pistol made nice, reassuring clicks. Chamber perfect and round ready. She took her purse, Jackie O's, and pistol back into the bedroom. There, the strange unease mingled with an acceptance that whatever happened in this room could not. Ever be as bad as what might be waiting outside. She stood by the fire escape window, naked and shivery, thinking of running and what that would mean if she gave up the four walls. To be inside was to be safe. She could not step out into sunlight. Her limbs ached sluggish. Her head felt dizzy, maybe still slushy from the drugs Alan had pumped into her to make her tell, to make her tell what? Something she didn't know. Something she didn't want to know. She felt she was half-dreaming and couldn't shake off that bit of stupor. It was like an overwhelming urge to crawl into sleep, to make it all go black.

She tucked the pistol under the mattress. Placed the shoes and purse right beside. Another look out the window: The sleepy South Bronx street calmed her. Nothing had changed.

She checked the pistol again. (All those reassuring clicks.) Snug in a place she could reach easy. One swift move. (She rehearsed the draw.) The urge to run. The urge to sleep. The wallet on top of the crate, a scrunch of dollars, a few silver rings he had not bothered to put on. She flipped through the billfold. His work ID: *Henderson's Department Store. Shoe Department.* The picture made her laugh: The sleeping man still looked sleepy.

"So he sells shoes," she said.

The voices that said *Run!* quieted down. She lay back instead and closed her eyes. At first, a twitchy bothersome energy that made her go fetal and small. Then came a thick blanket that fell like a sudden paralysis.

It was easy to be this tired.

4.

Before sun, there was gray sky. Reluctance of sun to break through gloom and brighten. The sound of trucks garbage cans air brakes. The shrill beeping of those *camiones dando pa'tras.*

The cranky bursts of rain did not restrain him. It was anytime better than being inside. The big windows, paint-smeared walls, the lack of a story line. Nothing to hear but that clock clock tick tick. There was no point staying inside, waiting for brainstorms. It was ritual it was almost duty: Monk might bring a bottle, Mink would provide the smokes. They would pick a nice crib somewhere and talk the sunrise up over the Bruckner Expressway. It could be rooftop, empty lot, a stop on a stoop. It always led back to Mink's rooftop nightcap, that would last until sunlight. Traditions, etched in steel.

This morning there was no Monk.

Mink had been on medium simmer ever since Monk had stormed out all door-slam. Wasn't even midnight. Mink thought fuck it, let it go, he'll come back, probably with some beers. But the hours went by with a loud clock clock tick tick, and there was no Monk coming back.

Mink's impulse was to storm Monk's building. Pound on his door and ask what the fuck was up with that? but he did not storm Monk's building because he knew if he did, he would only be doing what Monk wanted. Screw that. Wouldn't play that game. Mink instead sat at the long winding counter at the Greek's.

The Greek's was open all night. Cops went there. They sat in glum rows with their cups of steaming java, dreaming of a starring role in a major moment that would matter to someone somewhere in their dreary world. Mink thought often of painting them: three cops in a row, faces shapes geometric—sharp and brittle like glass. He could imagine painting a lot of things, but every time he was on the verge of inspiration, something would crop up, some disturbance emotional dismal, some ANYTHING that would block the road like a boulder across a mountain pass.

This time the problem was Monk.

"If I go up there," he told the Greek, "I'm just playing his game."

The Greek was a pudgy bearded man of few words. He gave every face regardless of race that same squinty-eyed appraisal. For fifteen years he had been there, running that big donut shop–luncheonette. He talked a lot these days of getting his white ass out of the South Bronx and opening a new place in Astoria, where he lived.

"Play his game, what do you care, don't be so proud," the Greek said. "People are here today, gone tomorrow."

Mink stared through storefront glass. Across the street, to the right of Monk's building, were Mink's big picture windows. One floor up, they stood out on that little building face like shiny gold teeth. The dark calm of the windows reminded him of the scary silence in his apartment, the murmur of a big empty space.

The landlord said he could have it, and have it cheap, provided Mink fixed it up himself. Low rent, long lease. The small building next to the big one housed a printing factory. The place was upstairs, slated to become a storage space, but some last-minute dispute led the factory to back out of the deal. Mink came along at just the right moment. He put in plumbing, a bathroom and kitchen. Wood floors. Knocked down some walls. Added those three big picture windows facing Prospect Avenue. They were a lot like the kind on those bone-white houses perched on hills in San Francisco. A skylight, central heating and air-conditioning

. . . When the landlord signed the cheap five-year lease he had no idea Mink was that artist bastard who appeared on OPRAH all those years ago. The landlord looked up the pieces in TIME and NEWSWEEK and there was that NEW ARTIST OF THE YEAR thing and all that stuff on the Internet . . . The landlord felt scalped, especially after seeing that color spread in PEOPLE magazine. Couldn't look the other landlords in the face after that, the court action just a face-saving gesture at best. Two years later and Mink was paying five hundred bucks for a space the Hilton would classify as a presidential suite.

In 1993, Mink Ravel Presario Melendez was the hottest young Puerto Rican painter to come out of the Bronx, south or south of no north, didn't matter which. He was borough-wide, city and state. His canvases of blocks and cubes spread like a virus. "*It defines the rise of LATINO ART and its importance to the new American tradition,*" the *New York Times* stated. "*It is the death of LATINO ART,*" cried HISPANIC, "*that of all the truly representative LATINO ART out there, the hungry gullible American public latches onto this.*" There was Kurt Cobain, screaming from the pain in his flaming guts while wearing a furry blocks and cubes T-shirt. There was that Björk moment when she jumps into an ocean full of fishy blocks and cubes. There were naked blocks and cubes and fuzzy blocks and cubes and rows of dancers spinning in front of spray-painted blocks and cubes. There was a famous sociologist who said that blocks and cubes were starting to define a generation; a dance club, a soft drink; and just when it looked like Coca-Cola might redesign its cans for South Bronx consumption, this young Dominican kid comes out with globes and spheres, globes and spheres. "*A new movement in LATINO ART,*" the *New York Times* stated.

Suddenly it was 1996. The wave had passed.

"Let go," Mink said, as Monk tried to scrape him off

the sidewalk. Mink fell again, rolled a little. Puked up some more pasta.

"Come on," Monk said, helping him up again. "I'm taking you home."

"Nah, man, I'm fine. I just fell. Gravel's loose there, man." Mink straightened his thin tie. Even from a block away, he could still hear the limos driving up. The chatter of people, the flash of cameras. Clacking high heels and the swish of costly dresses.

"You didn't have to come to this," Monk said. "To be seen here with all these ass-kissing idiots."

"It wouldn't have looked good if I didn't come."

"You think this looks better, getting piss-fucked and puking on the sidewalk? You can't tell me you want to go back there. You can't."

"I have to go back there. I just stepped out, right? I was dignity itself, bro. It was just the pasta."

"All those people asking where you been, like you died or something. Mink, the living ghost. And fucking MISTER SANTO DOMINGO with his smug face telling you how much he respects THE OLD SCHOOL. Didn't you get that? He was calling you old, man."

"He's moved on from globes and spheres," Mink muttered, ducking behind a parked car to puke up the rest of the pasta.

Mink met Monk at a reading back in 1993. It was a LA-TINO ART EXPO at the Seattle Museum. Mink had just flamed with a new series of paintings, while Monk was promoting his first book, *Ashes to Ashes*. It was the first spick thing Mink had read about the South Bronx that didn't sound like it was written in 1869. They were the only two Puerto Ricans in a show that was mostly Mexicans doing stuff about crossing borders. Monk read to a standing room only crowd, with blocks and cubes as a backdrop. They bonded instantly, two crazy spicks exploring space needle city. Rolled blunts in a hippie house with dread-lock white kids in the U-district, walking that jug of wine down Broadway in glittery old Pill Hill. Mink saw Monk get three encores at Elliott Bay Books. He had those Mother Mary eyes from some old painting, that black ski cap it seemed he wore year round on his head. Mink was bowled over by his writing: The harsh reality of it made Mink think Monk was wide awake while he was still dreaming, trip-ping funny pictures all glide. They talked for days and nights about art reality nationalism colonialism identity and this weird feeling of having stumbled across another spick that can speak fluent Americana. A week later Monk flew to Portland to continue his tour and Mink returned to New York, but they stayed in touch. There was no doubt for either of them that they both represented a "scene," a "new wave" or some wave of some sort. They kept firing each other up from a distance.

Monk's next book was the novel *Dust to Dust*. The stark reality of Monk's writing began infiltrating Mink's pieces. Gone was the whimsical tongue-in-cheek of his early pieces like CUCHI CUCHIFRITO, 6-TRAIN MOONFACE, and CAST YOUR VOTES BEFORE SWINE. Now came his famous BULLET-RIDDLED BLOCKS AND CUBES and his POSSE BOY BLOCKS AND CUBES. Mink and Monk—one was pictures, one was words. They became their own scene at just the right moment—when mainstream interest in things LATINO peaked simultaneously with the arrival of the crack trade to the inner city. Monk scored a two-book deal and a movie option, Mink sold paintings at six-figure sums. TV, newspapers, magazines. He joined Monk on an-other tour—in Los Angeles it was meetings with producers and film people. In D.C. a bitter fight with hotel staff af-ter they were mistaken for vagrants and thrown out of the lobby. In Philly they were both arrested for tossing a TV set out a hotel window (it was a Keith Moon thing). Mink and Monk got stoned in thirteen states of the union.

Despite writing a pair of scripts, the movie never got made, and the next novel somehow never got delivered. *Shadowtown, Featuring a Play on Words: The First Collection of Mink Ravel Presario Melendez, with Text by Monk Velasquez & Four New Short Stories Illustrated by Mink* was released in 1997 after a two-year delay. Monk's last book to date. He wasn't making appearances or doing workshops. (Nobody was asking him to, either.) The people who once lauded him for his daring now criticized him for being limited. There was a sense he would keep repeating himself. "*The Puerto Rican Donald Goines,*" somebody wrote, sending him into a deep depression. He rebelled. No traveling, no planes, no trips abroad. He would stay home to write that next book, whatever it was. He grew his hair long like an Apache. He shaved his head like a Buddhist. He had a walking stick, not bejewelled like Balzac's but carved out of oak, topped by a lion's head. Prospect Avenue was his turf, the place where his dreams sprang from. He felt free of the outside world there. He didn't want anyone to know he was a writer, almost as if he was ashamed. He never talked about it, and would get quiet if anyone ever did. Most people in the area that knew he was a writer had never even seen his books, much less read them. He preferred it that way. He picked up his daily fruits at Sancho's bodega, his early edition of EL DIARIO at Hector's newsstand by the subway, that first cup of coffee at the Greek's. He could stay inside and not come out, but he was no recluse. People knew him, and he knew them. He knew every story all up and down Prospect Avenue better than a trio of gossiping housewives. Two or three days out of the week—depending on his mood and his need for people—he could be found at Manny's garage just off Union Avenue, where he liked to work on cars, get greasy, share cigarettes and stories. He could still tell stories, but write them? There were scribbles, starts, a page here a page there, but no one thing driving him to the finish. 2001 made it four years since his last appearance in print.

Mink fell down the same hole. Blocks and cubes had been very good to him, but now he was completely identified with them. He could not possibly keep doing the same thing over and over again. His soul was hankering for some new way to say it. He busied himself doing what he later called "window dressing," living in Los Angeles for a year doing music videos. He spent another year in D.C. doing Beckett plays with a theater group, always in touch with Monk via phone, via letters, via e-mail. It was Monk that brought him back to 149th Street. Mink would never have ended up living down the block if it hadn't been for Monk telling him about that empty space over the printing plant. Things worked out grand—they drank away days watching Hitchcock films, playing Thelonious and Ravel. Late-night rantings always led to dawn. The quiet could come on his roof or a flat field overlooking the churning East River. To get a view of the South Bronx so moviola fresh. To discard the old, hang it like laundry from valleys of antenna wire. The South Bronx was the stuff of dreams to them, this big city this small town. They wanted to capture it to bring it back to the world in living kaleidoscope color. Maybe something slipped away while they slept. They vowed not to sleep again, so late nights always rolled into early morning. The parties got smaller, more intimate. "I'm getting a new agent, he's British." Monk buying old typewriters, Mink peeling latex off girl asses with his teeth. (The brushes were not in a giving mood.) More drinking under tables and what about that sudden trip to Amsterdam last summer? ("I must see van Gogh," Mink said, taking Monk and his friend Alex along. "He has something to say to me.") They did copious amounts of smoke at a Jimi Hendrix coffee shop near Rembrandtplein. Van Gogh's stabbing swirls make each painting more of a relief map than a picture, textured brutal thick. Books do not capture it. Van Gogh is not flat, Mink said, inspired and chatty—but he still did not paint.

What was that fight about last night? Mink had said something about how the urge to paint was strongest when he was nowhere near a brush. He was painting in his mind, without hands. This was part of his process, he told Monk. The moment he'd said it, Monk got off the couch and started to pace. A runaway train careening down tracks, skipping stations.

"That's a crock and you know it. Painting in your mind—yeah, right! Of all the sick shit you've said about art and creation, this has to be the sickest. Do you have to find a way to justify doing nothing? Zilch! *¡Que mierda! ¡Es que no estás haciendo nada!*"

The outburst made Mink get up from the couch like he had been bitten in the ass. Another runaway train . . .

"You're way off base, man, way off! It's all going on in my mind, man. You're just upset because there isn't anything going on in yours. You're the one doing nothing! You're just talking about yourself."

"At least I'm not sitting around making excuses." Monk headed for the door. "I can say it to anyone's face: I'm not writing. But you take the cake, man. Even I can paint in my head! I think I'll go home and do just that. Lie in bed with my dick in my hand and paint twenty pictures!"

Slam.

Those big *camiones, dando pa'tras.*

Mink walked out of the Greek's. He was no man of inaction and was thinking about what he was going to do to put things right. Should he have said such a thing to Monk—that there was nothing in his head? It could have stung Monk way too deep to hear the truth . . . More writers kill themselves annually than painters. It was a fact. No matter how much they fought in the past, Monk always came back with the counter-punch. It wasn't like him to not even call. Mink refused to be responsible for such a thing. He was imagining what Monk would say as he headed for his stoop, when he spotted Alex coming out of the building. Mink froze to the spot.

Alex looked dishevelled, shuffling along in old loafers, his hair tall grass wild. A sleepwalker, not looking right nor left. Alex was a good buddy of Monk's. The two were pretty tight. Monk was always talking about doing a book about him. Is that what was going on? Maybe Monk had gotten together with Alex last night to brainstorm for his book. This thought was enough to redirect Mink away from the stoop, to fall right into step with Alex. The slow walk to the corner, sun so bright. Alex gave Mink a wide-eyed stare like everything was happening too fast for him.

"I decided fuck it," Mink said. "I'm not playing his game."

A groan of approval from the group of red-eyed men as the riot gates on the liquor store rolled upwards.

"Okay," Alex said.

5.

Mink knew Alex because of Monk.

Mink used to throw a lot of parties, and weekly. There was that big roof, the glittery skylight, a South Bronx veranda decked with Chinese lanterns and lush plants of various persuasions. The perfect place for all-night *lechón* roasts and FANIA ALL-STARS. The locals could crank up a nice vibe and friends from downtown completed the show. (Mink used to bus in the white folks from a club downtown.) Monk was a regular who one night last year walked in with Alex.

The moment Alex appeared, something happened to all the women in the room. It started with their eyes, looking at him. They walked up to him, talked to him, got him drinks, followed him from room to room. Alex was oblivious and concentrated on the next drink. Mink and Monk were transfixed, watching the room empty of ladies every time Alex stepped out—kitchen, living room, the long blue hallway lined with Mink's paintings: He moved, they moved. Up on the roof, they started dancing. Amidst flashing lights he was mixing drinks, a line of women waiting to get *mojitos* from him. These ladies, whether spandex crinoline panty hose or combat boots, all were drawn to him—white not white class no class and even a few models. Monk talked about doing a book about him, Mink already with a possible cover—that sketch of his lean angular face trapped in a prism of female torsos.

It was a running joke with them, that he was never with the same girl twice. That changed last spring, when

Belinda came to live with him. No telling what buttons she pushed to get to stay, but there he was, time and again with the same woman. He brought her to the parties, was seen going with her to the movies, shows, strolls through St. Mary's, snacking on slices at the pizzeria. Mink and Monk placed bets on how long this would last. It wasn't that they didn't like her. She was smart, funny, unbearably cute. She came, and she came to stay. But there was something troubled about the Alex they found sitting in his apartment, surrounded by flowered curtains, fistfuls of daisies, and those embroidered *tapetes* she knitted.

Three months later, Alex was appearing at parties by himself again. Belinda was gone. Spotted him some mornings, sitting on the stoop. A vague stunned look and a cigarette. A mass of furniture outside the building one day. Carpets, two bureaus, a full-length mirror, boxes of books, magazines, kitchen stuff, knick-knacks, a bed complete with headboard and box spring. Mink took the love seat. It was cushy and retro, a sad bronze color.

A week after that, Alex was walking down 149th Street with a Dominican *trigueña* named Sandra, talkative about past lives and her penchant for *Santería*. Three days later it was Alicia, who dressed like Shakira but sounded like Cher. On the fourth day, Tina. (Monk kept up with his notepad.) Alex talked less and drank more. He withdrew, but the less he spoke the more women were drawn to him. He frequently forgot things. Sometimes a vague medicinal smell about him, as if his pores sweated 100 proof. What happened when, he didn't want to talk about. He could just stay quiet a long time until that moment of insight, muttered words after cigarette puff. Mink thought he was disappearing, a little unconscious, unable to add the parts, or unwilling. He seemed to be wherever he was by chance, adrift and waiting to adapt to the next swing, the down pitch of the boat. Was it the liquor? Only his cousin Benny could bring up questions like that. Most times Alex would just smile vague, eyes misted over like the addict fighting sleep. He had that look this very morning. There was nothing unwelcoming about it. Mink walked with him like it was all part of the plan.

The liquor store was air-conditioned. There was already a line inside. Three scruffies waiting for their fix. Smell of moldy cardboard. A thick glass that separated the rows of bottles from customers. The guy lurking behind the glass looked as shady as any drug dealer. The bells on the door tinkled shrill.

"Well, Sir Alex Rodriguez," Mink said. "Up at noon on a Sunday? I don't believe it."

Alex squinted. His T-shirt was inside out.

"Mink Ravel Presario Melendez." He said it slow, like he was memorizing. "How fun, seeing you without a Monk attached."

"We're fighting," Mink said.

"What's new about that?"

"What do you want?" the guy behind the glass yelled to the first scruff.

"Hey, speaking of, have you seen Monk? He didn't show last night. I'm a little worried about the guy. You know, on account of, he's been a little bit of a mess lately."

The first scruff stuck his dollar bills in a hole in the glass. He walked out with his crumpled plastic bag.

"I haven't seen him, no. I stopped by his door on the way down."

"What do you want?" the guy behind the glass yelled.

"I knocked but he wouldn't open."

"Ahh, man, you see what I mean? The guy's in bad shape. Did you call the cops or anything? Maybe we should call the cops."

Alex grinned. The third scruff turned and left with his goods.

"Cops?"

"Yeah, man. Fucking guy could be hanging from the ceiling already."

"What did you do to him?"

"Nah, don't you know more writers kill themselves annually than painters? It's a fact."

"What?" the guy behind the glass yelled.

Alex counted out the bills. He thrust them through the hole in the glass. "He's not dead," he said. "He's typing."

Mink felt a deep shudder. Turbulence rocked the plane.

"He's *what*?"

"He's hitting those keys hard and fast. You ever been on the island during one of those *aguaceros*, bro? Raindrops blasting hell on a tin roof. You can feel that shit in your chest."

"The typing?"

"The rain, man. The rain." Alex collected his bag of clinking bottles at the hole in the glass. "Do you always tune out when I talk about Puerto Rico?"

If Monk was typing, he was writing. He had six typewriters and he only used them for writing. The computer was for other stuff, like e-mails and scripts. Prose was what came out of the typewriters at Monk's house, and if the typewriters were going, there was prose. This feeling inside of Mink was like a burning and a freezing both at once.

"Puerto Rico?" They were outside again. "We weren't talking about no Puerto Rico. We were talking about typing. You said Monk is typing?"

Slow grin. A shake of the head. "Okay," Alex said, fishing around in his bag. "After I have a drink, we head up there. You can hear for yourself."

The sun climbed higher. A *piraguero* planted his cart on a corner by the bus stop, his block of ice gleaming like a diamond. Youngsters clutching towels and a big red cooler rounded the corner to the subway. A pair of moms parked strollers under the bodega awning to have a chat, heads bumpy with curlers. Clack clack clack, a pounding machine sound interrupted only by that little DING and then the sharp carriage SNAP back to more clack clack. Hadn't even reached Monk's floor but they could already hear the clatter batter. As they reached the door, a lull. A moment of quiet in the stairwell.

Alex pulled out the plastic pint of vodka. He uncapped it with a twist and took the first gulp. Shut his eyes a moment, almost breathless calm. Leaned up on the wall by Monk's door. When he opened his eyes, he looked grateful.

"Sunday mornings," he said, "I get the shakes some. The sense of never-ending *ñoña*. Maybe the blurry-vision thing. After that first dose, I have to just be calm a moment. Wait for the brains to come back."

He passed Mink the bottle. Mink waited. Would Monk hear them? Would he come to the door? Why that exciting sense that he was doing something wrong? Now he heard: another sheet of paper scrolled into the machine. Mink figured it must be that big gray Royal typewriter, that archaic paperweight that he noticed many times on top of the radiator in the living room. Monk must have moved it to the kitchen table for it to sound so loud. The typing began again, steady waves of clatter. It was action and speed, a solidly forward momentum.

Mink put bottle to lips. Took a deep swallow that burned a steaming path to his empty stomach. Bubbling lava. "Raindrops blasting hell on a tin roof," he said.

"I'm waiting for a book," Monk was always saying. On the stoop on the street by the coal-black bridge. "I'm waiting for a book." Squinting into the distance. This clatter must be the sound of that big locomotive thundering into the station.

Alex's eyes blank. Nodding slow like he heard a good riff. Mink stopped him from knocking. The typing slowed to a trickle.

"But I thought you—"

"Forget it," Mink whispered. The typing picked up speed. It was a motorboat now, chugging away from dock. Monk was doing something, and Mink—standing there like a peeping tom—was doing nothing.

He passed the bottle back. A warm fuzzy spreading out from his chest. The typing. Heavy rain thumping against an umbrella.

"I was going to ask him," Alex said, motioning with his head.

Mink slowly registered the words. "Ask him?"

"You both. You're out on the street lots of the time when I come back from . . . dates."

"Yes." Mink felt like he was reminiscing. "We all know about your crazy Saturday nights. We always place bets on whether you'll come home with a blonde or a brunette."

"That's just what I wanted to ask him. Ask you. Did you happen to notice? Last night?"

"Last night?"

"Yeah. What I came home with."

Mink accepted the bottle. Two, three gulps of dazzling vodka burn. "I told you." He passed it back. "Monk and I had a fight last night. We didn't get to the hangout part."

Alex shut his eyes. Trying to recall. Answers on a test. "There was this lesbian circus act," he said. "A Puerto Rican woman named Lourdes and a black woman named Sharon."

"So *whoah*. There are two women in your crib right now?"

Alex took a calm sip.

"Nah, just one. A blonde."

"That creep Monk. Now he owes me fifty bucks."

The typing started again.

Mink thought about how strange it was, how mystical, to be right outside while Monk typed, like they were sharing the experience, like he was somehow part of it.

Passing the bottle, celebrating the moment. A strange "being there."

"A white girl," Alex said.

"A white girl." Mink now dizzy swirl from his early-morning empty-stomach drunk, the vodka setting off fireworks behind his eyeballs. The typewriter clack clack. Like being on a train. "A white girl. Where did you pick that up?"

Alex shook his head. Tired laugh. "I don't know."

Mink chuckled through spinning fiery vodka burst. He had thrown some crazy parties over the years but could only remember one time he woke up with someone he didn't know. The tequila smokes and those heavy doses of Pernod. He left her alone for an hour and she stole three of his paintings.

"Hey, man, you mean you left some strange woman alone in your house? Suppose she steals your stuff?"

"What stuff?"

Mink shrugged, recalling the empty Alex hut. God knows how he ever got all that stuff downstairs. Here today, gone tomorrow. He never asked them for help.

"Hey, you like blondes, right?" Alex was looking at him. Something insistent. A pimp baiting a john. "I'm thinking maybe you know her. She looks just like one of those model types that come to your parties." Alex was already moving down the stairs. He capped the bottle and slipped it back into the bag that clinked with his other bottle friends. He was going down the stairs and Mink was following him. The sound of typing followed, lost in the stairwell. Replaced by pots and pans door slams and that lilting slow *bachata* creeping from old man Confesor's apartment.

"Come on up and see her," Alex said.

Mink felt a blast of melancholy. He couldn't hear the typing anymore but knew it was still going on. The sense of momentum stayed with him, made him hate the narrow stairwell, the fragrance of coffee and, somehow, burned toast. He didn't want to be alone now. He followed Alex, thinking about the last time the guy had invited him to come up and "look" at a woman. It was just weeks after Belinda left. Her touch had been everywhere. The colorful curtains in the living room, the tasteful doilies under lamps, and fresh flowers. She adored daisies, their bright chatter killing any semblance of bleak. What a difference after she had gone, so much tunnel and blank. Alex had taken him straight to the bedroom to meet the woman. There was a fat spliff, some laughs, too much tequila. It was their first threesome, a sudden falling in. The thought of it gave Mink a stomach burn.

"Maybe this isn't such a good idea," he said.

"Just come and look at her."

"But you know what happened last time."

"Last time what?"

Mink sighed. A definite advantage to blackouts. Alex moved fast, there was no hesitation to him. They had to go down to the lobby to cross to the stairwell on the other side. It was a big lobby, kept immaculate by Iris, the skinny beanpole daughter of the super. She had single-handedly found a way to restore the glittery old chandelier which had hung toothless for so many years until the day she found just the right crystal pieces to replace the missing. Now a return to the glory days of old, and how she shined up those big mirrors, frosted archaic and flowing up to the ceiling. Mink always paused to glance up at, to see himself faintly in the smoked glass. Up another stairwell to the top, the floors slick from a fresh mopping. Mink fought off thoughts. Liquor sometimes depressed him, robbed him of energy. He couldn't get that typewriter clack clack out of his head.

The apartment felt warmer than he would have expected for a place so empty. The living room was all windows, curtainless. A furry recliner in front of the TV. A VCR lay a few feet away, snaking its cables along the wood floor like umbilical cords. At the foot of the chair a bottle, empty but still standing post.

The bedroom used to be a dingy cream color. Once Mink saw words scrawled in black paint on the wall: YOU SPENT IT. Letters trailing paint in rivulets the way blood snakes along cracks in gravel. (Maybe a tequila joint dream?) The words had been painted over. It was all blue now, almost underwater but bright enough to include sunlight making the surfaces sparkle. It was an outdoor blue, a summer sky-blue, each time vaguely different: YOU SPENT IT. Or maybe Mink had dreamed the words, thinking of time SPENT doing *nada* and being SPENT or having SPENT himself doing *nada*, and he had done a lot of *nada* there. Talk and drinks and joints and a good place to end up after a party or maybe Alex was just inviting and he had three women who wanted to come along so

(Monk sometimes partook of)—patchouli girls in sandals. Kisses full of air. That temporary anna joanna bobanna mindless endless fuck—Alex and Mink after laughing— Mink could never remember a single name and wondered if memory loss was contagious. The room was the same, but the bed, wasn't the bed different? It hadn't been floating in the middle of the room like it was now, almost like

an island

some land of enchantment land of some enchantment, some moment waiting to happen. Stolen, snatched, something that passed by. What had escaped him? How had so many years passed into *nada*? How did he become thirty, how did his work become OLD SCHOOL? Though he had only killed time here on four or five occasions, he now felt the weight of time wasted, SPENT. Time that would not come back again. Brushes crispy dry. Oil paint flaking, old paper crinkling up. Time falls like a hammer.

"She's still asleep," Alex said.

The woman lay amid sheets like a painting. Like renaissance, like a well-lit stage. Alex was saying something. His lips were moving but Mink didn't hear a word. He was tripping island tripping time tripping PUERTO RICAN style which is from one hanging vine to the other, smooth and flow like Tarzan if Tarzan could be Puerto Rican, and why wasn't he? After all, jungle, vines, loincloth—Mink was imploding, looking at this woman on this island of bed, floating in the empty *nada*. A time trip. Snaps from a book. A coily haired blonde frolicking in the woods. It was Eva Braun sleeping there, lying on a hundred-mile island like she washed up on shore after a SPENT life with a madman. Mink was painting the curve of her ass jutting up soft hills, valleys of a mussed sheet. Nothing covered her from him—stormy winds, cream vanilla flesh. Cherry-red toenails. Scratches and cuts around her ankles (it had been a rough landing)—it's Eva Braun, he thought, sleeping on the island. Last time all she got was a bunker and that acrid almond aftertaste. A ripoff, a scam, a horizon of barbed-wire detention camps. A multilayered concept of some towering dimensions overwhelmed Mink hurricane style. White black red armband and it figures she would be sleeping—giants always sleep when they find a nice crib, don't matter who was lying there first, because to them maybe Puerto Ricans always appeared as inch-high Lilliputians

(I don't care what the story says, I DON'T WANT NO GULLIVER POPPING UP AROUND HERE! Giants are a problem. It's not so much where they go, as the collateral damage they leave behind.)

a ripoff a scam a tired slogan rolled out after a cataclysmic event, a whole train of thought. Mink walked slowly around, far to near, never too close, as if he could feel the invisible velvet rope. Could see every bit of her except for those bits Rubens covered with raiment and gossamer shit. She radiated words. Mink was looking at a painting. He was getting words. She was more than a painting. She was a whole narrative.

"Where did you find her?" Mink whispered.

Alex, against the wall, slid down to squat. Swishing on that bottle, liquid splashing.

"I don't know," he said.

Mink didn't think this was any time to joke. He shot Alex a look and saw those vague blurry eyes staring at her with as much question as answer.

"I woke up, and she was there. I thought maybe she was one of yours. A runaway from the Mink refugee camp. You sure she's not one of yours?"

"Oh, I'm sure," Mink said, because back then, when parties were rampant and white women would come up from downtown, they really didn't want to brave that subway and streets too much at that hour of the morning, so Mink would put them up, no problem. And for some reason many ended up waking in Alex's bed.

"One moment she's not there. The next, there she is. Does that ever happen to you?"

"Not lately, no."

Mink came close enough to touch. (No touch.) To almost breathe in her breath sleep. (No breath.) He changed his view, not sure if it was him moving or her, revolving.

"The feeling that your life is like slides," Alex said. "Someone slips in a new one while I pass out. I wake up someplace else."

She moved. A flutter of eyelashes. The swirling universe of freckles on her back.

"Look, if you don't want to tell me, don't tell me. You don't have to make up some bullshit story on my account."

"It's no bullshit." A vague smile. Alex was pleased that

Mink was annoyed, churning, involved. Could read how Mink was waiting, a word, any word, explanation, hope. "She's a dancer," Alex said.

Mink flexed his fingers like a strangler. She was a war. She was combat footage. She was a fucking death camp, ashes raining down from chimneys. Alex passed the bottle.

"She's a model," he said.

Mink swallowed the hot sting. He was seeing colors splashing canvas. He could smell the paint: a whole series. A sense of wonder at what he was seeing, what his mind was doing with the information.

"She's an actress," Alex said. Like pitching pennies in a fountain and making wishes.

Mink was about to make a crack when he saw the way Alex was still looking at her.

"She's white as a ghost," he whispered.

Mink waited. He could feel the splashes of paint slowly forming her on canvas, locking her in forever. He felt terror at the thought of her waking, of her walking away, of anything changing in that room, ever. He wanted the moment only for himself. (In his memoirs he would banish Alex to the outer peripheries.) He was thinking about what generally happened to the women in Alex's life, the women he had seen him with, either on the street at the party or in his bed: They disappeared, each making way for the next flavor. No telling how Belinda managed to stay so long. She succumbed to the disappearing virus. In this empty room everything vanished, even the furniture. He bit his lip.

"One moment she's there," Alex said, eyes burning, "and the next, she's gone."

He stared at her. Mink's pulse throbbed like techno.

Alex said, "This is around the time I wake the girl up and say, *Hey, it's time you go home. I got stuff to do today,* right?"

Alex sounded toneless. Mink waited. There was no way Alex could miss what was happening to him, was there? Mink suddenly hated him. He couldn't say anything. He wanted Alex to look at him, to maybe see it on his face. But Alex would not take his eyes off her. What was happening to him, the way he just sank against the wall?

"We should let her sleep," Alex said.

6.

the tall thin vodka bottle on the kitchen table.

there is no hanging with robert when he gets like that. cross-eyed with drink and horny as all hell behind that cheap smelly cigar. the big *patrón* in his white suit lusting after the slaves, thinking he's going to get laid even if somebody gotta get paid. that was why his fascination with alex the pussy magnet. that was why this sloppy friendship built on a pyramid of wasted weekends, this *amistad* built on booze and pussy. it was probably why he hired alex to work at the shoe store. alex for three years now slipping shoes on girlfeet while robert raked in the cash—the store was owned by his parents anyway, just a present for the unpopular fat kid who needed something to do. he didn't even need to come in every day anymore after his deal with the big department store that grew around and swallowed it. had alex to run it, alex to be there every day, drawing in the ladies with his indefinable something, something robert drove him crazy asking about.

　　—yes, but what do you think it is about you, he asked too many times last night, waving the cigar like he was doing an interview, and that was the thing: remembering last night. for all intents and purposes, he did. there was no blackout last night. he was almost sure of it.

the rain came down in sheets. her hot tongue zipped across his lips. she showed him the ring in her belly button. green stones on silver.
　　—that's because I'm irish, she said slurry, she slurred

blurry. scotch-flavor kisses. sitting up against him in the backseat of the cab. had to kiss her to get her to shut up. laughing spinning merry-go-round city. lights through the back window of a cab flashing. round glowy pinpricks through half-closed eyes. the feel of her through the dress was bony but strong insistence to the way she clutched him in mid-kiss. they were both riding in a cab going up-town. uptown to where? he was skunk drunk and she was drunk skunk so they exchanged numbers—no reason this couldn't happen when they were sober—some story like that. the cab pulled up to the curb, across from her build-ing. "the rain came down in sheets." he got out of the cab like he would walk her to the canopied stoop, but they fell drunken laughing through slip-slide rain. and her name was

monica

thought he was sweet for NOT fucking her. promised to call him but he knew like she knew. that she would wake in the morning, angry for a lost night, grateful she hadn't given anything away. his number scribbled on a matchbook. the reminder of an almost-cost. how she would rip it. toss it into the trash can like it would give her strength.

the cabbie was a mustache dominican guy who was scared of airplanes.
    —I just don't get what holds them up there, he said. someday they just gonna fall.

alex gave him a big tip for riding him up to the south bronx.

he came alone last night.
the truth came splashing, as luminescent as a jesus paint-ing sold on astor place with little blinking lights in them

to make them glow. monk had three of them. a jesus by the waterfall, a jesus in the valley with some lambs, and another jesus with disciples all lit up glimmering above his flat-screen TV. monk was usually the person he went to on sundays for clarity and commiseration. monk was a writer and so good with plot development and with filling in those blank spaces. alex thought about him again now as he sat in the kitchen, alone with the tall thin vodka bottle. the sound of her breathing filled the entire apartment. what could monk possibly tell him about this?

monica
a name scribbled on a piece of paper folded small, which he found in his leather pants. a name, a phone number. proof of reality, but in a way, still not an answer. all he knew from past blackouts was that coming out of one felt different than just waking after a big drunk. there was a black curtain feel, images with no connection flashing feverish. there was even a taste, of lead or something metallic. now he tried to distinguish between petty distinctions, red lights green lights and still no sense of what really happened because deep down still, there lurked a massive distrust of his mind, his memory, and any pat narrative. and so he had to admit that even if he came home alone or had the memory of riding back in the cab, anything still could have happened between the time he left monica under the canopy and the time he crawled under the sheets. (she was half under the sheets, clutching pillow tight. he thought he heard her whimper, saw her hands flex the way a dreaming dog gets twitchy paws from a running dream. running toward, running from.) it could have happend that he met her, but maybe only if he wanted to believe it. the flash of images came quite suddenly, clustered like after-thoughts: he was still negotiating a trip to the bronx with the cabbie when she got into the cab

it was the kind of confusion that sent him to the hall closet to fetch the wooden box. crafted in india, from a woman named sandra. she must have seen his restless nature at a glance and accepted she would not last but still gave him many things to remember her by, including a book on *santería* and this box to clear away clouds. sometimes bad spirits will come, she said. there were trinkets. rooster claw. holy water. a picture of santa barbara and a few cigars. bad spirits come to confuse, she said, and when they come, it's good to blow cigar smoke to diffuse and dispel. and for protection, he should ask for changó.

as he lit the cigar and slowly walked through the silent apartment, a new feeling in him. the open window presented him with an obvious answer. if she had been puerto rican and not a white blond woman, he might have even believed it.

she slept still. the curve of her back was to him. he puffed.

—changó, changó, he whispered.

7.

It started with a day in the office.

The captain was a gray hair who wore his epaulettes with a dismal gravity. Displeased with the ill wind that blew his way after my dance with Internal Affairs, we generally didn't talk much. It was all business with us, cordial and distant. I knew he tried to keep contact to a minimum, suffering those moments when we had to cross paths with the solemn dignity of a weary priest. So it was the other day when he came over to tell me there was a special agent coming to see me. It was no special briefing—he knew nothing about it, he said, only that the guy wanted my help and that he was coming all the way from Washington. I wondered if it had anything to do with Internal Affairs, but the captain shrugged off my questions with a terse request. "Just try not to give the department a shiner on this one." This was no tongue in cheek. This was his parting shot, his way of letting me know he didn't plan to be around for any of it. It put a rumble to my stomach that made me resent my visitor from Washington before I'd even laid eyes on him.

I wasn't so much "office" once. Once I was so much more street. Contact hard ground tenement brick. Puerto Rican face molding fit to shape. Tenement hard or candy-ass soft, all shrink to fit. All devil with no bite but a lot of *culo*. First it was to prove I was smart enough. Then it was to prove I was tough. I thought I wanted power to help people. That was why I became a cop. Contact with the streets in a new way. And not so much "office," like now.

It was nothing like now.

I was the cop spick ducking shells in 1991 when the

South Bronx was more like Kosovo. I collected bullet holes while they fresh-scooped teenage bodies off the sidewalks. Spick kids getting ripped by high-caliber shells when I was flush with first love. The new missionary returning to his people. I was the young priest in that old *Kojak* episode. At the bedside handing the kid a Richard Wright. Twenty years on the force. Gold shield. And so much more street.

I knew streets. I knew them like people and the faces they make. Every nook every route. Every backyard pooch barking at a cat. I came from there. I was connected, born and bred South Bronx bonafide. I knew those people in my files and the places they lived. Each one had a story better than Broadway. I saw openings, I saw closings. Better than Cagney Edward G. and Bogey. Bad endings and funny names. Droopy, Cesar, Gooch. Like I was battling cartoon characters. Snort, Debit, Spider. The men of my Puerto Rican time. The schemers the achievers the heads of state. The diplomats the soldiers the army generals. A whole generation, how nobody noticed. Came and went. The wind blowing ash free tumbling over ashtray rim. I didn't only see them climb to power and props. I always stepped onstage to bring the house down. To follow that simple Hollywood formula: There's bad guys and there's good guys. It was my personal arm wrestle, my eyeball to eyeball.

I did my job. I busted them. I busted them running, I busted them under the bed, hiding. I chased them over rooftops. I waited. Patient, parked down the block. They knew I was there. Building a file, getting to know habits, manners, style, face. I waited like an old lover throwing pebbles at a back window. I didn't need some impatient trigger fuck to come start piling up bodies in the name of the law. I did it by the book for twenty years, and it was working. Crime was down drug dealing wasn't so visible and the streets started to glow with people again, just hanging and gathering over there by the stoop . . . when this Dirty Harry motherfucker starts shooting people in the back.

Dirty Harry is a classic cop movie from 1971 directed by Don Siegel. It stars Clint Eastwood as a cop who takes the law into his own hands after a serial killer gets sprung on a technicality. The resulting murder spree inspired four sequels and made the vigilante cop a mainstay of Americana.

Two summers ago, drug dealers started getting popped. During arrests and mop-ups. Falling from rooftops, stairs. Cracked skulls after falling. Shot while trying to escape.

"He pulled a gun."

"He was resisting arrest."

"He turned in a hostile, aggressive manner," because yeah, some cops get tired of process. Of filling out forms in triplicate. Of taking time off from real life to testify in court, only to watch the guy stroll out the revolving doors. It starts small like that, almost by accident. The pushing, shoving. The first-time kick or handful of hair. It starts to flow out of hand. How the other buddies cover for you. For each other. A special club. The precinct rippled every time someone got gunned down during a street stop. The rush to files: Was it one of ours? (Correction: They were all MINE, four names crossed off, plus two who only looked like drug dealers. My alleys and streets invaded by a "special task force" doing sweeps as if to clean up my mess.) There were some late-night debates about it, hand-wringing wrenchers about where did loyalty lie and duty and other big words, but nobody wanted to deal with it. It was a problem for some other precinct, maybe some other cop. But these people that were getting popped were from my files, and I was from here.

So I went out on the streets. Treated it no different than if I was hunting down a psycho. I asked questions of people that the other cops didn't bother to ask. The streets talked back full blast. I used to think it had something to do with me being from here, but this was one of the biggest lies I ever believed. It was not the biggest of all, but hard to choose. I believed all of them.

I started a file on Dirty Harry. I packed that shit full and spent a drunken night with Lieutenant Jack, arguing. He said I should forget about it, wasn't worth throwing a career away. I respect him for having said it. I still don't hold it against him on days when I can't join in on their reindeer games. I walked that file over to Internal Affairs. They were not too happy I did that, or that the story got leaked to the *New York Post. (DIRTY HARRY COMES TO THE SOUTH BRONX!)* The *New York Times* started buzzing the commissioner's office. Resignations. The investigation took a year and a half, involved three precincts and led to five major acquittals. There were no riots. The people of the South Bronx went back to sleep as the story slid off the headlines without a squeak. Dirty Harry and his squad remained heroes to some in that Clint Eastwood/Oliver North kind of way, though reassigned—while "doing a Sanchez" became synonymous with squealing singing songs betraying buddies RAT FINKING. It was like throwing twenty years down the toilet. That first year right after everything was the hardest. There was talk that I was taking the death threats seriously. The captain said he had hoped to transfer me but found that no other precinct would have me. So he said I get to stay, suggested putting in for all that vacation time, as a favor to myself and the department. Prevent entanglements. "Scenes." In any case, he didn't plan on being around by the time I came back. "Let some new captain deal with it," he said, and from then on developed the ability to not speak to me at all, even when talking.

"So much for moving up the corporate ladder," Lieutenant Jack said. "Looks like I'm stuck with you."

Lieutenant Jack had a face like an orange, round and studded with pores. A real bear-hug Irish bastard who loved working the South Bronx. It was the early '90s when we started working together. His files as much as my files. Wasn't a murder scene crackhouse stoop shooting we didn't do together. Crack was the fast lane, the scam that scammed the town. Teenagers formed posses and shot each other to shit. A whole generation scraped off the sidewalk. Southern Boulevard Cypress 138th Street, all bullet-rattled window panes. Baggy-pant shootout boys lingered to watch the body wagons come. The staff at Ortiz Funeral Home got sick of seeing me turn up there, too many funeral parlors where posse members congregated to say *adios* to their foxhole buddies. I chased some, I jailed some. I scared some out, I scared some away. Back then, no matter how hard I tried, I wasn't as fast as what was killing them.

"You gotta let that stuff go."

Yeah, well, that's what Lieutenant Jack says. I can't forget. All those kids getting killed. You would think it was some kind of civil war. Kids armed and taking charge. And then the pace slowed. Was like the kids got bored. Spotted the truth behind the hype. The big dealers found their young audience dwindling. Like politicians record producers teachers Ricky Martín—they hadn't delivered. Dealers were no longer zipping by in big cars, popping caps across crowded streets. They learned to sit quietly. To keep a low profile. To share booty and bargain with rivals. Overnight, the face of the South Bronx changed. Empty lots got paved to fill up with rows of three-family houses, hedgerow lawn and suburb. The criminals moved indoors, got subtle.

For us, it was slow pace. Informers, alliances, betrayals. Endless surveilance. Took months to get inside, to know the workings and the players. It was all background scenes, establishing shots, and the long roll to end credits. That was my office, my street. My daily life for twenty years. Once there was an US vs. THEM story here somewhere. Once it was what I did for the South Bronx.

"And the New York City Police Department?"

I did what I thought was right. According to my training and my belief in certain principles. I put a stop to a gang. Nothing more, nothing less. But a lot of people didn't think so. I stood my ground and I'm still standing right here. My wife and I even bought one of those new prefab houses on

156th Street and Kelly. As much of a quiet treelined street as I could get and still call it South Bronx. But connections popped like high-tension wires after Dirty Harry. Dancing, spinning, bursting sparks. Reminders of special non-status. What was I supposed to be doing if I quit being a cop? My wife and I were talking about having a baby, and three weeks in Mallorca ought to do the trick. It would be a gray slow time. Neither here nor there. Time to end things or get things started. A gold badge tossed on the captain's desk. As movie-like an ending as possible.

But so much for Mallorca and great escapes and movie scenes rolling to end credits. I had started smoking again. Swiped loose cigarettes from everywhere. Menthols, kings, filter tips, Chesterfield Regulars. I had just about every type of smokable tobacco squirreled everywhere I could reach like pocket like shelf like desk drawer always a loose one someplace for a sudden drag. And to sit sometimes and smoke them in rows as if waiting for someone to walk through that door. An armload of facts, irrefutable. Maybe they had sicced some dark *yoruba* spick cop on me. Parked outside my house. Getting to know habits, manner, style, face. The pebbles striking my window at 4 a.m.

The agent had two bookends with him. Left them standing at the desk in the entry hall, faces impenetrably stone. Special agent? I expected older, salt-and-pepper hair, abrasive vocals. A face lined with experience and hassles, and not this young guy, hands sunk in the pockets of his long tan raincoat. I would have been more impressed had I caught him picking my lock or rifling through piles on my desk.

I hadn't even stirred my first cup of coffee. It rained buckets that morning and the wet was still in my bones. How I sat and started talking to him about cop life was beyond me. I didn't have visitors for a reason. Didn't have to scratch the surface much to strike a nerve. Nothing to hide, and that's the best policy. How it all comes spilling out.

"I'm Special Agent Myers," he said.

There was also that hunger for the raspy bite of that first cigarette of the day, which went with the first taste of coffee.

"Detective Sanchez," I said.

A calm, sure grip. Smile so *simpatico* in that AMERICAN HEARTLANDS kind of way. To trust that face the moment you spot it on the screen. Should I say CIA? It never pays to say. People get riled over the silliest shit these days. Three simple letters in an e-mail like FBI CIA or FALN (that's four letters), and suddenly there's a background check and a black car with tinted windows following you around. Funny clicks on the phone. That guy outside the bodega who for some reason says, "Smile for the FBI," as you head for your car. Too clean-cut to be a used car salesman. Too much energy for such a small space. Offered him a coffee and that was a mistake. Ripping those sugar packets and sprinkling sugar liberal, then stirring mad. Spoon clang clanging like the fucking bells of Rhymney. On top of which he asked me to close the door. By the time I got behind my desk, it felt like the room had shrunk.

I guess I talked to him because I saw him as a cop from somewhere else—Washington, not South Bronx—another plane of reality where the power was stored. Maybe the feds had decided to step in and order a real investigation into what was happening here. It was an opportunity for me to talk to someone from OUTSIDE of here, OUTSIDE of this narrow confining orbit. To check and see if I was really going crazy. A new federal investigation would mean more new noise at a time when all was a vague limbo, not here not there. Good guys. Bad guys. A hazy blur. I don't know now why I even bothered to raise my hand. I suddenly got the feeling from the deep silence that I didn't want to talk anymore.

"I know about your record," Myers said. "You came highly recommended."

The best time to light up that first cigarette of the day is halfway through that first cup of the day. Had to be halfway, give the taste buds enough time to get saturated with coffee. The coffee would be the right temperature. My coffee was not yet at the halfway mark, yet I was already thinking about that cigarette. I was even thinking about what kind: a filterless Chesterfield. That rough, abrasive first taste of smoke. No filter to soften the hammer blow.

"Detective Hanson at Four-Three. Detectives Peterson, Lemmings, and Bryan at the Four-O. The Bronx district attorney's office. There wasn't a single paralegal there that didn't know your name. And your captain." Vague smile. "He had quite a few things to say about you."

The open window faced a brick wall, a back alley of steel stairwells, and a basement grille. I was always going out there with Lieutenant Jack for a smoke, just standing on the grille and puffing away. Below were some glowy basement windows and hundreds of discarded butts. I was longing to go out that window.

"I know pretty well about your current troubles," Myers said. "But that's not why I'm here."

I had the sense that I didn't know whether to be relieved or disappointed. I had the sense that I knew deep down what he was after, and that troubled me. My seventh sip of coffee. As flaming burn as the first.

"It's very important that I find Anthony Rosario."

(Oh man. Another quick gulp of coffee.)

Drug dealers are born with real names like regular people but they develop street tags, alter-egos. Rap-star comic book villain names like Destructo, MurderMan, Sniffles, Ace of Spade. Names I became so familiar with that it took awhile sometimes to register, to put the real name to a face. It was as if the real name was a secret, something hidden. It didn't please me to hear Myers just blurt it out.

"Spook? You're looking for Spook?"

"A.k.a., Spook. That's right."

Silence. Deep cave.

"What makes a special agent come all the way from Washington to look for Spook?"

Standing ground again. Old habit. At first I thought he was here because of me. Now that he said "Spook," I saw that it was still ABOUT me.

"I'm involved in a top priority investigation. We've been following certain trails and one of them has led here. The things I'm about to tell you shouldn't leave this room."

My fingers found a cigarette in a drawer. Totally unconscious. Automatic. Rolled it around. Thinking about that open window and no Spook thoughts. I longed for Lieutenant Jack, for his cynical laugh and the way he made trouble seem smaller.

Myers pulled out a manila envelope from an inside pocket. He tapped it against a thigh, bit his lower lip. He handed it to me.

"This is strictly confidential," he said.

"Sure."

"Are you aware that over the course of a month, Anthony Rosario deposited over ten million dollars in four different bank accounts?"

"No," I said.

"Four accounts. A couple of names you might know. The other two are foreigners. Not from his organization. We were already watching them. They led us right to Mr. Rosario. We've been following the money since it came stateside."

I opened the envelope. Bank statements, phone records. Numbers dialed on Spook's cell phone. There were two names I recognized all right, trusted Spook workers. The other names I did not know. The room was feeling smaller and smaller.

"He floated the money into the accounts, then disappeared it. These two names." Myers came around the desk to show me on the sheets. "They are known to us as individuals involved in a terrorist organization that has recently been waging an undeclared war against the United States."

Bank statements. Deposits. Withdrawals. Phone calls. Transaction slips. Footprints in the snow.

"This organization has been flooding the country recently with money. Over the past six months we've snagged accounts in New York, Florida, Chicago, even Los Angeles. Closed a batch last month that used fake Social Security numbers. Unbelievable how banks let this stuff slip. A bunch of others we suspect but can't touch because there are laws, laws, we have them, don't we? And the more they protect people, the more these criminals use them to strangle us. We're onto the bank thing, so now they're trying to switch tactics. Last week we arrested two individuals using debit cards—individuals, again linked to terrorism—but every petty arrest we make generates a reaction. First, they were setting up accounts openly, with phony Social Security numbers. Expired visas, illegal aliens using debit cards . . . so we nail some. Now the method starts to change. Now they're trying to launder the money in, approaching criminal elements who are highly skilled at it. We know they approached the mob."

Myers, standing by my desk, now staring at the window as if he had followed my eyes. I had the cigarette in my hand. I had my hand up to my face. To sniff the bouquet.

"It was the mob that got us onto this thing to begin with. They told us right away. The mob is too patriotic to step into that. But a drug dealer . . . from the South Bronx? Who would even bother to look in the South Bronx? It's a shift in tactics. Like an animal that's aware it's being hunted. It reacts, it shifts, it has a brain. We call that a conscious coordination of effort."

The half-point to my coffee had been reached. The coffee was at the right temperature. Myers, spirited and antsy, walked around the desk. It seemed like he hadn't gotten to the worst of it yet.

"I'm sorry," I said, my words tasting sluggish. "I'm having a hard time seeing Spook involved in this."

"I can understand," he said. "But would you say his business has been so good over the past month that he would be making such a big deposit just coming out of jail?"

I didn't want to answer a question like that. My guts were tighter than a Dominican ass in stressed jeans. How didn't I see something like this? Was I so fucking lazy? So we busted him two months ago, raided some sloppy operation, didn't get much on him. Nothing that would stick when you have a good lawyer, and Spook had that. His "clean as a whistle" brother David made sure to hook him up every time.

"But where's the money from?" I felt testy, grasping for handhold along the ledge.

"You don't need to know that," he said. He was by the window, peering out into the alley. His voice sounded somehow gentle. "Anyway, it's not your fault."

"Why would it be?"

Myers took his seat again. There was concern creasing his face. "That you didn't know. You can't blame yourself."

There was just the ticking of the clock. Our eyes met across a strange distance.

"Unless you really do know every last little thing about the people in your files," he said.

It was one of those silent moments you replay later.

"Nobody could," I said, hollow.

Myers gestured toward the flip-pad on my desk, which also came in the envelope.

"Mr. Rosario met someone this last visit to prison. His name is Mounir. He's from Saudi Arabia. We know him pretty well. He's been especially talkative right now, since he's scared his old friends are going to kill him. He's the one who made the connection to Mr. Rosario. Just think: You're this two-bit drug dealer who just got his ass busted on some shit charge, and here comes this stranger, offering you a chance to launder millions of dollars. What would your attitude be?"

I wasn't through rubbing my face shut.

"I would go for it," I said.

"Okay, this is where it gets worse." Myers leaned closer. "They'll probably pay a certain amount for services rendered. Something reasonable for the trouble, but what if you start to think? Why take some small fee when you can have the whole ten million? Tax free. What if you think you can just run off with it, rip off a bunch of stupid foreigners, and disappear?"

"Ah, shit." The room felt too small, too tight. Even Myers had to stand up. Hands in pockets, he walked over to the window and stared across at the brick wall.

"These people," he said, "they're psycho-killers with international connections. Fearless, well-indoctrinated, with goals and a purpose that goes beyond people. Mr. Rosario might have picked the wrong people to fuck with. It could be they're tracking him down right now, him and everyone he's connected with. This guy has really botched it up for us. We've been following this money trail for months now. If they get him, we could lose all of it. The money, the trail, the people it would have all led us to."

"Maybe the money already got where it was going," I said.

"No. It never got there. We know where it goes and it hasn't reached point A. Mr. Rosario was just a pathway. He was not the final destination. This guy . . . Spook." The way the name bubbled off his lips made him grin a moment, before his face creased up again. I read it like concern for Spook. All of a sudden that sick feeling, an old adrenalin kick from those "first love" years. That feeling that YOU CAN MAKE A DIFFERENCE. That YOU have been chosen by providence to be at the right place at the right time to make that one special move. And maybe it was one of those big lies coming round to get believed in again. Or maybe it was just the goddamned truth. Staring me in the face as much as Myers. My destiny. My beginning or my end.

"I really need to find Spook," he said.

My stomach was burning. My ears, my head. I stood up too. Fished out my cheap-ass lighter and stepped out through the window.

"I think it's time for a cigarette," I said.

8.

blurry like this: swishy sudden camera movements at close range. shaky like hand-held. jump-cuts in elevator going down. heavy usage of drugs indicated, or: bad dream. to shake off one image replaced by another. to shake off another image replaced by

he was there when the elevator doors opened, standing by the reception desk. looked amazingly well-pressed in his business suit, business suit, what dirty stinking business was it? he looked at his watch when he saw her. as if he would dock her.

—what are you doing here? like she would walk right by him.

—I didn't come to see you, he said. had a way of chewing gum that brought some film to mind. robert blake, *in cold blood.* tapping with two fingers on the furry armrest.

—but you said you wouldn't, she said.

—but you said you would help me, he said. you said you'd get back to me. it's been three long days. you can't expect the federal government to sit on its ass and wait for you to finish doing your makeup. the wheels are turning. if something bad happens, no, don't turn away. if something bad happens, it's your fault.

—I'm working on it, she said. it's taking time. I need more time.

—time isn't something we have.

—I'll talk to him about it today. I promise.

—well, I've been waiting fifteen minutes already and he hasn't come in. you don't think maybe he got a tip from somebody, do you? you don't think maybe he ran off?

—he's not guilty of anything. he has no reason to run.

—since when is he the type to be late like this?

(he took out a cigarette. had just about every type of smokable tobacco squirreled everywhere he could reach.)

—there's no smoking in here, she said.

his kiss tasted like curdled milk.

they were in an alley. service entrance stink. wire gates. packing crates. his hands squeezed her arms hard. she closed her eyes.

—that's not how you kissed me the first time, he said.

—I was drunk the first time, she said.

he laughed. she pulled his hands off. bloodstains on her blouse. everywhere he touched her. he touched her face.

she ran. it was a long blurry hallway. water splashed in through cracks in the walls. she went up some stairs and pushed against a metal door. when it finally gave, water burst in. the streets were full of water. it was the great new york flood of 2001. the water was up to her waist and rising, brown brackish. people everywhere running, screaming. cars floated free and crashed into storefronts. dead bodies floated up in bubbles from subway entrances.

it was new york but it wasn't. it was park place, it was dupont circle. there was boston first federal savings bank on the corner. there was a T-train stop. people struggled to pack into its trolley depth even though it was already inundated. she fought her way through the water against the rising current. couldn't tell new york, d.c., or boston. couldn't tell uptown or downtown. she wanted uptown. manhattan was sinking. whenever she had been in that part of town and lost her bearings, she would check the horizon to orient herself against the world trade towers. she looked for them now, should have been visible. but they were nowhere in sight. a dented skyline. sideways swimming. looking for street signs. the buildings were not saying. she was swimming but not getting far. clear of buildings, she could make out the vast sweep of the atlantic ocean. just past the sinking skyline was europe. the eiffel tower, visible beyond the curvy waves. she was kicking through the cushiony warm wet, but the water was gelatin thick. she was sinking, a dark scramble into murk. she was fighting her way out of the dream. the airless dark pocket between waking and not waking.

—where did you find her? a voice asked.

—the feeling is that your life is like slides, the woman in the chair next to hers said in a man's voice. someone slips in a new one while you pass out. you wake up someplace else.

—she's a dancer, someone said.

—she's a model, someone said.

—she's an actress, someone was doing her hair. she was at sarita's, the beauty parlor, with the cotton-haired puerto rican woman who was a *santera* and gifted with insights. the place was packed. women in chairs everywhere talking spanish while blow dryers blew and spanish music spanished. sarita, snipping at her wet curls, paused as if receiving a message.

—you're going to take a long trip, she said.

after she told him everything, david drove her down 149th street. she could hardly take in all the frenetic traffic heading in all directions, so she took snaps. subway noise rising up through subway gratings. stores obscured by boxes of sneakers racks of t-shirts and stressed jeans. music pumping from electronic stores. cheap flashy strobes. fat black speakers sitting by the entrances wearing thick chains like bad niggas.

he stopped in front of a bank, his face grim with purpose. she almost wanted him not to do it, to not include her. if she didn't know then, she couldn't say, no matter what manner of drug alan gave her. once she knew, she would have to make a choice.

hesitation.

—maybe if your brother puts the money back, she said, they won't have a reason to bother him.

—yes they will, he said.

she knew it was stupid when she said it, but she had to say something.

—if he goes to the feds, they won't touch him.

she knew he didn't believe her, and she didn't believe it either.

—it's too late, he said.

in the bank, thick cushiony carpet. a smell of sterile and cheap colognes clashing. he took her down some stairs, right up to the lady behind the bars in the cage.

—my name is david romero, he lied. planted his key on the slick marble counter. I have a safe-deposit box here and would like to authorize my assistant to have access to it for me while I am away on business.

—you can't fall in love with him, alan said. *a puerto rican.* he said the words like he was spitting out teeth.

—you're not supposed to get involved with him, was how he corrected himself.

—that's not what you said at the beginning, she said.

—you'll be with someone, but don't fear him, sarita said. he has strong guardians.

—but where am I going? she asked, staring at herself in the mirror. her hair, for some reason, had turned black. a woman carrying a tray of curlers bumped into sarita. there was a clatter crash. pink curlers bounced everywhere like tiny bunnies.

the cell phone beeped its song. *oh say can you see?* she shook she jumped she searched her purse. she was dressed for the party.

—ava, help me.

—david. where are you? what's wrong?

—they killed my brother, he said. I think they're on the way here now.

she ran. always this thing with time: time running out, we haven't much time, racing against the clock, or else it was *sometime*:

—sometime you're going to have to choose, he said, again and again in his precise alan speak.

—we should let her sleep, a voice said.

no, the doctor said, giving her a shot of sodium pentathol. make her talk first. and he squeezed her face with his hand like he would squash a tomato.

—no, she said.

The windows were wide open. Blue sky almost touchable through that clean pane. The bed was at the perfect angle to see nothing but sky through both windows. No buildings, no rooftops, no sight of anything but blue sky and cotton clouds. These were dream windows, painted by Dalí. The chilly breeze made her pull up her blanket. A sick flat taste in her mouth.

Her eyes were wet. The strange blue room alternately calmed and panicked her. She sat up a little, clutched her folded knees. Wanting to hide, wanting to take it back. Something, everything, to blot out all the lines connected to her with an eraser.

There was the smell of coffee. The sound of water in the sink. Dishes. A man's footsteps in the hallway. Nearer, near.

She closed her eyes. The same way a little girl closed her eyes, and said, "You can't see me."

She was counting to ten.

9.

it was the dress that did it.

not the woman in his bed, for there had been many others after, to disappear in the morning with that first vodka
splash. women who left no tracks, no visible proof they
had ever been there. he could have dreamed them, but he
didn't dream belinda. and he didn't dream that dress.

hanging from shower curtain rod. eye level as he pissed and
flushed. there hadn't been a dress hanging in his bathroom
since belinda. was her habit, her mark of permanence.
(there was also: bra and panties. actually, a black g-string so
flimsy that just staring at it made it slip off the curtain rod.)

"changó, changó."
the cleansing tobacco rolling slow into the air, he especially puffing the dress. (how it shuddered from his smoke
breath.) maybe he should have been praying something,
but he only muttered *changó, changó* like in that song by
celia cruz

fought off the first wave of disconnected images with vodka
and ice. cleansed that sense of DOOM with that first bright
hit. that tumultuous puerto rican *aguacero* splashing the
windows clean.

the second ice-clinking swallow stopped the pictures. he
busied his hands making another vodka ice, then rolling a
cigarette slow calm. the cigar had gone out. maybe it meant

something spiritually. he parked it on the ashtray for another cleanse later. but now sat in the small kitchen, in the
narrow confined space with nothing but the ticking cat-
eyes on the wall as his nerves settled, free of turbulence.

equilibrium.
that was the thing people left out when they started the
rap on the evils of drinking. the equilibrium, the sense of
things falling into place. someone should tell benny about
the peace-and-tranquility part. liquor gave him that feeling
of invulnerability. popeye's can of spinach. he could slow
the pictures down, pick and choose, no rush. benny should
learn that shit before he preaches about the evils, but then
benny should know better. he was once a drinker too, even
owned a bar. used to toss them back like a pro, but he
mistook liquor for a new belief system, depended on it to
make him into someone else. benny was always looking to
change himself. he convinced himself that liquor changed
him for the worse. alex was not so convinced. drinking
made him normal. his blood, his nervous system demanded
it. "you can't talk a drunk off a ledge with promises of
bible," he said to benny, he said to belinda.

   —that did it, she said. you choose: the bottle, or me.
   was it such a problem, his drinking? did it have to come
up every time something went wrong? he tried it her way,
pouring another bottle down the drain. proof he was a new
man: but poses become roses, whither and die, crunchy
and dry. did he really choose the bottle? was it really a
question of choice? she had talked to him, endlessly, about
how she had been in relationships before and how this was
her last time, do or die. she would force it to work, with
her own hands force it with sheer will. she had talked to
him. she had always talked to him. she knew he was sick
of running around waking with strangers, but she felt the
liquor was what caused infidelity. it was like that with her

father, she said, it would be like that with him. alex tried
to tell her there was no connection, women came through
his open doors until he closed them, he swore he was closing them for good. but the fighting about drinking caused
more drinking, so alex one night opened his doors. sometimes it's the only way out.

> *you'll never have a woman again. you're never going to find
> love like you had it, like I gave it to you, like you spent it.*

it was a good speech, he wrote it on the bedroom wall. big
letters in drippy black paint, just to prove he would never
forget them, drunk or not drunk. alex had a hard time remembering how the rooms were then. it was far from him,
almost another life. some people have to fill a room with
clutter to remind themselves they're alive. the curtains
were all hers, the bureau. the big mirror where she used to
stand in her panty hose, adjusting those bra straps. boxes
of cosmetics, kitchen utensils, fashion magazines. bulby
ceramic lamps. flowered *tapetes*.

the last time he saw her alive she was throwing the vase of
yellow peonies at him. hit the wall with the impact of an
RPG, him flinching from shrapnel where he stood under
those drippy black letters. her face usually so calm, now
so furious broken, as she charged out the door, stooping
only to pick up her shoulder bag. going going gone. she
never called about her clothes, her furniture, her things.
"our things," she would have said, insisted. she never
called.

he tried her a few times at work, the investment firm
of debussy and stark, but she wasn't getting back. it was
what he told the police barely a month after she left, when
they came by to visit. it wasn't that he was a suspect, they
said, but whenever a daughter kills herself, the family always blames the boyfriend. the cops found it strange that

he never met the family, which had nothing but derogatory things to say with what little they knew about him. belinda never spoke well of her parents. she always said they were too rich and too narrow-minded and that was why she was more than happy to move here and write them and say "I'm living with a man in the south bronx." alex was the part of her rebellion that failed. a half-mad half-dominican blonde with *castellano* to her english, she had stopped taking her medication when she came to live with him. the details were sketchy now, intentionally so.

there was no memory of a funeral, of a gray day and umbrellas poking up amidst tombstones like black mushrooms. he didn't really remember the cops, just monk on a rainy day asking him about it.

—cops looking for you, bro?

—belinda, he said. they're looking for belinda.

—you mean she's missing?

—I mean she left.

it started with the curtains, and after that everything came down. blank walls, her pictures taken down. pulled out, torn down, bundled. paid this one-eyed neighbor from downstairs fifty bucks and all the vodka hits he could take to get the sofa-bureau-love-seat and bed down the stairs. he pulled up the linoleum, scraped at the dirty old floor until it was fresh beautiful wood, varnished fresh slick. the black drippy words in the bedroom gradually disappeared with each different color he applied. by the time he settled on blue there was only

YOU SPENT IT

before that one night, finally painted over, the whole house blue—detoxed de-spirited de-boned. a slate wiped clean. it wasn't that he forgot she was dead, but he forgot he was blaming himself for it. he forgot it was his fault. he forgot that as much as possible. only some things, some times brought it back.

he found her sitting up in bed, half-covered by blanket. she was facing the open windows, tucked into herself like a snail.

he came closer. her eyes were closed.

"Hey," he said.

Her eyes opened. Green still, but maybe brown-flecked in sunlight. To wetly wetly blink.

"Ten," she said.

10.

"Did you sleep okay?"

The running through the streets had been no dream. A firecracker kick drum. Shattering glass. Percussive slaps. Things twirl-spinning up to her. Running from one dark zone to the other. Bad dream—this guy staring at her. His face was not so instantly readable. He COULD NOT be connected to that pipeline, that snakelike curling around her fast: He could not—or she COULD NOT have picked a worse place. He looked at her like he didn't know her, was that it? It could be the best way to start.

"Bad dreams," she said.

(Her thing was still to not acknowledge tears, to never give them any attention.)

He puffed out a thin stream of cigar smoke that hung in the air between them.

"Changó, Changó," he said. Some private ritual that cut through all the noise in her head. Calmed her the way numbers did. The perfection of them. How things always worked out in the end, if you stuck with it and spoke the language of integers. He was leaning against the window as if trying to figure out a way to tell her: I know you. I know why you came.

"It's *Santería*," he said. "Changó is a Yoruba god, represented in Cuba by the virginal Santa Barbara. The African version of Achilles. He was born to fight but came in dancing. So why is it he ends up being adored as a woman?"

The scrape of his loafers. The soundless slow descent of planes over tenement rooftops. He puffed out more smoke.

"See, he had enemies. So the manly Changó disguised himself as a woman. Sometimes *Santeros* ask for his protection by chanting his name and blowing tobacco smoke to dispel bad spirits and confusion."

The pungent aroma settled in the room, thickening the air overhead. It gave off heat.

"And you're a *Santero*?"

Her words felt encased in Jell-O like she was still swimming up from dream.

"No," he said. Puffing away slow on that cigar, talking about a god of masquerade, a powerful protector. A god who knew the importance of wearing disguises. Had to be. Her god. Her dream—Sarita appearing to her and talking about protection. *Santero*, *Santera*. A direct link from dream to waking.

She closed her eyes. "*Changó, Changó.* Like that?"

"Yeah, but you need to puff."

He was close. Slow putting cigar to her lips.

(He would tell her: I know you. I know why you came.)

She drew in smoke. A cigar-tip sizzle, squiggly worms flaming up ash. He looked just like the type to play it slick. Could rely on good looks, lengthy pauses, and those brown dog eyes, staring. A hard-to-read granite face. No sculptor would have ever used this stone. Marvelous pretty, but horrid to work with. (Unyielding, easy to chip.) She thought she saw disdain, disinterest, compassion, curiosity, and no harm swimming there. He didn't seem too excitable. Could be the kind of person one might sit with and say nothing, and that would be all right.

He sat on the edge of the bed and took back the cigar. It seemed to be just for ritual, the way he stubbed it out before words, as if gathering his strength.

"Listen," he said. "Last night."

(I know you. I know why you came.)

"Last night," she said.

There was a moment of just staring and her hope that he wouldn't say anything. No words, just a quiet, safe blue room.

"I don't remember it," he said. "Sorry. It's a complete blank."

The soundless slow descent of planes over tenement rooftops.

"I hope you're not insulted."

"No," she said.

He got up and went to the window. The room throbbed with hesitation. He couldn't, she couldn't. Something just couldn't.

"This happen often?"

"Not like this," he said.

Seagulls seemed to pass awful close. Windows darkened with wingspan. A moment of mad flapping. Shrieks and cries. A voice that said, *Tell him.*

"I remember last night," she said.

He looked at her. He looked away. She hadn't meant to make it sound like that. No telling what was in her voice. No telling what was on his face. Impermeable, but not closed. It would all be guesswork, or he knew her. He was playing dumb. He was a silent player, in with the one-eye. He would probably stall her with coffee.

(There was a muffled gurgling.)

"The coffee's ready," he said.

"My dress is wet. Did you see?"

"Yeah. It's still wet."

"Do you have anything I can put on?"

He was scanning the clumsy watercolor sky, a pause to his every step like he was thinking it over carefully. A sense of going, of staying.

"The blue crate," he said.

She trailed sheet as she walked the floor. It slid off in a heap as she rifled through crates. A blue one, a red one, two red ones, a green.

"Why's it so empty here?" she asked.

"I don't remember," he said.

She checked his face. Joking, serious, hostile, what? He didn't seem to be scared of her, and if he was wondering about her, he kept it well hid. The coffee pot gurgled more insistent. It was hesitation again, a strange sense that he didn't know what to tell her and she didn't know what to tell him. He left. She slid into a pair of his jeans. A Red Hot Chili Peppers T-shirt. She walked over to the fire escape window.

The street below was sunny lit. Traffic flow lazy slow. A *piraguero* on the corner scraped his block of ice. She wasn't from here, but the place reminded her of Spanish Harlem. Coffee smell, tenement brick, pots and pans. The sound of Puerto Rican Spanish. The sidewalks glittered with broken glass. A Puerto Rican flag fluttered from atop a tin shack. A graffiti tribute to a girl named Magali who peered back from the brick wall with glowy orb eyes. A flow, a rhythm, the roar of subway coming up through steel gratings. She couldn't describe what the feeling was.

She had been very attracted to that Puerto Rican part of town. She was Upper East Side, nine blocks from Spanish Harlem. (Close enough to smell the *criollo*, Trudy always said, and not get burned. Whatever that meant.) She often headed up there on skates that first summer, drawing some attention as she sped up and down Muñoz Marín Boulevard. (Could have been all that loose blond hair trailing along behind. Could have been the shorts.)

She bought her fruits and vegetables at La Marqueta, haggling in her classroom Spanish with pinch-faced fruit vets that called her *La Blanquita*. She got her first real haircut at Sarita's, a beautician joint on 113th Street. White-haired Sarita was a *Santera*, and could foretell events. She did readings and all that, but everyone stopping by for a trim or a manicure could mean receiving any number of tidbits about upcoming events GRATIS. It was Sarita who gave her that 1930s haircut. She sat in the chair with no plan other than getting her hair cut. New in town, new face, new look. But what Sarita did was bring back her face. She stared at herself in the mirror like it was a time portal.

"I've always been attracted to that time," she said.

Sarita smiled. "We all have past lives. The things that attract us from the past are sometimes traces from places we've been before."

It was like seeing herself for the first time.

Sarita in her dream, the first time she made an appearance, and what was she trying to tell her? She rebelled against the idea of soothsayers, always did. Never really wanted to know what was coming tomorrow, but it seemed every time she saw Sarita, the woman would always say something relevant, something to come that could only be proven later. She hadn't been to see Sarita for months. She wished she had bothered to stop by, even though every fiber of her being twitched at the thought of believing in such things.

She sat on the bed, checking her feet for those stinging scrapes and cuts before slipping on her Jackie O's. A deep heaviness. If she spent more time thinking about it, she would never leave that blue room. It still felt safe, even with the man in the kitchen preparing coffee—or maybe because of him. It was foolish, impractical, dangerous. She wished she was good at talking. (A voice that said, *Tell him.*)

She picked up her purse and undid the latch on one of the detachable handles.

He had laid out coffee mugs, coffee pot, container of milk. Fresh toast. Cold cuts and cheese. There was a tall thin bottle of vodka. He was rolling a cigarette when she appeared in the doorway. She felt comfortable in his clothes.

"Looks good," he said, tucking in the loose fibers at the end of the cigarette with a pen.

She sat in the chair beside him. "As soon as the dress gets dry."

"Sure." He lit the cigarette. "You want I should roll you one?"

"I only want a few puffs."

Now came that feeling of hesitation again. His, hers. She clutched her purse. He seemed about to say something, but it was only cigarette smoke. She looked around the small, bare kitchen. A thousand words came to her and she refused to speak them. She was not going to play a role or do a dance this time. She would not be guided by voices. She was bad luck, the kiss of death. Besides, she couldn't even attempt to tell the story. She began fiddling with her purse.

"Hey," she said, "do you have any tape? Something thick, like maybe masking tape?"

He looked at her. Cigarette smoke formed rings. "What's your name," he said.

The ticking cat-eyes of the clock did not distract her. His eyes were searching her for facts. The strange thought hit her that he was somehow being generous. That he knew, and wasn't saying anything about fire escapes and open windows and women who slip into bed with total strangers.

"My name is Ava," she said. "Ava as in Gardner, not Gabor."

The cigarette was between his lips. A glimmer of amusement in his eyes or a show of welcome.

"I'm Alex," he said, extending his hand. The touch was familiar, no surprise to skin. He passed her the cigarette. She took her first puff but it only added wooziness, blurriness, a flat taste. "You need tape?"

"The strap on my purse is broken," she said, sort of holding it up.

"There's some gaffer's under the sink."

She crouched down, opening the metal door to the undersink. Movement was better than just sitting there looking at each other, just sitting there talking, and he wasn't moving. He was working those cups.

"Milk?"

"Oh yes, please."

"Sugar?"

She put the gaffer's tape on the edge of the table, noticing that he had dipped his spoon into a box of sugar cubes. There was something really funny about that. She laughed.

"Yes. Four cubes, please."

Plop, plop, plop.

"So, about last night . . ." he said, just about to drop in that fourth cube.

That's when she pulled the gun from her purse and hit him with it.

11.

and not always right you could be not always right and somehow still function still pull it off every day because it's a job NOT an adventure way of life or belief system

pads and memos and files to look up files to shift from PER-PETRATOR to VICTIM. Another name gone another piece of past obliterated stamped out no memory no trail as if this person never walked those streets

this is how I will always remember the South Bronx
that preen and whore-proud strut to the corner where she tempts the truckers. Short memory so she's never hurt long enough to do something about it. Spread sand over blood newly paved over streets. Make it look new make it smell clean. "It never happened here." Some people never remember what some people work so hard to forget. Make failure sound like success. Put fake petunias in the windows. Celebrate and go parade. Every June fools. A sometimes Puerto Rican tendency to forget. To shrug and say well

what can you do

swallowed Jonah whale peoples. Live your life SPELLED BACKWARDS is dog. Seats taken, better stand. A long way home and that train is a local. Why burn books that have never been read? He doesn't know about Puerto Ricans. He mentions Castro like he wants to speak my lingo but I don't give a damn about Castro and still think Gloria Estefan is a Cuban torture device. To distinguish between LATINOs.

When differences like that don't make a difference anymore then it's time to book a flight buy a house find a seashore far from. Good guys bad guys "when differences like that don't make a difference anymore," but no matter how you slice that shit it always comes down to the basic fact that Shakira was much better before she started to sing in English.

"What I know about Puerto Ricans couldn't fill a post-age stamp," Myers said. The city blurred through rainy windows. Cranky squawk of windshield wipers wiping. The two of us in search of Spook. "They're U.S. citizens. They love coffee and cigarettes. They play good baseball, like that guy THE A-ROD. They wave around a flag that can't be found in an atlas. I got that from a Puerto Rican guy at the academy. I'm not surprised he washed out."

The two of us, in search of Spook.

"You forgot salsa," I said, drowsy with listening with not, with driving with blotting out canceling all like-terms.

"Salsa music," he said. "Now you're trying to trick me. That's Cuban, right?"

The cigarette thing was a definite problem. Outside of those cheap opportunistic bonding moments with others, there was that stink on the fingers I hated so much that I was constantly washing my hands. My wife made me a special tea. She is sympathetic, having quit two years ago. She never banished me from a room or avoided my stink. On that recent sleepless night, she was there. Getting up from sheets to sit beside me in the dark living room. There while I finished the last two cigarettes, thinking

she's in on it. All of it. This plan, that old plan. She was there when I tried to forget. Names that sometimes fade into files, but I have this thing with faces. Streets retain the memory of them. Sometimes they are caught in the flash of my headlights. They peer at me from fire escapes and stoops. Any cluster of kids in hooded jackets could be them. I developed a brief drinking thing with Lieutenant Jack. Was just learning how to forget when Dirty Harry came. After that came the nether float of an iso-tank. Big words and phrases shrank to a hand-hold, to the slow stroke of her fingers across my face when nighttime black. I was no nation of millions. I was a nation of two. Together we searched the atlas for a country with a flag. A place where houses are sold to foreigners on very favorable terms. Beach. Sun. Spanish. One good down payment

and the rest was gravy. No more South Bronx do-not-pass-go. No more South Bronx do-not-collect-$200. No more South Bronx go-directly-to-jail. Just no more South Bronx

not as culture not as place not as barrier not as wall not as language not as space as condition as sickness as way of life. Not as reason for living not as big as you think—

not as patria

but as springboard. Jettison speed. The ticket in, the ticket out. The one sure place to hit THE LOTTO. It was lightning hitting that power station to bring the blackout we had all been praying for, only this was more than a looted TV set carried through shattered glass streets. I had the images already collected like film strips: the squealing of a stuck pig. A gold shield on the captain's desk. Beach. Sun. Spanish. "The check's in the mail."

"That's tough about the death threats," Myers said. My car moved slow motion through dark rain slick. "If the department gave half a damn, they would've rigged your phone up to a DSP-4000 with ripper autotrace functions and digital remote. Could show up at the bastard's house two minutes after he makes the call."

"I told you, they tried some of that stuff."

"They didn't try hard enough."

Establishing shot. Giving Myers those preliminary drives through turf. "Here's the church. This is the steeple." A game of fingers. The rain kept people indoors or clustered in door-ways on stoops.

"I don't even want to know anymore," I said. To me it was a collective rejection a bad rating a sort of pink slip. I couldn't talk about it while driving strange. I kept pulling to the left. The wheel wanted to go right.

"But the department should want to know, especially in a case where it's obvious the callers are going to be police officers. Police officers making death threats? Why wouldn't they want to look at that? Who is better equipped to carry out a death threat than a police officer? Who has the better resources, better access? How easy is it for people to accept that a cop did it?"

The theme seemed to be shifting, from death threats to cops who try to get away with murder.

"Damn." Myers searched an empty cigarette pack. "I wouldn't mind at all, nabbing a police officer who thought he was going to get away with something."

The sound of that crumpled pack reminded me. I reached into a pocket. The gas pedal was a squirmy fat mouse and I was going to squash it. I passed him a cigarette and lit mine. He could light his own—I passed him the lighter.

"I did that once," I said, more smoke than words. "It's not all it's cracked up to be."

We sped down Avenue St. John, the street that always sounded like a playground.

"Say, hey, what's the rush?"

"You said we don't have a lot of time." I ran a red light. Screechy right turn onto 149th Street. A bus honked long and hard. I could imagine cop cars in pursuit, blinking lights crazy zig-zags. Pedestrians jumping out of the way.

Myers laughed. "Man, that's the ultimate treachery."

"The ultimate treachery?"

"It's just that you can never trust words. You're a detective, you know that. Humans have a failing that they only believe what they feel sounds right. Nothing as outlandish as the truth. That Kennedy thing, they're still arguing about that! They could've shot that man with a bazooka and have it all on film and people would still swear it was lone-gun Oswald pumping away on an antiquated slingshot. Words? What's the point? I don't go that way. I go by gestures, body movements. That's the ultimate treachery."

There was a jolting buzz from his words. I enjoyed the car splashing through puddles, a slick almost slip-slide feel to the handling that made me go faster.

"Those little things. Fear, guilt, anxiety. All these have their unique physical manifestations. The way fingers grip a steering wheel. The beads of sweat on a man's upper lip. The way he starts accelerating the car wildly at certain points in the conversation."

I flinched from a bump. It was the car fighting me, the car. Red light. I went through. A batch of honks and one frenzied car squeal.

"Not my favorite conversation," I said.

"It's completely understandable. I don't know if I would take it so well. After twenty years on the force. A gold shield. And still, cops walking around calling you a traitor."

The car growled, the rain slapped the windshield all blur. The car wanted to speed. The car wanted to scream.

"I wonder what you would do," he said, "with ten million dollars."

It was not the first time I had heard that question. Did Myers somehow know that, the way his eyes were all searchlight strength?

"You tell me first," I said.

The storm raged over. Rain like a million baby fists pounding the car. I slowed down, pulled into a blank space. The seething engine, through with tantrums. The dashboard felt hot. I pulled the lighter out click. Put it pressed sizzle and lit cigarette number two.

Myers laughed. "Great," he said, saying nothing. And me saying nothing back. And whoever says nothing best, wins.

Which brings me to David Lynch.

A few nights before I met Myers, my wife bought the entire first season of *Twin Peaks* for a weekend marathon. I was hooked to Lynch's hypnotic story-telling style and his characters, especially a certain Agent Cooper (played in the series by Kyle MacLachlan). I couldn't help feeling this was who Myers wanted to be. Young, smart, inquisitive, spiritually gifted with the ability to locate answers in symbols and dreams. Cooper was a city-slicker who found himself in a small town, and loved it—unlike Myers, who seemed hardly interested in his surroundings. His empty face could go innocent or malicious, his eyes briny with sincerity or closed like a door. He tended to laugh when facing opposition, to joke when he didn't know an answer. Facts figures case scenarios like a long-winded lecturer like a loathsome FULL OF HIMSELF bore who needed to show there was no point in trying to stop him. Facts passed for cockiness and strut. I got the feeling he invented his own job, made it up on the spot, convinced others they couldn't do without him. Sold himself to some big hat with a problem. He was all job, jumping from place to place on the map. He was in service to some amorphous national entity that gave him no real connection to people, turf, community. He was being real or he was being fake. All faces fit perfectly. Yet with me on the street, he was different. I saw timidity, bits of humble and moments of fumble where he showed it was not his turf. He was NOT mister everyman. He did not BELONG everyplace. This time, he was the scrub.

Those first few days he was on me like glued. Took interest in every word every picture every nick and crook. Every scribble on the edge of my desk, every doodle on the side of the page. That my car was a 1998 Caprice somehow unsettled him. On the street, he stuck close. No major scenes, no fleet of cop cars, no flood of blue. Just Myers and me, knocking on doors, talking to people. (Sometimes the "Myers team," all two of them, put in an appearance as bookends.) Sitting in the Caprice and just watching. Who comes, who goes. "Stuck to me like glued." Coffee, cigarettes. The surreal aspect of me on South Bronx streets, involved in a case of national security. Hand-picked by some Washington yoohoo. I suppose I should have felt proud, elevated despite that MARK OF CAIN. "Still part of the team." But all I felt was

suckered

more like I'd been set up. My pockets filling up with cigarettes. Death threats? It was pretty funny how they always started to come in right around the time I had almost forgotten.

I had a hard time forgetting.

What happens when you fight to get in?
What happens when you get in?
What happens when you want out?

After three days, we still hadn't found Spook. No David either.

I should have gone to him first, Myers or no Myers. A costly mistake. I felt I led it all right to them. I had opened a door. It was me. I let something in, something ugly.

The South Bronx has always been a self-contained world to me. Take the 6 train, rolling down from green lawns of Pelham. Coasting through Westchester Avenue on elevated tracks. A turn and steep plummet into Hunts Point station. To speed under Southern Boulevard streets. Longwood Avenue, 149th Street, 143rd Street. Scraping against the Bruckner Expressway to Cypress Avenue, then Brook. The South Bronx ended right at 138th Street and Third Avenue, the last stop before going under the East River into Manhattan. That's where the planet mostly stopped. The world can go to shit south of that station, but up here—the same timeless timbales rhythms, the same girls dipping bare feet in cool streams of rushing hydrant water. It was the end and the beginning, that fucking 6 train. It was the Bronx troubadour spreading its snake length from south to south, bringing South Bronx to Park Place and back again. Could hear it pulsating in Willie Colón, in Eddie Palmieri, clatter boom bang and hiss of sliding doors. Could hear it on any salsa album from the late '60s or early '70s, though YOU CAN'T HEAR IT AT ALL on the Jennifer Lopez album named after the chugging Bronx local. 149th Street has its own sound like that roaring 6 train, that blast of steam pouring out of a crusty old radiator. As much small town as any city can be. The world and its events lay outside, distant. The South Bronx was any town in any spaghetti western, sleeping calm when the men in black pull up to the saloon. Bad guys make it easy in westerns: They wear black. They blow into town, and everyone knows. Ripples go through streets like stones skimming pond face. *Good guys bad guys* is a Hollywood formula. In the South Bronx right here right NOW, you cannot tell who is playing second base or outfield without a scorecard.

Myers needed that roster, the list of stats. He sucked out my intuition, the human side to the files the disks. He did not need my help with computer facts with cell phone data. He had the latest technology the fastest tricks. The electronic toys that read mail, hear phone calls, trace cell phones down to restroom cubicles in crowded malls. He had the machines. He had to show it off, as if starting the game with a display of force: It was a fucking bread truck. The old kind, big and boxy. Picture on both sides, huge Jewish kid face snacking on a slice of rye. *Levi's Bread*. Inside, knobs and screens with graphs that snaked and lines that swerved and a map in color and rows of blinking lights. His "team," those two always, those same two and never anyone else that I saw, working switches and knobs, earphones attached to faces as waxy as Ken, as inflexible as Barbie. A bread truck parked on the fucking Grand Concourse. What did he have to go and do that for? To tell me there were no FCC regulators hurling court orders at his ass, to remind me that his "team" was in that fucking bread truck meticulously working through the night.

You don't know what they're looking for, but you know they're looking.

I was no longer flattering myself that he sought me out for my expertise. In fact, I was striking out. Spook used a tried and true system of security. It wasn't hard for me to locate his squads, but this time he evidently went under with no security, no one with him. I told Myers that Spook was going solo, and this proved it. I knew his ways pretty well. I had my list of entrances and exits, particularly helpful during the Dirty Harry time. Chasing after Spook can be a real Tom and Jerry, but he would turn helpful if I was after someone else. Spook was just that kind of guy, ready-set to whittle down the competition. I guess he figured he'd take some dumb-cluck foreigner for the dough and invite him to come and get it. He could imagine some bunch of foreigners bumbling around every *cuchifritería*, searching that ghetto maze for a man with his own well-armed troop to protect him. The South Bronx is a complicated system of tunnels and trap doors, so maybe it wasn't so crazy for him to think he could get away with it. He just hadn't banked on the feds. I hadn't really either: Just what was with them? If Spook ripped off a pack of foreign terrorists bent on doing evil, the feds should be rolling with mirth that they got robbed! They should pin a medal on him, get him to work with them to set up the ringleaders, all U.S. Americans together fighting evil! Didn't they recruit the Mafia to fight Mussolini? Didn't they recruit the Mafia to assassinate Castro? What was so fucking outlandish about recruiting a spick dealer to fight for "his" country in a war on terror?

It seemed the thing that scared Myers the most was the possibility that Spook was truly alone in this. Dropped his security apparatus and did a fade-out with the whole bag. The money came and went. Spook opened four businesses, four bank accounts. He purchased four pieces of property, all in the South Bronx, each and every one the ratty kind of riot-gate shop stinking of rotted wood and empty shelves. These were his supposed investments in the scheme. He seemingly fronted the money from his own pocket, though looking at these pathetic properties it was unlikely he spent much. This was his goodwill tactic, promising these people not only a front for floating money but four locations in the South Bronx they could use for whatever purposes pleased them. This probably excited them, a home base with Manhattan just twenty minutes away on the 5 train. We were still getting down to the nitty-gritty of how Spook pulled the swipe, but it was clear the terrorists got sold four ramshackle properties in the South Bronx for ten million bucks. It was all they walked away with. The money had already passed through by the time the feds arrested the four losers left holding the bank accounts. Of the four, two were from Spook's family of regulars. Outer-fringers, Spook must have pulled them from a hat. He paid them each eight thousand dollars. Just another small business banking its money, right? They saw the money come and they saw the money go. Afterwards they still had eight thousand dollars in the bank. They also had federal agents asking them WHERE IS IT?

The other two were foreigners. Spook banked four million with them in separate joint accounts. They didn't even have eight thousand after it was over. They had expired visas, few documents, and fake Social Security numbers. They claimed to be Saudi Arabian students with very wealthy parents who had just gotten swindled big time. They were young, a little scruffy, and somehow accustomed to interrogations. Myers took me to see them at an FBI office downtown. They sure looked Puerto Rican to me in that way Arabs sometimes do. The two Spook regulars were pretty freaked out by the feds and were relieved to see me, a *compa'i* who could speak their Spanglish. They were a torrent of words, nothing to hide, talked volumes. They knew *nada* about the money or where it came from.

"And you believed them?"

"That's right," I told Myers. "People who don't know can't talk."

"So you're saying he likes to involve civilians, innocent types, people who don't know. Is that right?"

I didn't really get where this was going until later, when he and I were blowing down a couple of slices in my car. We were a few blocks from the precinct, going down the list of Spook people. Myers had his own list, drawn I imagine from his bread truck tricks, his electronic toys. Even with all that, he didn't have a knowledge of *cuevitas*, those little holes they go scurrying into when trouble comes, those loose lines of contact with the normal folk in the community who don't get picked up by bread trucks. I gave him my informa-tion. Maybe he would take it and go away. He was pushing for big raids. He didn't understand about the big splash and how it always causes a stink. You make a splash in one place and everybody else you don't nab will head into *cuevitas* so deep . . . could spend months looking and nobody on the street is going to tell you, not after a splash. Nobody likes so much noise. Sources dry up, the streets stop talking. There were times when it could do the precinct some good to be "seen" making raids, the sign of an active police force doing its thing. In most cases these raids were stage managed with the care of a Broadway production. Myers didn't know about that. His was a boyish enthusiasm that soon played itself out. I felt him pushing me. I sensed he was trying to get underneath me, lead me to make some admission. When I insisted this was a Spook solo number, he wanted to know how I knew, how I could be so sure. And yet we had spent the past day and a half looking up the people who guard Spook. Myers knew as well as I that none of them were with the man.

"But would that make sense to you? That he would swipe ten million bucks off some goons, then run off without his team to protect him?"

"The team wasn't in on it."

"But if he has no security?"

"How secure would you feel surrounded by a pack of hot-headed South Bronx gunboys? Would you tell them you have ten million dollars?"

My words slowed him down a bit. He seemed to launch countless little offensives, but once blunted, would lapse into moody silence. There was a lack of air. We had long ago finished our slices. I rolled down a window and lit two cigarettes. There was the tender touch of rain droplets appearing on the windshield like blisters.

"He probably figured it was easier for him to ditch the gang." I was blowing out smoke, relishing the warm harsh. "He can hole out someplace safe while the gang takes the blame, and maybe gets the bullets. Maybe we're playing into his hands."

"But you still think we can find him?"

"Yes."

"What about his brother?"

My stomach was churning bad.

"He's not always helpful."

"What does that mean?"

"It means sometimes he doesn't know."

"But what if he knows this time?"

I pinched my eyes shut. I could feel the next Myers offensive coming, that relentless assault of words. I felt tired just looking at him.

"I told you, he's clean."

"Clean. Exactly the type his brother utilizes to perfection. What better place to stash the money?"

"What worse place. His brother's? Didn't you just come up with it? How much of a stretch could it be?"

"His brother could be a front for the entire operation."

"David Rosario has never been involved in criminal activity. He wouldn't swipe a paper clip."

"He bailed Spook out of jail."

"That's right, a couple of times."

"Sounds like involvement to me."

"Hey, don't you have any brothers or sisters? He sometimes takes care of his wayward little brother. But not crime. He won't break the law."

"How about the fact that Spook shows up at his apartment? He was there three times last week. Why is it that, if we watch David, we get Spook?"

Some cold wind blowing from him. Somehow, some way my blood was turning to ice. I was burning and freezing at the same time.

"So you've been watching him," I said.

That's the thing about feds, Jack told me. They might know things but they won't tell you. Maybe not right off, maybe only when they want to use the information to make you do something. You don't have the information. In many cases you don't even see it. I expected Myers would get as cryptic as the Book of Revelations, but that wasn't what was coming.

"That's right," he said. "I don't have a big team, you know that. Three weeks ago I managed to place somebody with David Rosario."

"An operative?"

I was sucking on that cigarette too fast, or something else was making the surroundings shrink, all pressing in toward me.

"Let's just say *a good friend*."

"So if you have the information David has it, why are you chasing Spook?"

"I don't have the information that it's at David's. But I know it's the two of them. It's between them somehow and I'm going to find it."

His insistence, pressing against my temples, my neck. I started the car.

"You told me you wanted to trace the money to its source, to follow it on its journey through those terrorist arteries. To know who's who—who fills the trough and who feeds at it. You told me that just talking to Spook could give you valuable information. Now all you're talking about is the money. So what do you want? Is it the money, or is it Spook?"

He rubbed his eyes. "One leads to the other, that's right."

"So you want Spook to hand over the money?"

"The money's course has been interrupted." It was a night voice, a horror-movie narration. "The flow has to be reestablished. A lot of people went to a lot of trouble to set this up. A lot rides on this. There has to be a way to salvage this, to set the money back on its course." Black mask, red parted lips, and some tongue-flicking like in that Marilyn Manson video.

"Sounds like you just want to give it back," I muttered, more to my cigarette. "Is that right? Do you think you're going to get Spook to give it back?"

"The important thing is that we find him, and find him first . . . before the others do."

Who says Myers had to be wrong about David and Spook? The two of them could be in perfect touch, symbiotic, instinctive. And what about those "others" who are after him? Good guys bad guys? Arab terrorists running around on American streets? See the first *Back to the Future*, also the '80s classic *Into the Night,* with a young Michelle Pfeiffer and Jeff Goldblum. Could imagine talking to people on South Bronx streets: *Seen any Arabs around here lately?* So many Arabs look like Puerto Ricans. All they have to do is learn some Spanglish.

"They don't have to be Arabs," Myers said, sick of my jokes. "They could hire anybody to do the job—anybody."

The feds working to retrieve money stolen from a group of terrorists? This was not a plot twist I wanted to deal with. My wife rented the Coen brothers. *Blood Simple*: how one simple mistake leads to another simple mistake, and after that, does it matter how it began? I was on my fifth cigarette that day. Some days it's only two or three. Some days you hit five without thinking.

The 5 train is another South Bronx rhythm, cutting across the middle of the borough. Goes underground through Manhattan, all the way into Brooklyn before turning back. Climbs out to open air on elevated tracks just after that other Third Avenue station at 149th Street. It clatters past small shops, a post office, and the running track, before its first outdoor stop by the tall projects. The Jackson Avenue station looks more like a worn-out house suspended over traffic. The round bulby lamps along the platform glow at night like fiery lemon drops. The 5 train runs all the way down Westchester Avenue until it hits Southern Boulevard. Makes that sharp turn right after the Freeman Street station. Trains howl when they hit that curve, even though they hit it slow. It is an animal sound, dogs crying, flutes wailing, a sound that has always been and will ever be. I remember it when I was a little kid and subway cars were black and boxy. I remember walking with my father toward Hunts Point. I must have been seven or eight. I was holding his hand, and looked back at that wailing sound to see those train cars up on elevated tracks all lit up like a string of jewels and Southern Boulevard all covered in flashing lights and Christmas wreaths that hung across the street over traffic. These things have not changed. Christmas wreaths still hang over traffic during the holiday season, and the trains still play their melancholic pipes. The trains are silvery smooth now, hydraulic systems adding a rising whine to the clatter of a passing train. A different song for a new generation to learn. A straight line from past to present, the one true continuity in a place where the landscape changes constantly. The South Bronx has become more like a city rebuilt after a war than the old town whose stories are etched in jagged tenement brick. Change comes. Change kills the past.

On the third day, Myers excused himself. "It's not like I don't love you, but I have to meet with the FBI. They're trying to horn in." He had this habit of calling on the cell phone. "Where are you?" he would ask. I was driving under the 5 train. Spook had a million cousins. One of them told me he had just gotten a visit from him where she lived on Fordham Road, so I headed out there. I knew Spook had a place he used to rent on White Plains Road. I had barely scraped the door with my fist when it swung open. I quickly pulled out my gun, moving into the apartment carefully. The place was a mess. Drawers pulled out, clothes thrown everywhere, a floor lamp tipped over. Too late. I got on the horn and called Jack. I was too late. Cop cars under the el. Lieutenant Jack and I smoking cigarettes on the stoop.

"Did you tell Myers?"

"I left him a message," I said. "He's downtown."

"What do you think?"

I couldn't put the uneasy feeling into words. The door

was open but the lock wasn't busted. The place was ran-
sacked, gone through, searched. A broken lamp, kicked-over
table and chair, the general disarray of a fist fight.

"I think they took him," I said, now thinking about what
Myers said, about "others" out there also in on the hunt. If
there were "others," they must be well-informed, because
who knew about this place? How could some outsider sneak
into town, find Spook unguarded, and take him? We ques-
tioned neighbors, street people, *bodegueros*. Nobody saw or
heard anything. Lieutenant Jack and I snapped into rhythm.
It was almost the old days again. I took the opportunity
during another cigarette break to fill him in on everything—
clearance or not, I didn't give a damn because it was cop
business and I wanted him in on it, I wanted him knowing.
It was a calm cigarette moment for us.

"You really think this guy did it," Jack asked, "swiped all
that cash?"

"Sure he did," I said. It was mostly the cigarette talking.
"He took it and hid it."

"So the feds are looking for it?"

"Yeah," I laughed. "Isn't that a kick?"

"Good thing I don't know anything about it," Jack said.
We both laughed like two small town cops making fun of the
ways of the big boys. We laughed until the coughing came,
some cigarette gone the wrong way. Too deep an inhale. A
wet-eyed sting.

"They should pin a medal on him for ripping off some
creeps, instead of chasing him like a rat," I said.

"Maybe they would," Jack said, "if they could find
him."

I called Jaco, Wiggie, and Quique, three of Spook's district chiefs. I told them I had reason to believe Spook got
grabbed, but after leaving messages and talking to Jaco,
all I got was the feeling that they didn't know shit, either
about what Spook had been doing or where he would be
now. Spook had the habit of clearing out. He would go un-

derground for weeks. He was not the type people would file a missing-person report on.

When Myers appeared, he seemed glum. He kept his hands in his pockets and seconded my feeling.

"They took him," he said. "We need to search some of his other places. Did you contact his brother?"

"I left a couple of messages," I said. "He hasn't gotten back to me."

Myers pulled out his flip-pad. "What can you tell me about a guy named Santo Romas?"

Memory bursts. Quick flick and there was a cigarette. Like I was back on home turf. Click. Flash. Light.

"Santo Romas, a.k.a., Sancho P., a.k.a., Smooth, real name Louis Santo Romas. Fenced stolen goods, forged documents. Credit card fraud. Caught him a year ago when Spook tried to turn some ready cash into jewelry."

"Jewelry?"

"Diamonds, stones. Fine-cut shit. When cash needs to be shrunk portable size."

"Well, some flunky just arrested this character at Kennedy Airport last night. He had ten thousand bucks on him. Fresh bank stuff. He should've turned it into stones! The ATF thinks it's a drug case, but I think . . . a definite person of interest in this case."

I was feeling a funny tremor. A low, thumping bass note.

"Where was he going?" The cigarette was making me sick.

"Mallorca."

"Excuse me?"

"Miami," Myers said. "Looks like the guy thought it was retirement time. Maybe you should come with me downtown tomorrow to talk to him."

The headache was back, hammers pounding a spot right between my eyes. I stared at Jack across the street laughing with some cops. I felt suddenly cut off from him, from them, from an old life.

"We have a record of Spook calling him. Looks like they did business recently."

"You know that? You bugged Spook's phone?"

Myers smiled smug, a bit of confidence through the glumness.

"Sure," he said. "It's what led me to David Rosario. Every person he has had contact with, done business with. How could I not get on his brother? For a guy who isn't involved in the business, he sure did a lot of phone time with Spook recently."

Why was he talking about David again?

"Everything leaves a trail." He nodded significantly.

"And how long have you been bugging David's phone?"

Myers took a moment to answer. "This investigation is almost a month old."

The nausea was coming back. Fucking cigarettes. I puffed away.

"It would take me that long just to get permission from a court to use a wiretap," I said.

"Yes, my friend, we're all aware of cop speed. My motto has always been, *Once you have the equipment, use it*. Obviously, a lot of the material gathered would not be admissable in court due to methods used to acquire it. But who says we'll ever need to go before a court? We're moving at federal speed here, Sanchez. No reason legality has to become a speed bump."

Maybe a migraine. Lights too bright. The bad taste in my mouth made me spit. I ditched the cigarette, saying to myself now, *Yeah, for sure I will quit*. A Puerto Rican with ten thousand in cash will never make it past Customs.

"I'm going to head up to Kennedy Airport and bring the guy downtown," Myers said. "Maybe we can talk to him." As if Santo Romas would need a translator.

"Okay," I said, surrendering to some overpowering flow, an inevitable energy. Somehow I felt I was pursuing myself, across tenement rooftops, waiting patiently parked down the street. Those stones hitting my back window. There was a famous dictator who said it once. *What really happened doesn't matter. What counts is winning. After that, the winner can tell the story whichever way is better.*

I was saying that. It was almost a prayer.

12.

She was a dancer.

Leni Riefenstahl
was born in 1902, in the Wedding district of Berlin. Her
mother dreamed of having a daughter who would become
a famous actress. One day Leni went to a film audition
and happened to stroll by the open door of a dance studio.
She was enthralled, signed up for lessons. Convinced her
mother that this was what she was born to do. Soon she
was doing recitals and getting rave reviews in Berlin newspapers. She might have stayed a dancer if not for a film she
saw called *The Mountain of Destiny*. She was so enthralled that
she hunted down the director and told him that starring in
his next film was what she was born to do. It is not really
clear what she did to the director, but not only did she star
in his next film, *The Holy Mountain*, it was also dedicated *To
the dancer, Leni Riefenstahl*.

Leni danced her way through a couple more films,
though now she had become convinced that filmmaking
was what she had been born to do. She decided to shoot
her own film, wrote a script called *The Blue Light*, and after
many hardships managed to shoot it. The picture opened
to mostly favorable reviews, but the experience was dis-
enchanting. Filmmaking is expensive, and it wasn't easy
getting sophisticated Berlin producers to finance her
kitschy ideas about mountains and naked nature girls doing dances by shimmering moonlit lakes. If directing was
a man's world, then maybe it was time for a new world
order. When she went to hear Adolf Hitler speak in Feb-

ruary 1932, she was enthralled and wrote him a postcard begging to meet him. Just so happened that Hitler had already noticed her doing that nature dance by a shimmery moonlit lake in *The Blue Light*. He offered her a job he knew she was born to do, complete with the promise of an unlimited budget, unlimited access, and enough film to give her imagination free reign.

It was the opportunity of a lifetime.

Leni Riefenstahl insists to this day that she was forced into making films for the Nazis, but it is very likely she saw Hitler as that big producer she could charm into doing her bidding. She was carving a path through terrain just like the short guy with the mustache.

Was remembering so hard? Was telling the truth such a chore?

She stepped out on the fire escape.

The gun was in her hand.

She went down the steps slowly, knees trembly weak. She gave the bed a last look, where she had left him.

He was not moving.

He lay like sleeping. It brought a strange guilt. She knew he had been drinking, that coming back to consciousness would always be slow. She hadn't killed him. She hadn't hit him so hard. She hadn't. She had gone out the window and turned back. She watched him as he lay sleeping. Like she did the first time she came.

He knew nothing.

She righted the chair that had fallen over in the kitchen. Swept up the sugar cubes, wiped away the spilled milk. Put the roll of tape back under the sink. She decided not to tie him up. She would not come back, but rather jump into the next square and hope for more open doors. And yet leaving, and leaving him there lying like that. A churning disquiet.

"I was a bad dream," she said into his ear. "I never happened."

Now going down those fire escape steps.

"I never happened," she said. "I was never here."

Like using an eraser. Like taking it back. A record was skipping. A record was stuck.

She was a model.

<u>Anne Sexton</u>
was born in 1928 and lived all her life in the Boston area. Princeton, Newton, Weston, Cambridge. Roxbury—clatter of the T across cobbled streets to the Harvard Square station. The pictures, so many pictures. A dark-eyed beauty posing like Rita Hayworth, like a '40s sex kitty with big smoldering eyes born to stun to startle to take prisoners.

She carried a bulging portfolio of snaps, but modeling fell from her like dead skin. She got married instead, in 1948. To start out as one thing and become another. The search for definition, for a definition one can live with. You become something until it doesn't become you anymore.

Anne Sexton became a poet. Wife, mother of two, she tried to kill herself and in a mental hospital discovered she could write. Drumming out lines passionate strange. Poetry did not save her from suicide but it did save her long enough for her to write eight books. She had dark ghosts following her, but when she wrote, she was as courageous as ARMY WAR HEROES. She blew houses down with cluster bombs of words, with images that stuck in the mind like thumbtacks. She wrote about crimes that dropped on her as if from a high building. The poem was "The Legend of the One-Eyed Man." The titles of her books seemed to reflect the struggle between staying alive or popping the escape hatch. By her last book, *The Awful Rowing Toward God*, it sounded like she had made up her mind.

She carefully snuck past the windows on the lower floor. Street sounds. Buses stop and go. That kid going, *Yo Ritchie!* and the scrape of the *piraguero's* shaver against the block of ice. Down another flight. As she reached the window, she squatted. She strained to hear, pressed against sharp brick.

The window was open a little from the bottom. The blinds were drawn but the slats were slanted to let sun in. She could see inside, past the wispy smoke of thin lace curtains.

The room was large. There was a bed, a bureau, a small table. An expanse of floor covered in shiny red linoleum. She recalled the candlelight, the Mexican girl's fringed dress. The CD player sat on the bureau like a fat silver bullet.

The gun was in her hand.

Women are born twice, Anne Sexton wrote.

She was an actress.

Marlene Dietrich

was born in 1901 in Schöneburg, a district of Berlin. She was a spoiled young blonde, attracted to the theater. Her mother packed her off to study music instead in Weimar, the home of Goethe. Marlene soon tired of the violin and returned to Berlin, to sign up at the Max Reinhardt School to study acting. She appeared in plays and, in 1923, her first movie. In most cases, she was just the pretty blonde with the legs. By 1928 she had appeared in thirteen films, was married five years, and had a four-year-old daughter. She was nearing thirty by the time Josef von Sternberg cast her as his "Lola" in *The Blue Angel*. Her career had run its course in Berlin. No one seemed willing to give her a contract, so she took Sternberg up on his offer and went with him to Hollywood. They made seven films together, Marlene crafting the look while Sternberg handled the camera, the lighting. Marlene would never look more beautiful than she did through Sternberg's eyes. They both created a presence mightier than substance, a huge glamour myth that destroyed any semblance of reality. She would forever treasure those films, love notes from a man entranced, a man she could work together with. She saw them as fine art, beautifully crafted paintings, no matter how trite, no matter how slight. After Sternberg, she made countless films, throwaway pictures, legs, a face, a smoldering cigarette. She was under contract, a working actress going where the jobs were. "I sell glamour just as another sells fish or shoelaces," she said. Too much praise made her grumpy. It was nothing special.

While she was working in Hollywood, the Nazis took Berlin. (They would eventually take Paris, the other city she loved.) Marlene was not enthralled by Hitler. She had no illusions about what he represented. The Nazis courted her, offering her vast sums of money if she would return to Germany, renounce Jew Hollywood, and become a true Aryan again. She made what she later called "the only decision possible," even though her mother and older sister insisted on remaining in Berlin. While Leni Riefenstahl shot her films glorifying the Nazis, Marlene became a United States citizen. When the war came, she went to work for the USO, singing and entertaining American troops. The only way to beat the Nazis was from the outside. It must be painful to live abroad while your hometown gets bombed into the Stone Age.

The war wrenched Berlin away from her. It took her mother six months after its end. By the time she returned to Germany fifteen years later, she had remade herself from glamourous actress to glamourous *chanteuse*, living off old glory like a veteran wearing medals. She loved singing those old sentimental Berlin songs, but when she came back to Germany to sing them, there were protests and stink bombs. Some people hated her for leaving. Some people hated her for coming back. She never returned again, feeling spurned. She settled in Paris, and died there. She wrote her memoir, *Thank God I Am a Berliner*, in French. She sang her love songs to the city from afar, from Paris New York Rio de Janiero Moscow and Warsaw, where she walked to the monument and laid flowers for the dead. She fought for her country. She turned her back on her country. She fought for her country by turning her back on her country.

Safety off. Creaky floor. Moved past toilet, tiny frosted window asparkle with sun. Goofy flowered shower curtain. The living room canyoned out after that. Cushy furniture, thick curtains. Entertainment center—stereo TV speakers a wall of CDs a shelf of ceramic knick-knacks froggies carrying Puerto Rican flags an ashtray that said BIENVENIDO A LA ISLA DEL ENCANTO—"I thought I might see you again," he said, not even flinching.

Not a line on his face moved, so stone clear-eyed as he sat there at the kitchen table. Blazing cigarette tip. Like he was expecting her. Stared at her and not the gun, as if it wasn't there. As if you can ignore a gun if a woman is holding it.

"I was hoping it wasn't you, though. I was hoping it was someone else." His voice calm steady. Thin blue plume of smoke up. "Because if you were someone else, I would have dropped you."

The eye patch gave his face a sullen, frozen-stiff feel. A statue talking, the way he sat so bolt upright. He moved only to bring cigarette to lips, to tap ash into Puerto Rican ceramic. Pictures of palm trees, a beach. Those fucking tree frogs.

"I would've dropped you when you stopped in the bathroom to check out the goofy flowered shower curtain."

A blur of movement. Subtle enough she saw the gun.

Almost invisible so steel-black against black matador pants. In his lap, no sudden move. He had the drop on her; she had the drop on him. He exhaled like he detested such scenes.

"You should put the gun away," he said.

She did not take her eyes off the gun in his lap, the hand lying casually beside it on his thigh. Her arms aching, a rubber band about to snap, and she couldn't be sure about not squeezing the trigger. A sneeze would do it, a pinkie flick.

The coffee pot started gurgling. What is it with Puerto Ricans and coffee? It pissed her off to hold the gun in a stance like that while he seemed so remote and untouched by threat. The angle he tilted his head to keep her in sight of his one eye reminded her of a caged panther staring back. He turned his face a little to receive cigarette to lips. A slow, thin puff. *I have remembered much about Judas.*

She shook off the intruding Anne.

The kitchen was not large. From his spot at the table, he pulled coffee off flame. A simple movement. She almost shot him. The way he poured coffee into his cup a challenge, an affront. He was daring her to shoot him, or he just didn't believe she could. Puerto Ricans must be well accustomed to having strangers stroll through their houses. He took another puff, still waiting for her to tell him. She would not lower the gun. His did not shift from where it sat on his thigh, on its side with his hand by it so snug. "The gun kept going off," she could tell the judge.

The phone started ringing. He didn't move a muscle.

"Don't you answer your phone?"

That was her first question to him.

"I have voice mail," he said.

The phone stopped ringing.

She watched the limp gunhand. Not necessarily unvigilant. With his other hand he deposited his cigarette in the CAGUAS, CITY OF DREAMS ashtray, then took another hit of coffee. He always seemed aware of her even when he wasn't directly looking at her. He reclaimed his cigarette from the ashtray's slotted holder and took another puff.

"So, what are you?" He picked flakes of tobacco off his lips. "ATF? FBI? Some kind of narc?"

She was thinking: *I'm going to have to shoot him.*

"I figured you were something like that the first time I saw you with David. He's that kind of people. Attracts cops. Like flies to shit."

"I'm not," she said. The other words wouldn't come out.

"David draws bad luck like a magnet. He's not the kind of person who should involve himself in underhanded things. I told Tony. We all had a good thing going, man."

He was nodding like nothing could be plainer. The word flow seemed to psych him up, a wrestler pumping himself up before the big lift.

"What I'm telling you is, I voted no. I wanted nothing to do with it. You know that. Are you wired?" He seemed to lose patience. "Just what the hell do you want?"

"David's dead," she said.

It was a thin crack, cutting through stone. A semblance of crease, flinch. Cigarette hand moving hypnotic slow, close to lips, no puff, close to lips. Something sagged, she could feel it. Her gun retracted slightly, slowly, unconsciously, as the reality of the phrase sank in. *David's dead.* Final, blank. She was blinking fast. He took a good deep draw. A semblance of rock-hard, restored.

"I just heard about Tony. Two days I been sitting here, waiting for the other shoe to drop. You sure he's dead?"

It shook her. The images that came in waves. The gun was a useless dead weight.

"I just came from there," she said.

The phone started ringing again.

"Did anybody see you come here?"

"No."

"Are you sure? Were you followed?"

"I said no."

"Did you come straight here from there?"

"No!"

The questions shot out fast, as if he were ashamed to ask. The phone stopped ringing—a sudden silence, an elevator drop. He stubbed the cigarette out and, in the same motion, placed his gun on the table by his coffee. A desolate emptiness passed over his face like a shadow.

"What happened?"

The burning dizzy. The hateful need to use words. She decided fast: David had trusted him. She exhaled, sank into a chair. Her eyes—she blinked fast, wiped clumsy, not wanting to look at him.

One-Eye reached into a nearby cabinet. The bottle of rum looked warm, worn like old leather. The two shot glasses clinked in his hand. He poured rum into both, made a vague toasting gesture, and took his shot. Slammed his glass on the table CLACK.

"They figured out it was at his house," she said. "I was there when they came."

The shot of rum was a flaming breath, a deep kiss that left a gratifying tremor.

"They were stupid enough to call and leave a message. They said they had Tony, and he was dead unless he gave them what they wanted."

"Did he? Give them what they want?"

"No." The air went out of the room. "He gave it to me."

"To you?"

One-Eye rubbed his face with his hand, trying to blot out, stamp out, somehow erase.

"And it, it . . . what the fuck is 'it'?"

He got up from the table. The kitchen was too small for him to pace. He ended up against the counter, staring at the light brown wood grain.

"At David's house. I wouldn't have expected that. David always played the law-abiding citizen, always helping out his crooked little brother. And yet he was the one that pushed Tony into it. Tony loved that I-spy shit. He liked the underground. Magic keys, special codes. Safe-deposit boxes. An intricate pickup and delivery. Tony has a million cousins." He poured his next shot, standing. "I'll bet you ten million dollars that what you have is a key. A small key, maybe to a locker in a train station or a safe-deposit box."

She didn't say anything. One-Eye stared at her like he had already gotten his answer.

"So you ended up with the hot potato." He lit the next cigarette with a quick desultory motion. Dragged for all it was worth. "What are you going to do with it?"

"Not let them get it," she said.

"Shit. They're going to think you have it anyway when they don't find it. And here, you had to come *here!*"

"It was another promise I made David."

"To come to me? What for? I wasn't in it. I said no. I'm the only one they asked. Wiggie, Jaco, Quique, they don't know shit. I can imagine how they'll feel when they find out. The two brothers decided to pull a heist and run off, hit it big and disappear. Leave the organization holding the bag. Because that's what's going to happen. You know that. Once those two vanished with the dough, the cops would swoop down on us. It's the end of everything, a cheap-ass sellout of the organization. I told them I'd rather go it alone, just do a fade-out and start someplace else. I just wasn't into it."

"David told me if things went wrong I should come to you. He said you were the only person outside of Tony that he completely trusted."

"Didn't you hear me? I said I'm not into it."

"It was why he wanted me to meet you, that one time when we . . . when he picked up the ID cards."

She remembered how uptight One-Eye had been when she and David went to meet him one Saturday almost a month before. They had walked up the hill in St. Mary's

Park, bought *coquitos*, sat by the running track behind the projects. David told him she was absolutely IN.

"Well, I'm absolutely NOT," One-Eye had said. "Just don't mix me up in it." He'd handed over the cards so David could check them out. There was a work ID and a driver's license. Both had his face. Both had a fake name. How could One-Eye think he wasn't involved?

"You know what those cards were for," she said.

A huff of smoke.

"I make cards for a lot of people. It's one of the things I do. I tell you what else I do: A week ago he called me. Wouldn't talk on the phone, I had to meet him. Somebody was after him. *Don't tell Tony*, he said. I gave him a Smith & Wesson mini .22, with two clips." Contempt made his lips curl. "It's the same gun you've got." He closed his eye a moment, as if his whole system had shut down for meditation. "Why he didn't use it to defend himself is beyond me."

"He thought he could talk to them," she said, feeling her eyes burn. The rum was making her feel disconnected. "They had Tony. He wanted to stall, to bargain for Tony's life."

The one eye was a round black stone.

"I tried to tell him to run with me," she said.

The hesitation was now on her, the hatred of words. She was thinking she made a big mistake coming down that fire escape. What was Anne trying to tell her with that poem about betrayal and the Judas kiss? She wanted to take everything back: to go back up the fire escape steps. The need for tobacco reminded her of Alex, of his words about bad spirits and confusion. She took a cigarette from the pack and lit fast. *Changó, Changó.* The god of imposters, sometimes.

"Don't you get it? I tried to shield the organization from this! I can't help you."

"You don't have to help me," she said. "Help David."

"Why should I?" His eye went cold hard. "You going to tell me there are ten million reasons?"

David had said One-Eye possessed a lot of integrity to turn down a piece of ten million dollars. She could see it in his stiff bearing, the almost sneer, as if such fantasies were beneath him.

"There's maybe one reason to start with," she said. "The bastard who killed David also killed Tony."

She watched the eye go glassy behind the cigarette smoke.

"David wanted you to get this tape to Sanchez," she said, reaching into her purse. "He didn't have time. He knew you could get this to Sanchez for him."

"You know about Sanchez?"

"No," she said. "But you know him. You know if you can trust him."

One-Eye's face was blank. He picked up the tape.

"It's from David's answering machine," she said. His fingers were tapping on the cassette, clack clack clack. "The killer is on it."

"What's Sanchez supposed to do with it?"

"He's supposed to make a choice," she said.

One-Eye was packing for a real fade-out. A black 4x4 parked at the bus stop. Two young scruffs ditched cigarettes and moved in opposite directions across the block, taking up post. She was by the fire escape window, thinking: *Go back. Go back up the fire escape steps.* In a moment, maybe they would be coming upstairs to collect One-Eye, to collect her . . . ? For One-Eye had snapped into action, telling her she wasn't going to run around on her own like that. After all, the organization had a stake in this. This was more or less a family issue and she should understand that. The best thing to do was for One-Eye to deliver her to Sanchez. *Like Judas I have done my wrong.* The betrayal, the Judas

kiss? She was thinking of mistakes, flashes of her dream
with Sarita intruding like pangs of conscience. How she
whacked Alex, left him for dead. (Not dead, sleeping. She
made sure.) There was a sick guilt, along with the weird
sense that she had blown it. *You'll be with someone, but don't
fear him.* Looking deep into that glimmery one eye and feeling she had made a mistake. Maybe he felt that way too,
seeing her pull the gun on him right there in his bedroom,
where he was still packing the duffel for his flight.

"No," she said. "I can't."

"But don't you want to stop this?"

"I made a promise."

His face darkened with disappointment. "Are you going to go through with it?"

"Yes."

"You think it's worth it?" he asked.

"It's me they're after."

One-Eye was looking past her, at the fire escape window. "Do you know what you have to do?"

"Yes," she said. "David said you were a man of dignity.
So why don't you show some and turn around so that I can
go out the way I came in?"

"You're making a mistake," he said.

"Just give the tape to Sanchez."

"But maybe he can find a way to put a stop to this.
You're not gonna get away with ten million dollars!"

"Turn around."

"My people are downstairs," he said. "Don't do anything stupid."

When he turned, she swung the gun. He crumpled, hitting the floor with a bony clatter.

13.

David Rosario's apartment was a mess. Drawers, boxes, pots and pans. Turned over kicked down pulled out. Kitchen cabinets thrown open. The gray couch had its cushions slashed, the back ripped down to reveal its skeletal frame.

The desk. Drawers open, papers strewn. He must have just picked up those rolls of film from the developer's. The packets had been opened, the pictures scattered. Snapshots of him happy smiling. An office party. The blonde I saw in his office. The way they snug laughed in the snaps, all close.

I should have come looking for him. He never answered my calls. I must have left three messages on his machine at home. It was why the lieutenant found me squatting by the small table beside the desk. The phone was there, but no answering machine. I knew there had been one. I'd seen it myself that time I was here. It was missing.

"Are you sure?"

Lieutenant Jack's round face creased up. I showed him the short connection cord, still attached to the phone. The phone jack was about ten feet away. The connecting cord, which would have gone from the jack to the machine, was gone too.

The time I came here to see Spook, David let me in. I was trying to get Spook to help me line up some witnesses to testify against Dirty Harry. He was on the gray couch, while David went back to the little table where the phone was. The machine was a clunky old Panasonic that used regular audio cassettes. David had been clearing messages when I came. My messages would have been on the machine's tape, along with something else. The something else that probably made someone swipe it.

There were keys lined up on the desk, as if meticulously examined—and rejected. There was a lockbox designed for the storage of a firearm. It was empty except for a clip of .22 ammunition and a leather holster. I was still doing the math when Lieutenant Jack did the tour guide routine. He was a nut for ballistics and forensics. He had a good team. These guys could make a room talk.

The killers had picked the lock. It was a pro job. (The locksmith was on his way.) They'd busted the flimsy chain on the door and poured into the bedroom. David must have had his back to them when they came. They blasted a bullet into his back that exited through his chest and lodged in the wall. When he fell, they pumped another bullet into his head. The bullet went through the floor. Scared the hell out of Mrs. Garcia, who lives in the apartment below with her three cats. She heard a third shot. This one shattered the window, perforated the blinds. The bullet chinked off the fire escape, and lay in the alley in a white chalk circle.

That bullet was meant for someone else.

"That would be the blond girl," Jack said, popping another stick of gum. Jack tended to chew gum compulsively at murder scenes. He said it killed the stink. He handed me a photo, his pick from the bunch.

"Myers identified her. Ava Reynolds. Twenty-six. Works with Rosario at the ad agency. His personal assistant. Looks pretty personal judging by these snaps. Got a couple of witnesses that spotted her running toward Westchester Avenue. Barefoot. In a minidress."

Her face. A white chalk circle. His pockets were pulled out, his shoes removed, pants unbuckled. IDs, wallet intact. Rings remained on fingers. The energy on Myers was an intense bright light. He was the first one on the scene. The other cops rubbing sleep from pupils all cloudy dark. Only way was to keep squinting.

"If I had something and didn't want you to get it, I would hand it to someone else," he said. "I would try to stall the killer so she could get away."

"She?"

The sure confidence of him turned everything around him into sludge. I was molasses. We were all mollusks.

"That's right. Tried to stall them so she could get away. The killers knew she had it on her. The killers knew when they came in. They tried to intercept a pickup. It's why they came."

"But he had a gun," Lieutenant Jack said. "There was a gun here. He could have used it to defend himself. It's missing. We haven't found it."

"Gentlemen, I remind you that Spook is still missing and has not been found. It's a possibility that they contacted David, to get him to hand it over. They probably threatened to kill him unless David handed it over. Instead of handing it over, David thought he would stall while the girl made the getaway with the goods. It's possible."

"Maybe they called on the phone," I said.

"The answering machine is missing," Lieutenant Jack added.

Myers gave the phone table a look. "It's possible," he said.

"Did you get anything from your wiretaps?"

This was the first time I alluded to Myers and his bread truck in public, that is, alongside Jack. Myers squinted at me and glanced at Jack. There were other officers around.

"Unfortunately, we had a weird system breakdown," he said, not missing a beat. All Myers talk had a rhythm, a marching cadence. "We've been down for three days now."

"Tough break," I said.

"We have to think that maybe these people have Spook. They might have made him talk. They didn't come here for payback. They came to find the money, or whatever leads to the money. They knew it was here. And they figured that whoever had it here didn't intend for the money to reach its destination."

The pale totem face beside him, his fellow agent, never said a word. Never registered words or the sound of them. Stood looking about as if he was guarding his man. The other agent was by the door to the living room, same blank face watching everyone. It was like they were memorizing us. I just kept asking myself, if they were both here, who was in the bread truck? Was Myers telling the truth about the system being down?

I wanted the next cigarette. I swiped three from Sergeant Mooney, but no smoking at a murder scene. A dead body should remain as pure as possible, the air untouched by nicotine, by scents and smells. Skin is highly receptive, even in death. A bit of cigarette ash on a thumb does not only change its smell. It can distort a vast network of minute data, or worse: wipe it out. Yet I wanted the next cigarette. To light and puff. To block words from coming, from spilling out.

Myers seemed to have developed the ability to ignore Jack completely. Maybe he was trying to dismiss him as a gum-crack wise-ass. I'm sure Jack realized that. It didn't stop him. It made him worse.

"But he had a gun. Why would he not use it to pop these bastards?"

"He thought he could talk to them," Myers said. "Just think, if they're holding his brother."

"But maybe the gun would have kept him alive."

"He gave the gun to the girl."

"You know that for a fact, yeah?"

"It hasn't been found."

"Maybe the killers took it, what do you know? You think they swiped the answering machine too?"

Myers grit his teeth. "Maybe if they were on it."

"Quite a bitch, not having your gizmos in effect, huh?" At this moment I was so in love with Jack. His gumshoe style was the stuff of movies, every romantic image of a cop I ever had. He nudged me, like I was in on the joke. "What the hell? A recording will only tell you you're right. But are you going to recognize the voice? Is it someone we know?"

"They obviously thought so," I added, "since they lifted the machine."

Myers's face went flat with distaste.

"He gave the girl the gun," he said, as if overriding all previous assumptions. "And probably something else."

The token booth clerk at the train station was still on his shift. He hadn't seen a blonde.

The bus driver said it was before 3 a.m. He was heading down Westchester Avenue, under the el. It was raining hard. He had just hit the bus stop on Elder Avenue when the blonde got on. She was in some obvious distress. Wet through and breathing hard, she could hardly swipe her MetroCard from trembling. She was also barefoot.

"Barefoot?"

"She was carrying the shoes in her hand." (Because she ran for the bus, get it?) She asked for 149th Street. The bus driver told her she should stay on until the last stop, but she didn't. She got off at the spot where Prospect Avenue meets Longwood. The driver was pretty sure it was down Prospect Avenue that she went. Hit the street running like she thought a car might veer off and give chase. "Sure as hell the devil was chasing that girl," he said.

Could Myers know like I know? If the bus driver was right, then she got off at the perfect spot to hit 149th Street. It was a walk, but going straight down Prospect Avenue in the direction she took would have led her right to the spot where 149th crosses Southern Boulevard. It made me think this was no girl just running. She had a definite destination.

The apartment was starting to reek.

It was still dark outside. Officer Jenkins was taking pictures. Mahoney was dusting for prints. Officer Peters stepping right up to bat.

"Lieutenant, I'd like to know how my people are supposed to do their jobs with this guy running around getting prints on everything," he said. "Did you see him and his people earlier?" He hooked eyes on Myers. "This is a crime scene."

"I have gloves on," Myers said, holding up both hands. Covered in those rubber disposables cops use when they touch homeless guys.

"You don't disturb a crime scene like that," Officer Peters went on. "And his people took stuff."

"Okay, I took these keys," Myers said, holding up a plastic baggie. "Would you say these are safe-deposit box keys?"

Jack took the baggie and gave the keys a look.

"More like luggage keys."

"Just what did you take?" I asked, but Myers didn't hear me in the outburst of cop voices that followed. Procedural questions, investigative priorities. Departmental pecking order. Jenkins, Mahoney, Peters. Cops I had worked with. I looked at them now as if from a distance, images through a train window on a landscape I was speeding past. I might have said once that these men were my friends. But since Dirty Harry, they were just officers. Their eyes grew hooded and empty when they looked at me. Unlike Jack, they would not stand and smoke with me. I never asked them for cigarettes. (I swiped them.)

I watched them argue. Myers wanted the room sealed, while Jack refused to cripple what he felt was HIS investigation with federal meddling. Besides which, he pointed out loudly, he hadn't even been briefed yet . . . at least not by Myers. All this while David lay there, no longer able to say a word as we pawed through his possessions and walked through his space. The stink that was starting to fill the room was his only gesture of complaint.

It was now, while standing there in that veritable cop world, that David Rosario's murder started to hit me.

I had told Myers that David was clean. How was I supposed to stick to a story like that if David got caught handing the goods to the blonde? Got plugged just as he shunted her out the window. Myers had suspected him all along. That smug look he was giving me. He was right and I was wrong OR I was lying OR I couldn't come up with a good enough story to explain the edges jutting through the fabric. And how about him, would he have a good story to tell? Could he explain to me how David got murdered while Myers claimed to have planted an operative on him? How did this informant not tell Myers what was coming? I was dying to put him on the spot, but I couldn't bring that up in front of all these cops. It seemed more and more that there was something between us, a private place of stories and lies.

The time I met David here, he pelted me with questions. He didn't really believe I was hunting down a fellow cop. "I'm sorry," he had said. Shaking his head. "Cops just aren't too big with us." (I thought he was going to say WITH US PUERTO RICANS, an instinctive feeling I grew up with.) Good guys bad guys. Spook and David's parents have a nice house in the Puerto Rican furry green. Couldn't link it directly to dirty Spook money, but I knew. The two of them, crooked and straight, earned their folks a nice calm life in the suburbs of San Juan.

"You never give up, do you?" He'd watched me grill Spook about getting me those witnesses. Spook had been wary. Bitched about immunity issues, cop retaliations, worries about his street cred . . . David pushed him. I got my witnesses. After Spook left, I lingered awhile. A cigarette before the *despedida* at the door, something that can take a Puerto Rican a long time.

"Hey man," he'd said as I went down the stairs, "do

you think being Puerto Rican makes you a different kind of cop?"

I didn't know at the time if it was an honest question or a challenge, a dare, a playful gibe. It was better to think of it as a joke, and that's how I took it at the time. I gave him some shrug, some vague one-liner. Back then I wasn't even thinking about stuff like that. Now it was too late to talk to him. I wanted to rewind the tape and examine the question with him. I wanted to tell him that no one had ever asked me this. Other Puerto Rican cops I knew didn't talk about it. I almost felt trained not to answer his question, even though I had never in my entire life heard the word *spick* as often as I heard it at the police academy. It was the price of admission. We were too busy trying to be cops. I didn't get to seriously answer his question. I wanted to, now. I think if I had back then, the answer would have been different. Maybe he already knew better than I did. Maybe what he was really asking was, *Are you sure you should be hunting down a fellow cop?* That made me feel stupid, naïve, sorry. POLICE CRIME SCENE, DO NOT ENTER. A bullet in a chalk circle. A light rain. A deep gray street. A watery coffee. Myers and I watched the paramedics walk a stretcher into the building. Half a stale cigarette. A bad gig. I could imagine taking the fall for this. A few words from Myers could do it. *I found Detective Sanchez to be uncooperative, combative, and unreliable.* The captain would be happy to finally see me wash out. Was that what Myers was thinking? I can't forget the grin he shot me as cops argued all around us about procedure, as if this chaos pleased him. About him I was guessing, just guessing all along. I could put a picture of him together, only to have him change the pieces, rearrange his face, his voice, his manner. I was growing two faces myself. One face to Myers, one face to Lieutenant Jack, who was simply trying to solve a pair of murders. In the old days we would have immediately side-by-sided. Now my legs were made of lead, my instincts no longer based on cop procedures or cop speed or even cop BELIEF. That comic book stuff about how good guys inevitably triumph over bad guys. How all parts fit together snug and there are always answers. Spook missing, probably dead, and David murdered right under my nose, almost as if that freak cop had returned to do a sequel. That's another thing that happens in comic books: Super villains who get snuffed in one issue may reappear a few issues later, just as powerful. Maybe it was just my instincts gone bad. I stood with Lieutenant Jack, popped a stick of gum, made cracks about the feds like we were high school brats razzing the teacher's pet. I felt I was going into mourning. Jack was the last piece of my cop life left. I could feel his energy bubbling over with mission. He had been briefed by Myers, in the loop but still skeptical and un-impressed. Who knows what the fuck Myers told him. Cops like to keep things basic. The more complicated things get, the less they believe it. This business with the ten million just didn't swing with him. The blonde was a witness who might be able to identify the murderers. But if she was an innocent witness in fear for her life, why not just come to the police? She could walk into a station house or flag down a cop car. That she was clearly not doing this already soured him on the whole business. Myers was impatient with him, brusque, matter-of-fact.

"I should go back to working with captains," Myers snapped at one point, when frustrated by Jack's questioning. (He would find it hard working with our captain, a man who rarely left the office.) It looked like in many ways he was still trying to avoid involving the locals. His thing was with me. He knew something about me. Him and his fucking bread truck, his twin zombies, his silent team. What did he need me for? I hadn't found Spook and I couldn't save David. Wasn't I just talking about the captain? He seemed to have the same opin-ion of me and my record of failure. "This doesn't seem to be working out," he said, but he meant ME, ME.

I hadn't seen the captain at a crime scene for a long

time, even Jack was agape. What brought the captain here now was probably not concern, but the FBI, which he had spent part of the morning talking to. (They must have roused him out of bed.) Myers's face went blank when he saw the three agents approaching. The captain addressed me with enough solemnity to bend my cigarette, had I been smoking one.

"Detective Sanchez, this is Special Agent Anderson from the FBI," he said. A tall, white-haired guy with a face like the rock of Prudential shook my hand, steel hard. "Special Agent Richards, Special Agent Dupreé. This is Detective Sanchez, Lieutenant Jack. I believe you already know Special Agent Myers."

Anderson's piercing blue eyes were stiff on Myers. He didn't waste time on formalities.

"Myers, just what the hell have you done? How did you get your nose so deep so fast in this case, and how did you manage to botch it up?"

Myers answered smooth swift, seemingly routine for him to field hostile questions. "It's not botched up yet. It's your butting in that's causing the problem."

"You don't have jurisdiction," Anderson said. "Did you forget that? Even if you solved this case, you can't possibly walk it into court. The judge will throw it out the moment you show him how you compiled your information."

Myers grinned. "You don't know that. You're hoping it's like that."

"You should know better, Myers." Special Agent Dupreé smirked like he was making a dirty joke. "You can't bug the natives. You can't watch them, listen to them, or triangulate their cell phones. You can only do that to foreigners."

"And Puerto Ricans aren't foreigners, last time I checked," Special Agent Richards quipped, giving me a wink. Was that supposed to make me feel better? These bastrads probably knew all about my record. They had a way of looking at me that made me feel diseased. Or it was me, the same paranoia. A net had fallen over me, and though there was plenty of air, I couldn't breathe. The apartment, so full of cops, was not the place to air this shit. The captain suggested we go outside, not even bothering to give the body a look. Out by the stoop, the words started twice as fast.

"Can you say EXECUTIVE ORDER 12333?" Anderson seemed to be reprimanding a child. "American citizens have been murdered here. This is where we step in."

"An American citizen murdered by foreigners," Myers said.

"You don't know that," Dupreé countered.

"Murdered by people we know," Myers continued. "You're stepping in a little late, I think. You don't fool me, Anderson. You tried it in D.C. and now you're here again, making another shoddy attempt to shut us down when what you really want is to confiscate our information."

That was it, I was through waiting. I lit a cigarette. All eyes turned to me. That's the thing about smokers: You light one, we all light one. I didn't have a pack, so I dug in a pocket and held up a handful to takers. Lieutenant Jack lit the round with his Normandy 44 Zippo. I don't know if it was rude. Everyone but the captain and Anderson lit up. Myers, calm and unfazed, held the cigarette more than smoked it.

"Let's face it, Anderson. You dropped the ball."

"*We* dropped the ball?" Anderson's eyes looked like they were full of boiling water. "How about you? Wasn't Ava Reynolds *your* idea?"

"That's the blonde," Jack said, nudging me.

"Will you—?" Myers coughed up smoke. "Not everybody here has been briefed," he said, giving the captain a wary look.

"You mean you want New York's Finest to locate this girl for you, and you haven't even told them about her?" Anderson laughed, his eyes mocking.

"Tsk tsk," Dupreé said, wagging a finger, joining in the laugh.

"No problem," Anderson said. "I briefed the captain on the way here."

"You what?" Myers tossed down his cigarette. "I demand you tell me what you told him! Captain, what he said just isn't true."

The captain stared back blank.

"These officers," Anderson went on, "are involved in a homicide investigation, and now that this is a domestic case, I'm going to make sure we find this Ava Reynolds. She's not going to disappear like some of the others in this case."

"Nobody's disappeared," Myers said.

My ears were definitely perking up now. I knew agencies competed. Sometimes teams within the same agency fought each other as viciously as street gangs. They battled over access, information, and scoops just like reporters, stalkers, and paparazzi. Which team gets the goods, which team gets the ear of the district attorney? Does the D.A. have a favorite team? The different agencies responsible for protecting the country do not communicate well, they mistrust each other, and they generally work independently. The cops are the last people to be let in on anything.

"This office should have been notified. We could have gotten the Rosarios with warrants." Anderson stepped awful closer. "Instead, you chose not to involve us and play spy games. Some stupid hook-and-tail scam like you pulled in D.C. It even looks," he said, casting a glance at Myers's bookends, "like the same cast as last time."

"Anderson, why don't you lick my nuts?"

"Gentlemen," the captain said. I liked him right then. He seemed the father figure cutting in between battling siblings. "My people haven't all been briefed."

"It's about the girl," Anderson went on, staring Myers down at close range. "She's no innocent bystander. She was working for Myers."

Now the blonde came charging into my mind like an

icepick. I could see her smiling away so snug and close in David's arms in those office party pictures. Could see her watching me, those two times I visited David at the office. The strange penetrating stare of her and how she seemed to be sizing me up. Now I thought hard, of David, David trusting her, David telling her, David pulling her in with him. For some reason for whatever reason she was inside that strange secret. And so was I, so was I. Did she know? And if she knew, how didn't Myers know? A burn to the air, a burn to my cigarette.

"Man, did you come all this way just to drop that bombshell?" Myers, hands in pockets, grinned furious.

"She was supposed to set up the Rosarios," Dupreé said, looking right at me, right into my eyes, something cops don't do very often these days. "But it looks like the bunny just up and run off with the prize. Ain't that about right, Myers?"

There was a slight Southern twang to Dupreé. Myers didn't say anything.

Dupreé laughed. "Man, you and your people should stick to overseas tricks."

"She's no agent," Richards said with a scowl, sucking down that last bit of cigarette nub. "She's a contract player."

"There's another word for that type of contract," Dupreé said, again wearing that dirty-joke grin.

I felt buzzed with a sick nausea, a need to crack someone, anyone, in the face. I wanted silence when the paramedics walked David's body past us. I wanted slow motion so that I could take my time and digest it, frame by frame. I should have been up there with him, working to find the answers and maybe receive any clues he might want to give me. It was a different feeling for me now. The room was full of cops. I didn't want to be in there anymore. I didn't want to talk through the stares and feel that hesitation when I gave orders or opened my mouth. It was a dark feeling. I was sad for David, but now I felt I was in danger. The *good guys bad guys* paradigm, the sense that I had crossed a line starting with the day David asked me a theoretical question about what I would do if I had ten million dollars. It was all questions with David. He had boxes full of question marks. I should have never answered. Maybe I was being hard on myself, but something I did got him killed, maybe something I didn't do. David went by with as much ceremony as a laundry pickup. He took my old life with him, that one wheel on his gurney jiggling round spin. I wondered if he knew about her, if she knew about me. I couldn't decide. Not about her. Not about David, Spook, or Myers, who was pulling an envelope from an inside pocket.

"Look, you want jurisdiction? Here's mine, gentlemen. You give the DD/I a call. Tell him what you told me. You get him to tell me I'm off the case."

Anderson didn't look at the letter. He passed it to Dupreé.

"Who hired you?" Richards asked, "Kagan? Kristol? Somebody at the PNAC?"

"Don't be ridiculous."

"Why are you after it, Myers?" Anderson kept pushing. "Even if you get it, you can't bust anybody. You need us for that. And we probably can't use your evidence."

"That's what you say now, in public," Myers answered, taking the letter back. "I have my orders. His ways are not your ways."

"I don't think Myers has ever made an arrest in his life," Dupreé cracked with a smirk. Myers seemed to ignore him, but seized on that keyword.

"Yeah, arrests! Listen, Anderson. Why don't you go downtown and make some arrests? You know who they are already, right? Go arrest them, make a big splash. Afterwards, we can meet at the Senate hearings in Washington, which is where the agency will take you after you blow this lead we've been working on for months. Go ahead. I dare you. Your courts will just let these people go. You're lucky if you can bust them on visa irregularities. Why don't you just do it?"

The captain was wearing a wry smile that I hadn't seen for years. I nudged Jack.

Anderson stepped so close to Myers I thought he would spit. "We'll find her," he said. "I'm sure she'll have a lot to say about you."

"Not if I find her first," Myers said. It was an under-breath, muttered. The words stayed with me for a day and a night. Words like a pledge, like an oath. The captain walked the agents to their car. Myers made FBI cracks. The cops laughed with him. Suddenly he wasn't looking so bad to everybody, more like a Joe next to those feds. I felt jealous of the easy camaraderie that grew around him, even if momentary. I was wondering why Myers would think I was the path to the blonde. The captain seemed to wonder the same thing. Talking to me and Jack seemed to rob him of all energy. He authorized Jack to give Myers whatever he wanted, whatever it took. As for me, "Find the blonde then," he said, "just try to find her alive, not dead." (The captain was still good at those *indirectas*.) "Then this guy Myers can take the whole mess with him back to D.C. and leave us the hell alone." He felt the case was already beyond us. Jack could talk as much as he wanted about finding the murderers with that old fire and verve, the captain gave him that closed face too. To me, Jack seemed a child, a happy puppy. He was alone with his enthusiasm. The captain went to talk to Myers, who had crossed the street to take a call.

"We have a murder investigation going," Jack said, "and that little bastard has taken all the fun out of it."

I couldn't tell if he was talking about Myers or the captain. Back when, we would've been Heckle and Jeckle, burning with the desire to solve this murder. Now I just stood beside him, feeling tired and empty.

I was thinking about a man named Roman. His manner was of tall thin aristocrat, of hardly ever speak. His black shirts, his eye-patch. People call him "One-Eye." Like Wiggie, Jaco, and Quique, he was one of Spook's district chiefs.

I'd tried reaching him over and over again since Spook dis-appeared, over and over for a few reasons I wasn't sure My-ers didn't know about. I couldn't tell him, that first time in my office. I knew about Spook. When I saw the accounts, I had gone straight to David. I was on the trail. I was stick-ing my nose where it didn't belong, or maybe it was where it belonged all along. I wondered later what an honest cop would have done with this information, realizing now I had passed the point where such terms carry any meaning. I thought I would just ask questions. I hadn't expected to be on the receiving end of a proposition. David just came right out with every fine detail. He laughed, it was a kick. "We're swiping the money from criminals!" More information than I had bargained for. No walls no barbed wire no tollbooth. A door was simply opened. I had expected evasions, having to duck verbal dukes, avoid tank traps. Instead I got some Asian defense tactic, which calls for letting your enemy defeat himself with his own momentum. You side-step his charge, maybe grab a piece of him EN PASSANT and help him along. Into a wall out a window down some stairs. Only this was no defense. This was an invitation.

David then took me to Spook. I told him it was madness. He told me it was a ticket out. The kids could keep the drug trade. The only person in the whole organization he brought into the deal was Roman, an old friend who was already phas-ing himself out of the business. Those couple of weeks I tried to talk David and Spook out of it, I approached him. Roman said no. To him it was a cheap-ass sellout of the organization. He fought, like I did in the beginning, to get them to give up the idea. By then, the laundering job was already on, the cash flowing in, before the swipe—"Call the feds," I said to them. "Tell them you want to make a deal." But Spook and David didn't think that was the way to make ten million bucks. In the end, Roman stuck to his guns and backed away, no doubt making contingencies for the troubled times to come. I didn't back away. I made contingencies too.

Roman was not "in" it, but he knew about it. I'm wondering if David told that to the blonde. I'm wondering if the
blonde knew about him. She had asked for 149th Street,
then ran straight down Prospect Avenue. Prospect Avenue
crosses 149th Street right where it ends against Southern
Boulevard. I bet if I had put it to Jack, he would've come up
with Roman. I hoped it might take Myers a little longer to
connect the dots—I was counting on it. Myers was all over
Jack—where was the manpower to do all these searches?
David's office had to be sealed and searched. Ava Reynolds's
things had to be seized. There was her apartment too, and
what about the girl herself? I plotted her course on a road
map. From the moment she left that bus on Westchester,
a straight line ending some place near 156th Street, close
to the last sighting of her . . . a good place, I said, to begin canvassing the neighborhood. Cops carrying pictures,
maybe a few of my detectives to do lay-and-waits.

Myers seemed a little distracted, his momentum shot,
when Jack just came out and asked, "So, was this chickie
one of your agents?"

Myers was unable to speak for a moment. There was
nothing on the street but cop cars and pigeons. The sidewalk was wet again, vehicles dotted with drizzle. Dawn was
dingy and dirt-streaked. I kept seeing that rock-faced Anderson, laying words like landmines. I kept seeing the blonde.
Those first lingering stares of hers, the sense that she knew
something about me. Had she really been in touch with Myers, was Anderson right about that? Myers hadn't contra-
dicted him. Again the thought: If David trusted her enough
to lay the prize on her, he could have mentioned me to her.
And she, in touch with Myers, could have mentioned me. I
couldn't light another cigarette fast enough. Myers looked
needy. I lit him one too. When he took the cigarette from me
and nodded his appreciation, I felt an odd kinship with him.
I sensed about him an intense loneliness, suddenly. I don't
know what it was, just a sense of standing outside locked

gates. Something to prove. How those days were over for me. When I saw how he pulled up the collar of his raincoat and didn't answer Jack at all, I felt included in some secret world. When Jack moved off to consult with some officers, it was just me and Myers, smoking side by side in the airless gray.

"Why does Anderson know you?" I asked. He shrugged, his eyes getting blurry. A high school student reminded of homework.

"He followed me from D.C. He caught the tail end of my last op. Couldn't raise a stink there so he followed me here. You have no idea how personal this all is."

"You're going to have to brief me again," I said, sounding reluctant, like I was trying to spare him. "Anderson covered a lot of turf."

He looked at me a moment with round, glassy eyes. "You're not insulted I didn't tell you, right?"

"Nah," I said. "Part of the job."

"I'm glad. I would hate if you—"

A cop car suddenly let out a string of beeps. Cop laughter.

"I meant to tell the lieutenant," Myers said sluggish. Tossed down the cigarette. Stepped on it, ground it into the sidewalk with his shoe. "I didn't mean to be rude. I haven't slept. He's a good cop."

"I know." I tossed my cigarette too. A nice flaming arc that sparked the street. "He's my favorite."

"Anderson only knows the half of it." Myers became more animated now, some of the old verve returning. "He makes good guesses and knows just enough to fuck up the game. This whole thing he pulled today." A dismissive wave of the hand. "He did it on purpose, to discredit me. He's still about three steps behind." Myers winked at me. "He hasn't even gotten to the Sanchez part."

"The Sanchez part?"

"That's right. There's a Sanchez part. He won't find her

because he doesn't have the Sanchez part. He hasn't even gotten there yet. That's why we'll find her, while he's bumbling around getting court orders for a few cheap wiretaps."

My stomach was a knot. I closed my eyes for just a moment, almost fell into a dream.

"So. You still think David Rosario was clean?"

I looked at him. It was a soft voice, tinged with sadness. There was no mockery on his face. I could see he didn't expect an answer.

"Don't worry about it." He looked out at the empty street, hands deep in his pockets. "I seem to have misjudged somebody too."

I felt he was talking about the blonde. I knew he was talking about the blonde.

He was looking at me. He spoke softly. "You knew, didn't you?"

Cop car let out another string of beeps. Electronic farts. Cop laughter.

"She told you?" I said, though I couldn't look at him. Anything was better. Gray brick. Parked cars. A brown dog happily lapping up water.

"I can't believe everything she says. Not now."

"I tried to stop it," I said.

"I know." He wouldn't take his eyes off me. "You see why we have to find her?"

"Yes," I said. Were we now in the same boat? Would eliminating her make everything okay? Is that what it meant? Sometimes the heaviest things in a relationship are those things never spoken, never admitted, the words never said.

"You should go home, get some sleep. We can meet in the afternoon." He smiled. It was slow, tentative, real. "You brief me, I brief you."

I nodded assent. I said something, or was I dreaming it? Did I tell you my wife's name is Milagros? The name means MIRACLE she was still with me after four years. She could sense when I was disturbed, couldn't sleep. She has those deep spiritual qualities that dark-skinned mountain women are supposed to have. Her fingers, soft stroking, could send me into a trance. There was candlelight squirming on the ceiling. David being wheeled by in a gurney just wouldn't let me sleep. All light was too bright.

I sat in the living room and almost finished my pilfered cigarettes. Milagros brought over the chessboard. Some little diversion while the sky lightened and the tea kettle boiled. I kept thinking: *I don't want to find her, I don't. I want it all to go away. I want to sleep and forget.* The strong scent of *jengibre*: She cooked up a strong tea, a potent blend of leaf magic that soon had me in bed with fluttering eyelids. Her touch . . . savory waves shimmery nymphs. Hendrix when he plays slow, and mystic. Her whispered words tranced me dark.

"Maybe the answers will come to you in dreams," she said, like she would breathe spirits into me.

14.

Memory blitz. Or memory something, the tune was a recurring swirl through dream. The drum was a heartbeat. It was feverish dark when the images started to play. Something was trying to snap him awake. He fought it, wanting to catch that glimmer of song before it faded off into the distance. He knew it had something to do with Belinda, with permanence, with a dress hanging in the bathroom. The drum was a heartbeat. Snapping to: like waking up under a table. Shiny boy shoes and girl calves. Donna wears a toe ring. Amanda has an ankle bracelet. A flash of sick came over him. As if time tripping, he had gone back to the prom, to that dizzy moment before he threw up.

Jarred awake, or not. Unsure, dream or UNdream. Fire escape window all lit up silvery, yellow, bronze. Pain, or fever. From time to time, an electric jolt, a lightning bolt.

Ava was on the fire escape. He could see her outside sitting, maybe on the sill maybe right by it. Squinting from sun, her hair all golden. "Ava as in Gardner, not Gabor." With his fingers he found the tender spot, the bump at the back of his head. There were brief pain sparks. Barely a memory, just black after the last snapshot: images cascading like falling postcards. There was a cab ride with Monica. The blonde in his bed. Mink: "Where did you find her?" The tall thin vodka bottle on the kitchen table. Changó in a minidress. A fat roll of gaffer's tape. "Yes. Four cubes, please." A laugh. "The rain came down in sheets." The warm breath in his ear: "I never happened." She was going out through the fire escape, or she was coming in. "I was never here."

Ava came in through the fire escape window. She climbed in only as far as it took for her to straddle the thick sill, her legs dangling down. Half in, half out. Her purse slid to the floor.

Jolted awake, all images scattered. He rolled off the bed, lightning bolts flashing. Left corner under the mattress where he kept the toy baseball bat. Had that shit since he was ten, sturdy old wood stained and chipped but still a potent weapon. Easy to swing, a Babe Ruth autograph visible on the fat end. To hold it felt good. To hold it felt right, but standing so fast from his roll was wrong. There was a thick gelatin feel to his legs. The sense of swirling sick came back.

"What the fuck?" he said.

Her eyes were wide and startled. Her hands were up.

"Easy," she said.

He was awake, wasn't he? The floor felt gummy under his feet, clinging to him sucking him down making him slow. He was not moving very well, his muscles sluggish. The room seemed smaller than before. Her eyes were very large, sucked the space from the room.

"Why'd you whack me?"

The sick pasty taste in his mouth, the ooze of facts and pictures. There was no way he could trust any information right now, not senses not sight not this strange dizzy and those clanging bells.

"What are you doing here?"

Bells?

Ava's eyes were pinned to the boy baseball bat he was waving around. Her hands open before her like that reminded him of a painting he had seen somewhere with Mink. It was in a museum. Maybe Spain. It was a religious scene, the tender pink hands of a supplicant.

"I can explain," she said.

That set off the bells again. Words words they would be coming soon and coming fast, words to explain to cloud to clutter to conceal to correct to trick to fool. Words coming was hardly a good thing. What Alex needed was not words. It was that tall thin vodka bottle sitting on the kitchen table. That first cold splash of sting would waken the senses all right. Splash mold off rocks, blow barnacles off steamships. To hear a muddle of words with that unlubricated brain would only make things worse. He needed that drink! But he wasn't going to get it with Ava sitting there on the sill. He didn't trust her one bit and there was no way he was going to turn his back on her and give her another crack at his head.

"I don't want to hear it now," he said.

Before she could react, he pulled her off the sill. She was reaching for her purse, which had fallen. That's when he gave her a conk on the head with the toy bat. She fell forward, onto the bed. She tried to sit up, to shake her head clear. It didn't work. She fell, she fell.

"Now we're even," he said.

15.

I was on a train. No idea about where it was going. It must have been a very high elevated track, or no track. Out the tinted windows, no land or houses or streets. Nothing below but ocean. Wisps of cloud stroked window glass like sand.

The train car was moderately packed. I was swaying dizzy from height, wondering what train to where. I couldn't speak, couldn't ask anyone where this train was headed. The chatter swooned around me, all butterfly wings with no substance. In the middle of this sat Spook and David, huddled together like conspirators. They were talking loud enough for me to hear. I found myself sitting across from them, squinting from the sharp sun that cut through clouds like pinpricks. I wasn't even sure they could see me until David looked right at me and said, "Hey, did you ever wonder what you would do with ten million dollars?"

"He's not getting ten," Spook said, throwing me a look. "How much do you think a spick cop is worth?"

The conversation was familiar. I remember once telling David I used to dream of having my own island. Was that my answer? I couldn't say now, I couldn't speak.

The train stopped somewhere, a station high up in a cloud bank. Misty cumulous was everywhere. Couldn't see tracks. The platform was a narrow thin wafer suspended in the cottony white. More people came on, talking that language that I still didn't understand. The only people I understood were David and Spook, sitting and talking like there was no one else in the car. I would have thought they would clam up in front of a cop. Maybe they knew me better than I did, right then.

"Ten million dollars," David said, rocking back and forth like a Muslim.

Spook rocked with him. "Yeah." He nudged David. "Hey. You know what? We might as well be the Romero brothers now."

That was the punch line, the kicker to the tale that sent them foot-stomping hand-clapping train-tilting laugh. Train tilting train tilting and then I was sick.

Her hand was cold on my forehead. I puked into the toilet.

"Another message," she said.

I shouldn't have taken that nap.

Milagros made a quick green tea.

The Romero brothers are a pair of Puerto Rican boys from the South Bronx. Milagros reminded me I had read a piece about them in yesterday's DAILY NEWS that said they were worth ten million dollars.

I was reaching for a cigarette when

to quit. To just quit. An elevator going down. A gold shield on the captain's desk. It seemed every time I made up my mind

always a new cigarette would find my fingers. Coming across one I forgot in my pocket. (Jack had slipped me three on the stoop.) It was no longer a challenge to wear the mark of Cain with distinction. Each time I almost forget, a phone call comes in. *You're going to die, Sanchez.* Maybe she doesn't say anything. I see it on her face. She hangs up.

"Wrong number," she says.

Myers talked a lot about betrayal about traitors about that Vonnegut book *Mother Night* where a seemingly American traitor is in reality a great American hero. Traitor, hero, traitor, hero, a theme song a constant refrain. It was him or me: I had Myers on the brain, a weird growth that screwed with my ability to keep to the story with a sense of chronological accuracy. I was getting flashes: a window five floors up. A look straight down. A blonde in a chalk circle. Myers in a state of blank shock. He liked jokes about the Kennedy assassination. ("How many shooters does it take to screw an asshole?") He kept bringing it up in those sudden phone calls as if he was working out some problem. Big questions about improbabilities and conspiracies and how there are always mistakes made and evidence seeps through YET THE PEOPLE WON'T BELIEVE IT won't go there won't accept it because America is NOT based on facts. America is a belief system—Myers rambling and I rambling just like him, a manic word fix while thinking of the just-after when I am sitting before the man with the face like the rock of Prudential.

And I change the subject, I say, "We were talking about Vonnegut."

And he says, "No, you were talking about the money."

Myers never talked about the money. It bothered him to mention it. His face creased like there was a bad smell. I couldn't see him doing something just for money. That couldn't be exciting to him. It was more about the chase, the daring bits of Tarantino-speak between bullets, the victorious conclusion to another campaign. He was the point man, the unsung hero who worked in the dark for the big boys. He was the one who carried secrets. He had the magic truck with the special toys. Even the FBI knew that and wouldn't like to admit it sometimes hired strange fellows to do the strange deeds that probably repelled them but might be called for in order to preserve freedom liberty etc. And when making a point like that during what can only be taken as an interrogation, the best course is to radically and quite suddenly change the subject.

"We were talking about my father."

My father was not a cop. He said there were other issues back then, about identity and culture. Becoming a cop
wasn't big on the agenda if you wanted to express your
PUERTO RICAN. He is still to this day uncomfortable around
cops. He grew up in '50s Spanish Harlem. There were Italians in that neighborhood who kicked your ass just for being
Puerto Rican. A lot of those Italians became cops. One of
the reasons back then why Puerto Ricans didn't become
cops so much. It was a far simpler time.

I would rather think of something farther. Not a blinking
dot on any dispatcher's board just yet. No high window no
five floors down. No bread trucks no path to follow. To quit
means to just vanish, disappear without a trace. Not so easy
in today's U.S.A.

Things I found out about Mallorca on the Internet:

1. 3,640 sq. km.
*2. Mallorca is part of the Balearic community of islands
off the Spanish coast. It gets 300 days of sun a year.
Palma de Mallorca is the capital city. Approximately
half of the island's population, or about 320,000 people, live there.*
*3. Balearic Islands: Mallorca, Menorca, Cabrera in the
north; Ibiza and Formentera in the south.*
*4. Valldemosa: where Chopin and George Sand spent
the winter of 1838–39.*
*5. Palma de Mallorca: in 1983, declared the capital of
the Balearic Islands, recognized as one of Spain's au-
tonomous regions.*
*6. Cathedral la Seo: constructed from the fourteenth to
the nineteenth centuries, in Palma de Mallorca. Antoni
Gaudí redesigned its interior in the twentieth century.*

Some people run away and they don't get far. Either
they have no idea how to run or they have no idea they are

already caught. I was thinking a lot about that "already caught" bit. More like a setup than I had planned. My pockets full of death threats. A place where houses are sold to foreigners on very favorable terms. Beach. Sun. Spanish. Milagros whispers: "Try not to force things." There's an art to letting your enemy's momentum destroy him. Do nothing. Wait, and a door will appear: La Puerta del Mirador, Cathedral la Seo, Palma de Mallorca. A door to the sea, designed by Guillem Sagrera. How I found Mallorca on a late-night surf. Milagros was half-right. This wasn't the time to wait. There was no combination of something else to think about. No drugs to make the mind go slow and careful like grunts in a Michael Herr book. The persistent sensation: a ghost tickling my elbow. I felt watched, observed, tracked. A red blip on someone's screen.

"Maybe I'm just being paranoid," I said.

"Just because you're paranoid," she said back, "doesn't mean they're not after you."

It was the cell phone.

"Where are you?" Myers had supposedly been called away by Anderson. Twenty questions, or: "Tell us what you know." They'd have better luck interrogating a turnip. I was glad to see him go, but I hadn't lost him. He hadn't lost me. He called so much I had to put the earphone on so I could drive. "Where are you?" was his way of hello. Every time he asked, I didn't believe him. I felt he knew where I was. He only asked to see if I would tell him.

I was driving away from. No point in being seen. I was making those sharp turns. All of a sudden there was this bread truck. I swerved LEFT jumped the curb CRASH and rattle. The tires could squeal—I wasn't about to slow down. What if Myers had lied? What if he hadn't gone downtown?

That made me stop driving.

I jumped out of the car. On my knees outside, doors open, checking under seats. Pulling out vinyl mats. Glove compartment, cup caddy, ashtrays armrests seat belts. Fucking sun visors. Those little furrows and crannies along seats and doors. Windows up, windows down. I was breathing fast, slamming trunk and hood. The cassette player came on. *"Roadrunner, roadrunner. Going fast three miles an hour."* A Jonathan Richman slow drawl.

I checked rims, hubcaps, fender, and hood. Ran my hand along the grille. I felt up every inch of my black Caprice. Strange looks from the peds as they spotted me on my back, getting a feel of the undercarriage. The giggle of gaggles.

"You lose something, mister?"

I drove over to a shop on Bruckner, where I got some Pedro to put it up on the hyrdaulic. He kept asking me what I was looking for. "I'll know it when I see it." That was a lie. For all I knew it was some gummy paste, an ink stain, a minute chip hidden on a paper clip. Bottlecap, bread crumb, empty cigarette pack. How does so much junk accumulate in the backseat of a car? I fully vacuumed after the car wash. I floated under soap suds and big brushes, stupid nauseous. I smoked three cigarettes and laughed defiantly through each one. I laughed at myself, at Myers and ten million dollars and a blond woman, running. Through caffeine buzz and nicotine burn came acceptance: The car could be bugged, but I wasn't going to ditch it. It might be easier to lead him toward something than to try leading him away from.

"Where are you?"

Somedays you wish. No car, just speed. Traveling down those South Bronx streets like in a video game where the POV is just street and houses speeding by, no car but driving fast as easy as. To speed down streets so fast no one can catch you ever again. Dream that.

No sense of boundaries. The thing about growing up here was that there was always a line a ceiling a fluttering tape that said POLICE LINE, DO NOT CROSS. Doors could remain shut a whole lifetime. Could turn walking a beer can down the street into a blatant act of rebellion. I understood fully about people making their own rules, searching out their own breaks. I knew them, I chased them, I put them behind bars. But good guys bad guys? No such luck that life could be so easy. It was like reading Marvel comics. Some people always get away with it. Some people never do.

You can wake from a dream and wish you were still dreaming. You can wake from a dream and go back to sleep in hopes of picking up where you left off. You can wake from a dream and not rememeber a thing about it. Or just fuck it, jerk the steering wheel to the left, violent fast. A radio call, a nightmare sound. The other shoe drops. A sudden surge, all landscape gone spin. The wheels chirp a little. A line of trees, and you know you're on Jackson Avenue. The cluster of sand-colored projects jutting into sky. Shiny silver train cars rattle by on tracks above.

The cigarettes seemed to be making me sick, but I had two left and I was going to smoke them.

The 2 train shared the same elevated track as the 5 train, at least until 180th Street, where the 5 veered off toward Dyre Avenue. The 2 continued on up White Plains Road. Both trains passed through Manhattan to Brooklyn, the 5 taking the east side while the 2 took the west. It had a bad reputation, passing as it did through the heart of Harlem and some rough turf in Brooklyn. It was once dubbed "The Beast," but that was just bad press. The 2 train was a trooper that sped express through Manhattan's overcrowded west side with ease, that went local through Harlem and Flatbush instead of cruising by and leaving people stranded. It was a heart-of-gold train, as tough as any veteran New Yorker with a tall tale. It roared into subway stations like a tantrum, but by the time it was side by side with the 5 train on elevated tracks, it was mellow. Clacking down the track, a pretty girl in heels walking fast. The clatter of trains like the clatter of dominoes. A group of old men playing under a bodega

awning. The arrival of cop cars flashing lights and those PO-
LICE CRIME SCENE, DO NOT CROSS tapes did not disturb
their play. They were surprised when told someone had just
dumped a dead body on the corner while they were playing.
They didn't see a thing. Those fucking domino games.

At fifteen minutes past 1:00 on a Sunday grown muggy
and gray, Spook was found garbage-bagged and dumped on
the corner of Jackson and 152nd. Lieutenant Jack was the
one to call me. I don't know where Myers was. I left a message. After that scene with him, I felt I was being pushed in
a direction I wasn't sure I wanted to go. The inside dialogue
never stopped. The blonde was creeping into my thoughts. I
could see her eyes following me to the elevator.

Lieutenant Jack seemed brighter-eyed than I had seen
him in a long time. He now had his homicide, his sense of
mission. Knowing Spook and many of the central characters gave him the feeling of being personally involved.

"It's strange," he said, popping the customary stick of
gum. "This was the one guy I didn't expect to see like this. A
big shot like him, swatted down and dumped like garbage.
It's almost the end of an era."

Yes, the end of MY era. The mess they made of Spook.
The mashed-up face the rope burns the way they slashed his
throat from ear to ear. They do that to people who "sing,"
who tattle, who tell tales. What a mess they made of Spook.
With all the hideouts and all the security, he was murdered
and dumped on his own turf.

The street now taking color. Rainy grays washed out.
With sun bursting through clouds came faces, from this
way from that from all over tenement streets. That Spook
was dead, going fast from ear to ear across town. Fingers
punched numbers on cell phones. Cars started up. Wiggie and Jaco arrived by 4x4. There were screaming wailing
cousins. Quique tried to reach Roman but only got his voice
mail. It made sense that he was hiding. As the only person
from the group "in on it," he could be thinking maybe there

was a trail to him. Soon Lieutenant Jack would ask about him. Soon Myers would do his own math. Roman, who had wanted to stay out of it, was now conspicuous in his absence.

The others knew something was coming for them. They didn't know what it was. (They were right. The cops would soon start raiding all their asses.) They clustered around, tossing up bits of information. Seen in the area: two white men in business suits. That wouldn't help much, considering white men in business suits look alike to most Puerto Ricans. Spook was being secretive, Spook was avoiding his people, Spook was seen with a white guy who looked like a narc—all patches and bits, nothing solid, nothing secure. I sang them a different song than the lieutenant. Hard cop, soft cop. LATINO cop. I kept hoping Roman would have the common sense to put in an appearance, at least so Jack could question him and take him off the suspect list. Already briefed by Myers and me, he would soon take his cop thoughts to the next cop place: What if someone inside the organization got wind of the ten million and decided to make a move for it?

The meat wagon comes.

Cops start to push. Sometimes when a body lies there a long time, people start to get angry about how it's lying there. Cops don't like people fucking with the body because it's evidence, so sometimes they push. People push back. Some cop panicked and got on the radio. Three more cop cars arrived with staccato shrieks, as if sonic beeps from a cop car would ever break up a crowd.

I didn't let them wheel Spook by me, this time I left with the body. This time I felt sure I had to make him talk to me. Somehow or other he had to tell me what happened and there had to be something somehow that I could read, pick up, a clue a sign a feeling. The coroner could tell me, couldn't he? We could find the answers hidden on him. But at the morgue, I was having a hard time finding a coroner to work on him. Would the day go so fast? Three hours before anyone would even touch him. I set off with Jack, a squad of cops along to hit two of Spook's nearby hideouts around Jackson. These were rooms, small apartments, spaces cluttered with old junk that didn't say much to us. Where was Myers? Had he somehow gotten what he wanted, as Jack was saying?

"Maybe he's already hiked his ass back to Washington," he said, but I didn't think so. I knew there was something Myers wanted and it had to do with me. There was no way to fight the feeling: I did it. I let something in. I opened a door, and maybe now it was up to me to stop it.

When I got Myers, he sounded harried and hassled. Anderson had him locked in an office somewhere. "I'm talking the whole shit," Myers said. "They shine a light in my face. They shove bamboo shoots up my nails. They're really grilling me. It's been a waste of a day. There's so much to do, and I still can't get out of here."

"What do they want?"

"I told you, they want information."

I filled him in on Spook, that I was rushing an autopsy and had searched a couple of his nearby cribs. Myers was not going to speed down like Agent Cooper to look for minute clues, the bits of dirt under a fingernail.

"I don't want you distracted by all this," he said. "The lieutenant will do just fine. Finding Ava Reynolds right now is the most important thing. Did you start the canvassing?"

"Yes. Some cops, some detectives. Lieutenant Jack's handling it."

"You make sure and look in on that. I don't trust the lieutenant to be as motivated as you when it comes to the girl. Don't get distracted by cop business. This isn't the time to be a cop."

The words froze me. Again that feeling, of hot and cold. I was searching my pockets for a smoke. (*Nada.*) These same words, that same phrase, coming back to me like a hammer blow. Again I could see her eyes, the widest, greenest eyes I had ever seen. As big and round on that small face as any character in a Japanese cartoon. This was a game, a sick game. I was puffing fast on a piece of cigarette, found broken in some pocket.

"I hate to tell you this, but I don't think there's anything Spook's body can tell you. They finished with him. It's very probable he talked, led them to his brother."

"But who led them to Spook?"

The Myers laugh, sudden like a cough. "You did," he said.

"What?"

"Who knows? He could have met them. He was doing business with them, wasn't he? I'll tell you something right now that I just found out here. The FBI was trying to hire him. Trying to hire the both of them."

"Seriously?"

"Yes. They approached David Rosario about it, just around the time the money vanished. They could have approached his brother directly. You see what I'm saying? The more people who get involved, the more teams. The more teams, the more information gets thrown around. There could be a mole at any point along those lines of information. They could be tapping any source at any point. We can't be sure."

"And what if you're the source?"

Myers laughed. "Great," he said. "My team is too small."

"They could tap your lines, find a way into your information. And goddamnit, that's *my* information."

"I hate to say it, buddy, but these people are sophisticated." There was a sudden interruption on his end. "Hey, I have to get out of here. We've got a date later."

The line went click.

The thought that it was my information that got them killed grew stronger. I would rather believe it was a mole, a leak, a tap, not that other idea growing in my head like a poison mushroom. "This isn't the time to be a cop." And that brought me right back to the blonde.

I had been to David's office several times before Ava Reynolds started working there. Fischer-MacMillan, an advertising firm on 54th Street. I had gone past the imposing woodgrain reception desk many times. The alley of cushiony cubicles, the name plates made out of CDs, everything familiar enough. Odd how just when all this begins, David finds himself needing to hire an assistant. The first time I saw her, they were both outside his office, she typing furious into a laptop. She saw me and stopped typing, face quizzical and edged with a sense of recognition that I found baffling. The last time I saw her, her eyes stayed with me every step of the way into David's office. They were with me when I stepped out. When I waited for the elevator, they appeared in person. She stood there, not saying anything. She waited until I got into the elevator, then slipped in just before the doors closed.

The elevator ride was one long drop. Her eyes did not leave me, so close so large so green. The glowing orbs in a science fiction movie that force people to tell the truth . . . maybe a kind of scopolamine . . . Her hair, what was with that hair? Everything around her wanted to go black-and-white, until we were both in a 1930s movie.

"I know why you came," she said. Words, there were words. She was staring at the rows of buttons on the wall. Down, we were going down. The elevator made muffled beeps.

"I know you're trying to help him," she said, "but it can be done."

It was funny to me how she had the same tone David had, only more insistent, more sure. It was as if she was continuing the argument I had just lost with David.

"No, it can't," I said, with the same passion I wasted on David. "The feds are bound to come. If I picked up on this, they will. Especially this kind of money, and the people that come attached to it."

"What people?"

"Terrorists. Criminals. Republicans. Whatever the fuck they are! The people the money's getting stolen from!"

"The feds are already here."

She pulled out a key and stuck it in a slot on the button board. The elevator came to a halt. So did my stomach, two sickening jolts later.

"It's more the reason," she said, "to do it."

"Now hold on." There was not even room to pace. Her eyes took up all the room all the air. "I've been trying to warn David off." Because the button hadn't been pressed, the money hadn't gone missing the first time David told me about the plan. By this time the money was gone. I didn't think they would be able to give it back, but maybe they could cut a deal with the feds to scam the terrorists and set them up. I couldn't tell her all that, or the reason I was try-ing to warn David off—I knew damn well once those two hit the ON switch, I was in it. I would show up, as involved as anyone, no matter what my final decision was. I didn't know if she knew that. David just wanted me to keep my mouth shut. Look the other way, then, should the feds get the ball, block the kick.

"Don't you know what it's like," she asked, "to have a personal score to settle?" The way her eyes flashed told me I wouldn't have to bother answering.

There was a sudden loud buzz. A red light flashed on the button board. The speaker crackled.

"Hey, number two. You stuck? What's going on?"

She quickly opened a small compartment and pulled out a phone.

"System training for a new recruit," she said, hanging up the phone. She closed her eyes for a moment, exhaled. Her face flushed bunny pink.

"There's someone coming to see you."

The burning in my stomach moved to my hands my ears my eyes felt like I had smothered them in onions. A sudden paralysis: the feeling this Ava Reynolds was more than just a David assistant.

"Who are you?"

"He's not just a fed, he's worse. He's a bulldog. If you can derail him long enough—"

The buzzing drilled through everything.

"Hey, number two! Pick up the phone! What's going on?"

"There's no time," she said, turning the key in the slot. The elevator groaned. The buttons on the board blinked mad crazy like slot-machine time.

"This isn't happening," I said. "I'm not hearing this because we're not talking about this. I'm a fucking police officer."

"I know what you are." It was a soul-weary smile, a sense of shrug. No explanation necessary. She nodded. She hit the *M* button. Her eyes went hopeless.

"This isn't the time to be a cop," she said.

The elevator buckled and began a speedy drop. I felt words crowding me. I suddenly wanted to explain, the way I couldn't to every cop every Puerto Rican cousin every commander-in-chief. I just couldn't break the silence in that falling box. I wanted to stay there, the two of us going down fast. I was inside something, pulsating with life. It was that perfect moment when you feel everything is in flow. And then she messed it up by opening her mouth.

"David's counting on you," she said.

Barely had the words hit, the doors slid open. People were already pushing in by the time I managed to swim out into the open space of the elevator bank, to see she had vanished like a mirage, that bad dream that good dream.

The murderers were real pros. Dissolved locks. Gloves, drugs, electronic equipment.

"They pumped him full of scopolamine." Richards was

the medical examiner who did Spook. "It's an old-style truth serum drug used by the OSS in World War Two." Truth truth who was telling the truth? "Amnesiac drugs." Of the anticholinergics group, including atropine, hyoscine, and glycopyrrolate. Not to be confused with the mild stuff they give you for motion sickness. "In larger doses, it can cause irreparable brain damage."

The Buick Skylark used to deliver Spook was stolen from 146th Street and Grand Concourse. Fisk, Jack, and Tedder went through the car inch by inch. Seen in the area, two white men in business suits. Who hasn't seen white men in business suits these days in the South Bronx? On Jackson Avenue, I spotted two FBI agents standing on a corner like they were hailing a cab. I recognized that Dupreé fellow smoking a cigarette, laughing a joke. They weren't fooling anyone. They might as well have been wearing sandwich boards. I don't know what their angle was. My angle was: The bus driver said she asked for 149th Street. She ran down Prospect Avenue. I drove down that same way to where it ends slam against 149th Street. I parked there, lit that last cigarette, and stared at the building across the street.

It was where Roman lived.

I thought one trail led to the other. I wondered if it would seem that simple, that clear to Myers. He could connect the dots any way that suited him. I wanted to believe that Myers didn't know what I knew, but I wasn't convinced.

Of course, Roman wasn't home. I left more messages. I knew I could find him. Spook had been the same when he went under, sometimes leaving a face on the corner, the stoop, the bodega. Just a dude chewing on a plastic straw until you come along. It's no push-button thing. You have to hoof it, talk, share a cigarette. You have to know the route, know what door to knock on for answers.

"Where are you?"

I was speeding crazy swerve, back to Jackson Avenue. I

had the earphone plugged in so Myers was an insect presence as I drove.

"I'm at the fence, right by the grassy knoll," I said.

"And what do you see?"

"Just some fucking motorcade. Did you know there are FBI agents crawling all over Jackson Avenue?"

"That's right," he said. "They want to jump in now that the stakes are getting higher." He sounded breathless, like he was climbing up some back stairs. "They planted FBI agents outside the Ava Reynolds apartment, in case she goes back. There are FBI agents arriving at both Rosario residences. I suppose it doesn't look too good for them if some foreign terrorist mob is running around slaying Bronx residents." He chuckled. "Like that does any good now."

Lunch break? Mad, desperate chompings on something soft, breadlike. A flaky crunch.

"Man, I'm glad to be outside. It's been nothing but the stink of offices and the people who work in them. Staplers, paper clips, fax machines. Secretaries rubbing oil on their panty hose."

Roman would have called for his crew, for that black 4x4 that was his ride of choice whenever moving was necessary. I expected Old Man Santero to be in his bodega, as always. His son owned that Bronco, and if it was gone there was a good chance he was driving Roman around in it. The old man was always good for a chat, but this time the bodega was gated up shut. It couldn't have been just because it was Sunday . . .

"These people," Myers said, "work in stretches of fifteen minutes. You say something they don't like or expect, and they call another break. All morning it was like that, all afternoon. I'm glad I got myself this chili dog. Some real Puerto Rican food."

"Myers, a chili dog is not Puerto Rican food."

"Sure. *Chili con carne*. That's Spanish, isn't it?"

I was driving again, now thinking about the next checkpoint. The next place I could check for an open door to Roman.

"Anderson has a tape fetish. Looks like he wants to add some of mine to his collection. They've got nothing and they know it, so they're putting the squeeze on me and my operation. Now I'm the one that has to do the tidying up. They're going to involve your captain and your department. They're going to want to talk to you as well."

"Me? What the fuck for?"

My car shuddered as if I had just rolled over a body. Two bodies. I was doing too much speed. The wheels were squealing again.

"Well, you're the expert, aren't you?"

Eyesight blurred. Snapping the earphone off would not solve the problem with words. Words would still be there.

"Or maybe it's just that you appear on the tapes," he said.

What was I reaching for? Hands, pockets, steering wheel. The crack of a lighter. The breezes were turning mean. I rolled up the window. Swirling newspapers gum wrappers plastic bottle caps. There, burning in my stomach. Blaze blaze fire dizzy storm. A cigarette-sick knee wobble, a pasty sweat.

"So I'm on the tapes," I said. "So what."

"That's exactly what I said. So what." Myers, punctuating his contempt with those damned munching sounds. "It's no big deal, just you calling up every one of the key players in this investigation on a rather frequent basis, sometimes at odd hours of the night."

Strong winds, rattle of cans bottles paper products. Rain storm coming. Skies gray all sudden like an *aguacero* appearing over *el monte*. What do dreams of downpours and floods mean? I made a sound into the phone. I don't know if it was words.

"They haven't heard a single strip." Was he lighting a cigarette? Click click blaze. "I'd rather blow up my truck than let them walk off with it. Their snooping around would only derail this, and who needs that right now? So you see, Sanchez. It's between us."

"Between us," I said. A lump in my throat the size of a tomato. A sudden wave of static, or did Myers click off?

I pressed down on that pedal gas daddy gas no stopping for red. The only sound I wanted in my ears was surf. There was an airline stink to my car. The last puff from that ABSOLUTELY LAST cigarette was all filter. If he knew, why didn't he just corner me from the beginning? Somehow or other I must be serving my purpose. I couldn't figure out what game he was playing. We were headed for that big talk. I was headed toward Roman. How was it Myers didn't know about him? When his call came in, I thought it was Myers.

"It's Roman," he said. "So Spook is really dead?"

"That's right, Roman."

"Am I next?"

"I don't know."

"Someone came to see me today," he said.

I didn't want him to say more, not on the phone, not these days with bread trucks running around. Why hadn't Myers just come right at me? I figured a cop would have. Maybe that was the reason . . .

"Did she come to stay?"

"No," Roman said curtly, "but she left something for you."

Now I felt a fiery panic that went right to my accelerator pedal.

"I'll be right there," I said.

David, David, what were you thinking? There's never an easy way to become a millionaire. What went wrong, why didn't I just do my job? I was tired of my job. I fell through the cracks. All the king's horses and all the king's men didn't give a fuck if I came, if I played, if I stayed. I was out of the club two years ago. David knew it, he felt it. He almost told me I was making a mistake going after Dirty Harry. After that, he saw I was only going through the motions. Office, not so much street. Death threats. A roomful of cops, and not one single bastard to have a cup of coffee with. Only Jack to step through the window with for a smoke. Only Jack. The one person in all of this that I will truly miss. How it would hurt him to know—David showing me those pictures of Mallorca. Sun. Sand. Stitch. The guy's name was Stitch. A small-time musclehead who stuck to small-time shit. Smuggled stolen goods, ran credit card scams on the elderly. I knew him well because I knew Roman, and one led to the other like shit leads to flies.

I swerved sudden braking, to stop smack against curb sharp like a diamond. The street was streaked with blue light like a film set. I was running fast up some rickety back stairs. I took the steps two by two fast, footfall thumps like sonic booms. The super used the room as his office. His name was Montero. He was an old man who didn't want trouble, so he allowed Stitch to appropriate the office from time to time for his business needs. I never made trouble for Montero. His information always helped me track Roman. I never made appearances there. I wanted the house to stay "safe." It didn't matter much now that I made a racket on the stairs. I was sure I was expected.

Stitch opened the door. It was a small room, no window. A lone bare bulb on a string. A table, some chairs. Roman was working the hot plate. There was a coffee pot on it. Flames glimmered underneath like crooked teeth.

Roman looked sharp in his black suit. The eye patch seemed to keep his face stiff. He dismissed Stitch with a vague motion. We both listened for the thump of his steps on the stairs going down, waited for the slow creak slam of the storm door below.

"What took you so long?" he said.

Roman liked long silent moments when he could just sit and stare. He never liked to be the one to start anything. He could play that calm parry-and-thrust like a haughty duke. But this time I could tell he was nervous.

"Are the feds after me?"

"They're after the blonde."

"Yes, but because of the blonde, are they after me?"

"Not yet," I said.

I was trying to take my mind off the slow puffs he was taking. I could hear the paper crackling with burn, taste the smoke at the back of my throat. The immediate dry mouth sensation. He lost some of the stiffness, which I suppose passed for relief.

"Fucking David, man." There was a mixture of grief and fury. "He got me into it. He got you into it. She wasn't supposed to come to me, you know that. If you think I would've hung around waiting for you, you're crazy. I'm only here because of him."

His one eye seemed to unfocus. It was a dark pebble. An extra couple of puffs on the cigarette. He felt the back of his head with his hand.

"She came to my place. Snuck in through the window, no less. What am I doing, leaving my windows open at a time like this? She pulled a gun on me, the same gun I got for David!"

The coffee pot was a steaming locomotive. It was hard to see where Roman's one eye was looking. At me, past me, beyond me. Fuck that. I snatched the pack of cigarettes off the table, tapping out a few. (Something for the jacket pocket.) That perfect little tube rolled tight—I pulled the filter off. I reversed it and lit the filter side for a straight tobacco hit. The first puff the first puff

electric tendrils spinning hot fiery swirls—I closed my eyes a moment. I wanted to say a hundred things at once. His mouth was moving. I wasn't hearing words, just sounds just a feeling like the one that hit me when I was locked in that elevator with Ava Reynolds. I was in something, a part of something. No blinking lights on a dispatcher's map just yet. No clear, defined path. Roman took the coffee pot off the flame, while I felt myself dissolving in wisps of cigarette smoke. Roman poured his coffee black, not even sugaring it, and shot it back.

"She must've thought I was going to grab her or something. She bonked me, man. Knocked me out! Crept back out the window."

"Could you tell where she went?"

"Nah. I didn't have the time for a search. I was making my own move just then."

"But why did she come to you?"

"David." His eye went glassy. He winced as he passed his hand over the back of his head, where maybe there was a bump. "He sent her to me. It's the only reason she came."

"She didn't want your help."

"No. David wanted you to have this."

He reached into the inner breast pocket of his jacket, then held up the audio cassette. The moment I saw it, I knew what it was. It was a black cassette with white letters that said INCOMING MESSAGES. It was one of the tapes that came with that old Panasonic answering machine.

"Did she happen to have the machine with her?"

Roman was touching his head and wincing. "Next time get a messenger service."

"She mentioned me directly?"

"That's right. Like she knows all about you."

I held the tape in my hand, bombarded by images that flashed like the speeding cars of a train. I could see those last hectic moments. A mounting nausea. I could not extinguish my cigarette even though I had lost the appetite. (You start something, you finish it.) The small cassette player was blue, with speakers on either side like a shrunken ghetto blaster. I put the tape on, right in front of him, because he was in on it too. I needed him to be in on it. I started to think about the moment in any investigation when the path becomes clear. Milagros talked about waiting for a door to appear, but the Buddhists kept the best for last: It's not one door, but two. Not one straight path, but a fork in the road. There's always a choice to be made. I pressed my cigarette into the ashtray but it would not go out. The sizzling embers spun like snakes and kept reigniting the tobacco. I rolled it I stamped it crushed it down to torn paper and black ashy fingers. I could not keep the stink off. Roman only had one eye, but I could not look in there. It was full of flames. A fine, cold sweat on my burning face. Roman behind the cigarette was the scientist watching me climb the walls of my petri dish. He had seen my face during the Dirty Harry time. He knew, the instant I heard that voice on the tape. His words were more confirmation than query.

"*Coño* meng," he said, "so you know the murderer?"

At first I couldn't make sense of it. Why would Myers phone someone he was about to kill? Was it just the usual reckless American arrogance, a man with RIGHT on his side and no time for bothersome little details? Maybe he hadn't even planned on killing David but had to correct his mistake, realizing the man had something on him. Myers swiped the answering machine after all. It might not look good for him to be on there saying, *"They've got your brother and you're next, unless you give me what I want."* That careful phrasing hardly made it a convincing case. I was frozen, I was pulled this way, that. I listened to it again and again, over and over, until Roman shut it off. I couldn't see walking it over to the captain, who would roll his eyes and curse his luck. Internal Affairs or the FBI would probably be the same song and dance, plus how would I explain my role in all this? I felt sure David wanted me to have this tape because he wanted me to do something about it.

"Son of a bitch," I said. "We have to get to the blonde."

"And what?" Roman scoffed. "Stop her? Join her? I'm not the one who trusted her." His legs were stretched out under the table, crossed at the ankles. Boots of Spanish leather. "David trusted her. He's dead. Do you trust her?" He got up from the table to face me. "I don't want to hear this shit about ten million. That's theoretical. I've never been religious and I don't expect no manna from heaven. Tony and David are dead. I saw you go after a cop once because he was shooting spick kids in the back." He pulled out a cigarette with an angry motion. "I want to know just what the fuck you're going to do about this."

Flash as he lit up. Why did he have to bring up Dirty Harry? Was he trying to say that because I went after a cop I was NO COP? LESS of a COP? That I had descended to a lower level and was no longer the SAME as a cop? Where did that leave me in the eyes of someone like Roman? Did that at least make me human? On the street there is a different justice. Nobody waits for the cops to come. Nobody even expects them. People prefer to take care of things them-selves. Looking into that one flaming eye, that round glowy pit, I finally got the message. Cops are sometimes outside the loop. The bulb on a string was moving. I felt the urge for a cigarette and fought it off.

I was thinking about her now, in a totally different light. Anderson's words, Roman's. How it seemed Myers disap-peared just when I had questions to ask him about her. If he planted her there to find the gold, maybe it wasn't that she "went" with David against Myers. Maybe she just took the gold. She could have set up Spook and then she could have killed David—it could have been her

somehow someway she could have set them both up to get knocked out of the way because she was working Myers all along

"You think she killed him?"

my question spilling out, no thought no real look at the facts but trying to find that personal level. A slow bewilderment on Roman's face, the eye blurring with thought.

"I know how to find her," he said.

16.

Waking from dream. Or still dreaming.

Or not. Barely memory of dream, just black after drinking. Sharp jumpcut from then to now. No sense of sleep. His body wasn't rested. He could have been dreaming if not for that pasty sick taste in his mouth. The need to piss, bad. That was what woke him.

The woman in his bed did not wake him.

The chair creaked. He had fallen asleep in the chair. He had planted it just right so he could watch her. Sat on it back to front and, leaning there with that long slim bottle to finish, he fell asleep. Or it all went vague and dark and then there was now. No telling how much time no telling even when. At least it wasn't a work day. He was almost sure.

It was a purple sky, a calm airless evening. Streetlights glowed dull and sleepy. He felt the bump at the back of his head. Again those brief pain sparks. He looked at her lying there across the bed. She was still in his clothes. He told himself that he wasn't going to turn his back on her, but it looked like he'd killed her with that one bop of the toy bat. It really looked like he had laid her out with just one blow, and so he felt safe to go take a leak, making sure nonetheless to take her purse with him.

In the bathroom, the dress still hung from the shower curtain rod like a limp flag. He flushed the toilet, splashed the slowness from his face, rinsed the metallic taste from his mouth.

He placed the purse on top of the wicker hamper.

The shower he took was brief. The stream of water set

off minute brush fires in his head. He dried off with the only towel hanging there. Then he picked up the purse. He examined the strap. It was detachable, with a locking hook on either end.

"The strap on my purse is broken," she had said, holding up a loose end.

"Shit," he said.

He spilled the purse's contents on the blue furry bathmat.

The shoes came first. The delicate curvy arch. Manolo Blahnik. Since when was he with a woman who wore those? Shoes were his business. They were the first thing he noticed on a woman. Generally.

The lipsticks, compact, assorted makeup items. A CD slipcase. Daffy Duck plushy. All into a pile.

The cellular phone. He put aside.

The Smith & Wesson .22 pistol, with spare clip. He put aside.

The yellow envelope had writing on it. Inside was an ID card pinned to a letter. *This Document authorizes Ava Reynolds to have access to safe-deposit box 6315 on behalf of David Romero and Fischer-MacMillan, Inc.*

The ID card was from the same company and had a picture of a wide-eyed, clean-cut Puerto Rican yuppie type. The letter was addressed to a bank on Third Avenue. Alex checked the address again, then put it all back into the envelope.

The gun had a metallic oil smell and hadn't been fired. It felt strangely familiar, as if his skin recognized it: She had hit him with it. He could almost feel the sharp sting of the metal striking him. With that, she had blanked out the rest of his day better than a tall bottle of bourbon. He thought carefully about what it could mean, that she bopped him. He'd had enough strange incidents with women during those hectic, near-forgotten one-nighters. He knew it was better sometimes not to overreact.

He thought about calling the police, like anyone would. Most people in distress will think of calling the cops if there's a spot of trouble. But Alex was a Puerto Rican who lived in the South Bronx, and that meant that any time he was in trouble he had to hesitate before calling the men in blue. It's just something to do with the way things go wrong between cops and Puerto Ricans. Something in the tone, the approach, the lack of communication skills on the cop part, and once they are in your house—BESIDES if a spick from the South Bronx called the police and said HELP! THERE'S A WHITE BLOND WOMAN IN MY BED, a battalion of cop cars would arrive within moments, sirens shrieking tires screaming. The people Alex knew always tended to be more DIY about such matters. It was usually better not to involve the cops.

He was still thinking about this when that blinding flash—the snap of a twig—the falling down fast slow, bathroom floor speeding up to face. Trying to turn to rise through churn to see through fiery snakes and ladders, a veritable falling star

she was holding the toy bat saying I'm sorry, I'm sorry and as he faded she was moving over him, pulling pulling

17.

because it was a soul-weary smile, a sense of shrug. No explanation necessary. She hit the *M* button. Her eyes went hopeless. A tiredness, an anger, some little girl some little boy a little lost when I looked in there

because she asked the question

because she slipped into that elevator fighting. Same David voice same David tone and she was more than herself because she was fighting for him, almost a cause a flag a sense that now (finally) she was on the right path

because she looked at me with eyes that knew me, and from the first time to the last time there was no sense of needing words. She wanted to tell me. "There's no time." She knew my crippled, fallen state. Or she would not have said a word. No reason for her to tell me

because she worked for the killer, if that is what he is. She worked for him up until when, what moment, when did she turn? Myers clearly didn't want to talk about her and didn't stay to chat, but there was burn on his face, the echoes of her slap

because Roman met her in the park with David, the three of them slurping on *coquitos*. Roman likes to do his crimes in private and here was David, bringing an audience. She sat like she was memorizing them, playing the clingy girl-friend, somewhat hand in hand. Roman insists. He didn't trust her then and he doesn't trust her now.

"She could've lied," he said. "First got in with David real tight. Got inside him, got inside the scam, got this Myers to bump off Spook, and then David."

"But how did she get Myers to make the phone call?"

We were playing ASK EVERY QUESTION THAT COMES TO MIND no matter where it leads, what conspiracy theory, what magic bullet. There was that feeling of running down a long hallway.

"It was part of the deal. She's there when they come to the apartment. She hands it over, get it?" Roman lit a cigarette with a flash. "But instead, she runs off. David gets plugged. She gets the ten million."

Now rain now sun. Sky goes dark, then bright. A pair of cell phones clamoring for attention. Rain, sun. The witch was getting married. The 4x4 following us was a dark cloud in the rearview mirror.

"But if that's true, why would she bring you the tape?"

My question sucked out the air. I had Roman in my car, bugged or not. Better for Myers to hear. What would he make of it, what would he think? Lies are funny things, the way they build their own traps. One must keep meticulous records.

Roman seemed to think long and hard. I felt like he was trying to build a case.

"She came to me," he said, "because she needs you to take Myers out."

Myers. Guilty not guilty, true hero or rogue. The insect presence in my ear. Lieutenant Jack noticed he was missing lately, wondered if maybe the guy got what he wanted and hiked his ass back to D.C. I knew better. He was a living presence, everywhere at once. I took it for granted he could hear me, see me, follow me on an illuminated map. I wasn't going to lose him. He wasn't going to lose me. There would soon be Anderson's rock-hard face, maybe the personification of what was left of my conscience. He could've said, "Why didn't you come to me?" He wouldn't bother. He already knew why. That elevator-drop sensation that stone-rock Roman face, clearly having second thoughts about everything, but it was probably just resentment.

I was tired of pretending there were choices anymore. I was shooting down a path. I was growing a new face. No time for stray thoughts. No raindrop-on-windowpane moments, no need to stay sane to join the crusade or be part of the bunch. This was independence day this was the end of the collective security of the group.

The theater was just off Van Cortlandt. It still had an old marquee. Its battered face must have been the thing of postcards once. Regal, archaic, The Majestic was an old Bronx movie theater that closed down in the early '80s. It stood alone on a block flanked by empty lots and a couple of tenements whose businesses on the ground floor were all shuttered. There were no movies playing on its big screen, the rows still standing but bereft of seats. It was an empty space, dusty and rotted. The front was cinder-blocked up, but that wasn't the way in. A tenement next door had a small business, a funeral parlor. It shared a basement entrance. That was how Roman brought me there.

Roman ran this little operation from the top floor. Fenced goods, stolen property, a whole warehouse. Boxes, crates, car parts. One area was full of CD burners stacked in tens, jewel cases by the crate, and a complete rig for running off cheap pirate discs. There was pop and hip-hop and scores of *bachata* compilations that his scurrying merchants sold at five bucks a pop from every sidewalk in town. In the office, he had laminating machines, printers, two color copiers, and an entire offset printing setup. Another room: boxes of passport stamps, blank state IDs, DMV stickers, and even a box of blank credit cards. These were the money schemes Roman was into now as he slowly phased himself out of the drug trade. He was "moving on," away from instability and danger to lucrative and less aggressive forms of quick cash. Pirate CDs, forging, stolen goods. Car parts! There were also weapons, another department he was phasing out. When the police raid this place, they will see the mixed assortment of automatic weapons, pistols, and those three grenade launchers as an arsenal for an army planning an uprising. Roman was Puerto Rican. There was no uprising. It was about making money.

The funeral parlor was a front. It was run by three old guys who probably never buried anyone in their lives. The entrance was solemn and tasteful, but once past that coffin showroom it was all warehouse. In the basement, walking past thick pipes and a boiler, what stuck in my mind was the elevator. It was steel, no walls, just a solid platform big enough to fit Roman's 4x4. On coming in, we actually had to walk through a part of the elevator shaft. Down there, a corridor, a rusted yellow pipe. It jutted out of brick and disappeared into the floor. I lost Roman a moment, then noticed he was a floor above me, fiddling with a little yellow box on the wall.

"What are you doing?"

"The elevator's broken," he said. He fiddled in the box some more. There was a loud clatter boom and the platform far above my head started moving. It was a few floors up. It was coming down right at me. There was no clearance in the shaft except for that small corridor. I made for it, grateful that the big steel door was open. I barely cleared it before the platform landed. I mounted it, and rode back up to Roman.

"Very funny."

"Accidents can happen," he said, "even to cops."

We rode the platform up two more floors, to the very top. A dingy skylight. A long corridor. The floor was bare planks of wood, like on a construction site. Inside a cage, piles of computer equipment. He unlocked the door and started rooting around in some boxes.

"Spook loved intricate systems, these sort of Rube Goldberg setups with people instead of cogs, each one filling a role that makes the machine work. But nobody was really aware of anything outside of their small, limited role."

Roman seemed to be reminiscing as he thumbed through blank ID cards in one box, photostats of card faces in another.

"Safe-deposit boxes were his favorite. He loved to pull tricks with them, you know. A key that leads to a box that leads to another box with another key that leads to a box with a code word, an address, or phone number. He had scores of these little deals set up. Paid people just to hold a package, to hold it until one day someone comes to the door and says, *Afghanistan banana stand*."

"Plus, he's got a million cousins." I thought I wasn't smoking, but the minute Roman lit up, it was fire time.

"He must have worked this the same way. I didn't add it together before, but when David came to me for those ID cards, I wasn't thinking it had anything to do with the swipe. I still fell for that clean routine."

Now he was looking through a box of plates, the masters of cards he had already made. Most pro forgers ditch this stuff, but pride in good work sometimes turns them into collectors. And sometimes Roman does refills.

I was a cop, madness, a wonderland bust, a sea of officers flooding in behind me. Once it would have been a big moment. Now it was ridiculous paltry, proceeds going to charity. I could leave it all to Lieutenant Jack. He deserved the collar for busting an operation we never bothered to fuck with.

"You think he set this shit up the same way?"

"Sure."

"So she has a key?"

"A key. Or something leading to a key. I'm pretty sure of it. And she'll probably use one of these cards to do it. A fake account, a letter of authorization . . ."

He handed me a couple of plates. I felt a weird shudder, involuntary. A ghost tickling my elbow with a feather: The name on the card was *David Romero*.

Roman exhaled, as if a weight had been lifted. What else? Regret, as if deep down he felt he were helping the wrong side. I didn't know about sides. I had reached the fork in the road, the big choice. Was that Myers on my cell phone again? I was not building a file this time. I was not walking it over to Internal Affairs this time. I saw nothing but closed faces, a huge system of tacit agreements and secret handshakes. I felt alone again, much more than before. If I tried to trust a cop, trust the turns and twists of the system, where would that get me? I was implicated. I needed to sit with Myers and find out how much. Was this what he planned? Was this his plan, her plan all along? Roman had a point: How could I be sure she wasn't working for him still? I needed to look in her eyes again, to weigh the feeling, see if I had read her right the first time. Maybe her rebellion was my rebellion . . . I had to start thinking like her. "This isn't the time to be a cop." I could see it clearly now, that gold shield on the captain's desk. Maybe Myers wanted me to think if I handed her over to him, the slate would be wiped clean. "It's between us." I have suddenly ended up working for him. I am the new recruit, the next member of the team. What could Myers possibly do for me, reinstate me as a cop? Get my respect back? Stop the death threats, the stares, the cold shoulders? What could she do? Pay me. Carry the plan through to the finish. David and Spook talked about moving the money out of the country, where the trail would get blurry and fade amongst the many varied jurisdictions. "I once dreamed of having my own island," I'd said. The Great Escape, Steve McQueen vaulting over barbed wire on a motorcycle. "Well, maybe not your own island," David had replied, "but . . ." Sun. Sand. Beach. Spanish. My wife and I have already booked a flight for our vacation. A nice hotel, Valldemossa, "The Hotel Vistamar." An appointment in a bank in Palma de Mallorca to confirm an account, a down payment on a house in Port de Soller . . . ridiculous . . . "You can make up your own mind then," David added, a nice stiff payment just for looking the other way, stalling for obstruction. This was something else. Right way, wrong way. A Hitchcock movie where the good guys kill the wrong guy. There was only one way to make it work. I had passed the fork in the road. (I was fooling myself.)

Roman's stare was empty, drained from thinking. He must have been traveling those same roads.

"You can't do it, Sanchez . . . you can't save yourself. And I can't save the organization." His last puff on that nib of cigarette. "You still want to find her?"

"That's right," I said, handing him the plates back. "How long would it take you to run off a couple of cards for me?"

Roman sighed, took the plates. We went back downstairs on the elevator, to the office.

The talk came in whispers. Walking streets hunched over from breezes shaking trees. Traffic backed up. A black 4x4 circled the block. Roman was running from *cueva* to *cueva*, collecting all his nuts. He checked the windows he checked the doors. Last thing he wanted was for his boys to get a whiff of some ten million. The thought nagged at him that should some money come to him after, he would have to kiss this world goodbye. It was all toast, all glimmery ash. Something going down, the natives can smell it. Bosses heading underground, visibles scurrying into holes. Spook's organization was falling apart. Every branch could smell a raid, a police swoop, a big bash. Someone said it was the cops who knocked off Spook, some old score that had to be settled. When the head of an organization is killed, it ripples the whole populace around and within. All sends signals all makes a statement. Even if the cops put forty-one bullets in a guy by mistake, it's the signal, the statement: forty-one bullets.

Roman couldn't see any way any how that he would be attached to the money. He couldn't see any way any how that there would be a payday, a reason to risk his neck, maybe even less now that Spook was dead. He had said no then. He was still trying to say no. When I told him my plan, he was furious. There was no way he was going to set himself up like that.

"The cops are coming anyway," I said, "and besides, it's not you I'm setting up. You're just the bait."

"I'm telling you, man, I don't like it." We were both outside the theater, watching the traffic flow through calm purple dusk. I felt stupid, out of my league, searching for a way to convince him it was in his interest to throw in with me and not just vanish. He could do that. I could blather about accounts, Mallorca, and money to come, but I already knew that was no way to get him. It was really not the reason. In fact, he had very little reason to throw in with a crooked cop who thought he would try to make good.

"Forget it," I said, brushing him off. I was walking to my car. "Go ahead. Disappear."

"Hey, wait a minute."

"No. Look, the more I think about it, the more I see this is just my personal business. I got myself into it. What I'll have to do now is just about me. Not you. You're right. You weren't in this. So go, disappear. I'll try to keep them far from your ass."

"Hey, you hold on."

I don't think Roman has ever grabbed a cop, not by the collar up close like that, right up to his flaming eye. It froze me. It froze him.

"I don't know about the money shit. I'm telling you, if you throw in with that girl expecting a payday, you're going to get ripped. But I still want a piece of the bastards that killed Spook. They took a piece of my life with them and somebody's gotta pay for that. After, I'll disappear. Just don't try to buy me."

"I'm not."

He released me gradual, a sense of shock. A slow coming to himself. The return of the stiff hard to his face.

"Just tell me." Was that disgust curling his lip? "Just tell me you know this guy is the murderer."

The spread of that hard burn from my face to the rest of my body like a heat lamp. I could phone Anderson, just to make sure Myers had been with him all this time, but what would that prove? The guy had a team. I had only ever seen two, but who knows how many more worked for him? Did people even know they were working for him?

"I know she thinks it's him." Roman pacing his words like a prosecutor. "I even know she wants you to think it's him. What about you?"

"But he's after me, don't you see that?"

It was more than I had wanted to say but the only words I could press out. All of a sudden I couldn't stand it. The tenement windows all lined up like a jury. The thought I was being watched the whole time, my actions framed on video, my words on spools of tape, and this asshole pushing me around on these streets that I know like every deep wound

and those stupid young smirking bastards I pushed him I pushed him choke so sudden he falling in my grip and it was ME feeling like the one-eyed freak in the country of the blind and it never occured to me that I could be king that I could be running this town—the bad closing dialogue from a Clint Eastwood film—the typical American hero taking justice into his own hands. Roman's head made a wood sound every time it hit the wall hit the wall hit the wall. All he knew was the old script, the black-and-white scheme that kept life simple. Good guys bad guys. Some stupid shit too about standing up for what you believe in, and that's not always flag queen country. I pushed him up against chain-link.

"Listen, don't be grabbing me like that again, okay? Because out here I'm still a cop. You got that? You still walk two steps behind me!"

I hit him again, didn't I hit him? He slid down chain-link, a slow sidewalk crumple. I must have kicked him. Those boys on the street, "Wattup, yo?" They know I'm a cop, they come running they want bark like dogs they want pull guns like big-time hoods they don't do nothing just come to a skid and I look at them and I kick him again and this big curly head yells, "Hey, are you making an arrest? Are you making an arrest?" And tenement windows swirl the same like eyes the same smells the same dusky gray I remember from 1993. "I'm still a cop," I say, some dignity, some straightening of the suit. Some looking down. I drag him up to his wobbly feet. And they still step back, but not so far back like they used to once.

I let go of him. Roman's eye dizzy blurred. He was trying to catch his breath after I winded him, gasping like a marathon runner. I walked away from him. I walked away and lit the next cigarette. How did so many find their way into my pockets? The pecking order of these streets and how I hate it. Better for Roman to be seen getting beat by a Dirty Harry than for them to think their boss was consorting with the enemy. The car door slam obliterates all sound. The tick ticking of no clock. The tweety chime of my cell phone.

"Where are you?"

The same buzzing insect in my ear that would not go away. A voice trapped inside of me. The part of me I created.

"I'm shooting some film at the grassy knoll," I said.

"What do you see?"

"Three shooters," I said.

You can wake from a dream and realize you are still trapped in someone else's dream.

PART TWO

*It is my bad luck and my supposed biggest happiness
to use things the way that I want to. How sad for the
painter who loves blond women but can't put them in
a painting because they don't match with the fruit
basket. In my pictures I use all the things I like.
How those things feel about it, I don't care.*
—Pablo Picasso

18.

It had always been colors. It started on canvas, unrolling outwards by itself. Contours appear. Things would take shape with no heavy mental prodding. A vague feeling, that had been enough. Desire. A handful of brushes clattering in a tin can. He would work until the acrylic got thick and it felt like he was painting with gravel. It was raw instinct, all rhumba cha-cha voodoo. Back then, every time he splashed colors, something happened. He blamed Monk for bringing him interminable concepts, these sociological undercurrents. Dry days and blank canvases immediately followed, as if trying to be specific stifled the crazy wild that led to birth.

Now it was new, this throb this pulse, almost an old feeling except that this was no chance encounter with colors, no splash-and-see: It was specific, it was theme and concept. It first drove him to sketch with pencil and charcoal. Sometimes it was just the fine lines of her, sometimes shadowy contours. Sometimes sometimes. Page after page hour after hour no sense of day passing. Into night phones ringing answering machine squawking. A bed becomes an island. A shiny wood floor, the gleamy Caribbean. A whole sketchbook filling with his many variations on a theme. To set up the easel was one thing, stretch canvas, hammer and nail: To paint was another. Tinkering with empty cans and paint tubes. The picture windows darkened with night before he began.

Past 2 in the morning, Mink completely forgot to call Monk. Monk likewise did not call him. There would be no restless search for meaning as they killed the hours waiting for daylight.

The blond girl had started to appear on canvas. Blanket of beach. Sun. Sand. Heavy-lidded sleeping. Didn't know if she could wake—for starters, he hadn't seen the color of her eyes. He could always ask Alex. Would he even know, bother to notice, bother to care? It would be just like the guy to ditch a prize piece like that, especially now that Mink would probably need some sort of release form. He couldn't just steal her, sleeping like that. He would have to ask her. The fear came not from the idea of seeing her again but rather from the worry that Alex, in his instant-woman wisdom, had by this hour already dumped her. He was thinking about that when he noticed the skylight above beginning to glow with first sun.

LIGHT

light was strange coming through the stairwell windows. glazed honeycomb glitter. sunlight bright but no bite. air chilly from floor to floor and in the lobby a strong breeze that ruffled paper napkins chewing gum wrappers. a good moment to pause. the building had four separate stairwells and a huge lobby. monk's place was front left, third floor. alex was front right, at the top. what stairwell went where depended on what side you were facing and how drunk you were. which was how alex was most times he sought monk out for clarity.

this time alex was not drunk. he was not fighting off the effects of blackout. the moist dress was in his hand, swinging like hair.

alex only knocked twice. the door opened right away as if monk had been "right there." his eyes were liquidy clear. the moment he spotted the dress, his face changed. he touched it, verified its realness. a smile, slow gradual like a stoner.

"Come inside," Monk said.

TIME
it wasn't time that was the problem it was the distance. the distance from someplace else. the place you are meant to be. something tells you when you're there. it's a mixture of signals, a certain grace. there are no sudden close-ups. no violins rising to an emotional crescendo.

more like a sense of recognition. the way light shifted against those windows. signs leading back to a place. stored in memory cells. leaking from some past life. the place you had run from. a place to run back to.

this thought. made the shutters come right down.
she wasn't into remembering.

she wasn't into astrology. she didn't generally believe in what she couldn't see, and didn't seek out tarot card readers, psychics, or seers. up until her experience with sarita, she had been skeptical. past lives? she only remembered one. a spoiled rich girl looking for kicks. gave her heart to a maverick agent. liked to see her perform. he was frameups, corporate scams. information gathering. formed his own team, made friends in hide places. flew off to texas for three weeks and came back a new man. talking about oil and national security and a new american century. gets work with cia to track money flowing into the country, money linked to terrorists. past lives? a succession of names, different faces. she makes like a doll she makes like a hooker a thief a liar. she makes like a lover she makes like a friend. time and time past, one job over she would do it again because she sort of hated him and liked him those long fuck nights when she could take what she could get, and he would get so wound up if she talked about quitting. "don't say that, don't ever say that." a child about to smash all his toys. and maybe she liked sometimes feeling like a possession, though she prided herself on her independence, her fast land life "in the service of your country." she was always morbidly fascinated by men who pimp off the women they love. it's the same even in the name of higher ideals. that last job—she expected a frame a setup the typical police raid at the end of the show, but when the curtain call came, four people were dead and she was through with it. she woke one day and didn't recognize herself in the mirror. that is, she did not see a person. she saw she could not place that current face with any she that she knew

that her name that her life was fake always a role, an empty pose a set of characteristics adapted not felt, not lived, not real. and if she always asked who she was when she looked in the mirror, she never got the answer like she did in the mirror of sarita's beauty salon when that young woman in the '30s cut looked back at her. almost black-and-white she was, shimmery soft focus. past lives? it was anne sexton she found one sunny afternoon, wandering the bowels of harvard's massive library

or was it wellesley, or was she thinking princeton? didn't matter which. she hadn't registered.

that skinny anne so slunk, so hiding from glare. beneath a stack of books like the last chicken in line, pecked bloody. a little battered but no less a firm spine, a hard cover, a crisp newness to every yellowed page. it was anne she chose that day while in search of something she couldn't identify. she opened a book and found, for the first time, words that would not go away. she could recall the page number remember the words recite as if burned into memory every letter every crinkle. she had known this closeness with numbers, but never before words. anne expressed her. she knew the words before she read them. they were not transformations, but confirmations. the discovery of her photographic memory came only through anne, through her poems, her letters, her life. like practice. rehearsals. training. "you can go far with a brain like that," some voice said. she took retention tests. disorienting quizzes. a black room. slides that flashed in an eyewink. whole pages of information, absorbed. swallowed, spit back whole, line for line. better than xerox. no microfilm to hide, no tiny camera to be confiscated—no documents ripped from the lining of a handbag. and she could lock her face like a safe. "imagine, you wouldn't even need a camera." that was trudy talking. "you've already got one in your head." ava started to think about her head as a camera loaded with film, each frame a memory, a moment, a piece of past. what happens when you run out of film? every head has only a certain amount of frames. once this camera runs out of film, it simply puts a new image on top of the old. ava found herself rushing to anne so that every bad moment was replaced by a poem, a page, a segment of her life. it was almost an exchange. soon memories would become poems, anne words. anne life. she didn't want any more bad moments to blot out, no more dead bodies to feel somehow responsible for. that people were killed was never part of the deal. the night she told him, "I think it's better if I try it on my own," something people used to say on THE LOVE CONNECTION when the date went wrong—he went ballistic. The first time he beat her. he was sorry, he cried like a baby. took trudy to talk her into joining the team in new york, they could just try, that's all, and if it didn't work out then they could still have new york

and that was what made her say yes, and this at a time when he was becoming more unbearable. not even dates anymore, and since the killings she didn't want him touching her. she couldn't see anyone else, he was too jealous too crazy—and she was in the room when he pulled the trigger pulled the trigger. "the realization that she's outlived her usefulness is one of the worst feelings a hooker can have," he said. "you are so much luckier than that." (the slap that resounded, and along with it, his laugh. him playing the star-spangled banner at every seventh inning stretch ruined being an american for her faster than fascism.)

but new york—she had been attracted since birth
the skyline was so deeply embedded in her mind it seemed a mirage, maybe atlantis or some marvel comics city. the world trade center was the first place she came to see, to stare straight up at those towers reaching deep into sky. she skated in the pretty park down by the water, strolled the walkways that reminded her of minneapolis. shopped in the bustling underground mall that led to the world financial center. and she, walking amidst the hustle of suits and ties, decided this time she would not just play a role, pick up a life, and discard it at the end of the play. this time she would become a person.

she saw that person in the mirror of sarita's beauty parlor.

LIGHT
the light was strange coming through the bedroom window. prismatic color almost like stained glass. churchlike, serene. a choir should have been singing. no hassle for monk to pop a few more oranges in the juicer.

"That dress really looks familiar somehow," Monk said. Feeling it again like braille, touching its intertwined rose petals.

"You on your way to work?"

"Yeah." The juice was a cold, sweet splashing blast down his chest.

"You got time for a quick cup and a smoke?"

there was a strange energy in the apartment. something was going on and this made the walls nervous. the bomb shelter had now become a headquarters. the big typewriter sat on the kitchen table. stacks of paper, a box of blank white taking up a chair, typewritten sheets spilling across. no sound of typing but somehow still the echoes of that ratatat and it was on monk—his energy now flowing fast, not the laid back gradual like before. with their cups and their smokes, they sat in front of the bedroom window. it was quiet there and for a while there was no need of words. the bedspread behind them lit up rosy with sun. the two rocking chairs they sat in creaked gentle. it felt momentarily like sitting on a *balcón* in puerto rico. prospect avenue instead of palm trees. the wheeze of a bus instead of *coquí*.

"I had a strange night last night," Alex began.

Monk lit his tobacco, stroked his stubble.

"I felt sure I imagined it." He touched the dress absently, which he had hung over a shoulder. "But then there's the dress."

Monk rocked faster, his bare toes gripping the sill.

"Does this have anything to do with that blonde I saw going up the fire escape last night?"

Alex felt the strange urge to jump out of his skin, to scream, to grab Monk and shake him. Something inside him wanted to get out, get born, get on with it.

"You saw her?"

The creaking of their chairs in rhythm.

"It was pissing rain," he said. "Almost 4:00. I would've normally been with Mink, but he pissed me off so I came home. I was looking around for something, I don't know what. Restless window thing. I had just lit a bowl of fine *chiba* and was watching the rain come down. I leaned out the window to check on the stoop in case Mink was down there, but there was no Mink."

Alex was imagining her climbing the fire escape in the dress, which he hadn't yet seen her wear. An odd thing, having seen her naked first. An odd thing, that the dress should be hanging from his shower curtain rod like something intimate.

"I could've swore I caught a glimpse of something down there. I craned my neck to look, and I swear I almost dropped my pipe. It was a blond woman, climbing up the fire escape, slow and stealthy. When I saw you holding that dress, I thought, fuck—I've seen that before. I couldn't see the color too good at night, but the pattern, something about it I could see. I could see she was barefoot too."

Alex sipped his coffee, puffed on the cigarette. An even, steady calm. A solid rhythmic rocking. So safe it was almost cradle. Could sleep now. She had those strapless, bit of a heel clackies on. He knew from first sight that they were Manolo Blahniks. How funny, how she kept them in her purse.

"Bro, I craned my neck out so far I almost fell out."

A ripple of laugh. A sense of relief. The feeling that all were present and accounted for.

"I saw her go up to the very top. I lost her up there, somewhere near where you are."

Monk's eyes, wide and mystified, now turned all their curiosity on him. He was never one to hog the story, for he especially liked people telling their own stories.

Alex took up the thread, waking up with the blonde, dizzy uncomprehending. Met Mink, took him upstairs because why, because maybe Mink, being real, could confirm she was real. "I tried your door on the way down," he said, "but you were typing."

"That's what happened to me," Monk said. "All this time I couldn't get to work, it was like something was in the way. Last night, that blowout with Mink . . . I just haven't been writing. I was looking out the window like I always do, like I'm looking for something. I think I found it. I stayed at the window for a while, thinking maybe I would see her again, or thinking I had gone nuts. Then I thought, yeah, right! She was climbing up to Alex. And then, this buzz. I went straight to the typewriter. Thirty-eight pages later, my back hurts, I have neck pain, my vision's blurry . . . it's glorious." Monk's face creased up. "Hey, what about Mink? What did he say when he saw her?"

Alex smirked. "He asked me where I got her. His eyes were all lit up. He kept circling the bed like he was checking out a Rodin."

"Hmf." Monk was rocking twitchy. He stopped suddenly and smiled. "Maybe my boy got himself a buzz."

"It could be." Alex almost thought Mink was somehow angry with him at the end. Couldn't tell why. "He sure left in a hurry after he saw her."

"What about when she woke up?"

Alex didn't find it easy to tell the story. It wasn't that he couldn't remember. It was that he could. Monk was much more used to having to drag the story from him, bridging gaps, connecting the dots. As it rolled out to Monk that she bonked him, that he bonked her, and that she bonked him again, there was a look of wonder and amazement that Alex had never seen on Monk's face.

"You're shitting me, right?"

"Nah, man. She bonked me." Alex showed him the back of his head. "I bonked her. And the second time, she . . ."

A radiant burst of images. More like dream than real. The fire escape was glowy with moon. She was that dark outline, moving at night. She was against the wall, looking at him. He thought he was dreaming. He still thought that. She took her shirt off, slipped out of the jeans. A smooth, female shadow.

She said shhh when he murmured, tossed, turned. Had

a calm, careful touch. She undressed him with the stern precision of a nurse, then got into bed with him. It happened slow. It happened in parts. Time-lapse photography, how a rose grows. Her skin felt fresh, a cool chill. He could make out her eyes, dark staring.

He touched her wet face.

"Why are you crying," he'd asked.

She touched his fingers. Then she turned, spooned into him. Still kept the hand.

"I'm worried about you," she'd said.

She was gone when he woke up. He'd had no sense of having slept but the jarring feel of having awoken. The sun was too bright on the gleamy floor. There was no air, a thick gelatin feel to his legs. He touched the back of his head: sharp flashes of pain. A sense of stupidity, of blankness. The apartment seemed emptier than before. There was the thought that he had already done this scene.

"It sounds to me," Monk said, "like you're having a relationship."

TIME

it wasn't time that was the problem, it was the distance. the distance from what? something hidden. not lara croft as portrayed big-lipped and big-titted. this was something worse. filling those blank spaces along the way with bravado. big time to chant poetry. build dams. shore off streams and fissures. landscape out some land. go out and cowboy some indians. not care much where or who. the old life was over. every room a new big inning. "a blonde always deals from strength." yes, but that was trudy talking. swallowing the myth of sex as power. madonna's pelvis/ britney's tan tummy/jennifer's *culo*, but was that freedom

and power or the weight of obligation? serious life training. mariah carey slashing and UNslashing her wrists. the
suspicion very strong that there would be no amelia earhart this generation unless she sported a bare midriff and
did a booty dance.

it was the usual blonde battle with casting.

her head was okay. no blood no pounding no deep sting.
no sense that she had been wronged. maybe more of a feeling that she had it coming—the tears had been unneces-
sary but unstoppable, a mad wave as she dragged him from
the bathroom, and it felt like murder, like murder again or
some death about to be, all because of situation because of
her because of something she brought with her, and if she
could ever stop dragging people into her shit she would be
more than grateful more than happy to for once not be in
the middle of some grand death play—

and, as if she could be the kiss of death (didn't he call her
that once?), so above caring about the havoc she wreaked
in her wake (the snake that bites the tortoise because that's
its nature)—no remorse meddling with what must be, but
who said it must

who says she couldn't change things flip them around become like a person?
and yet when she knocked alex out again she saw herself
reacting from instinct from training from fear. of having to
say of having to explain of alex calling the police—and that
would mean alan—a gut reaction a quick fix that left her
miserable and all sudden, alone

the least she could do
put him in bed check his wound make sure he wasn't dead.
a panic a fear again of being alone. a cold compress a whis-

pered prayer. she undressed him she undressed. she got into bed with him. contact insuring he didn't sneak up on her he didn't run off just in case it would occur to him to make a move she was as close to him as a wife and to be sure she could feel his every move

(she had his hand, and kept it with her)

tied connected no separation no space in between so no escape no running no fear of him and when his eyes closed with sleep she would not ask

was she holding him or was she holding onto him?

19.

and no feeling
as good as that first bite of a *perníl* sandwich from Julio's
on 149th Street just off Wales. That toasty bread crushed
down crunchy crackle the meat stringy soft hot like flaming.
That sudden flavor attack of a curl of salty pigskin snap
crackle crick with every munch

(he was being real or he was being fake, and that was the
key. The *perníl* sandwich brought color to his face. Not so
pale not so wide-eyed hungry now, but that mind of his
working like a calculator.)

I told him he should have some real Puerto Rican food and
that's why I started the fucker off with a Cuban sandwich.
(A little payback, a little inside joke.) He haggard he looking a little slow yet the energy in his eyes pulsing wicked.
I thought a beer would loosen him up. What are the truest
words spoken in American culture? It's not "make my day"
or "it's quiet . . . too quiet," heard in westerns and war
movies. The truest words spoken in American culture are:
"Cover me." Every American alive knows them. Every American alive knows what they mean. They are the symbol, the
call words of a fraternity. A brother turning to a brother for
help: "I got your back." Words that say we're American. No
matter what color what culture what stripe, that we are there
for each other no matter what. Americans standing up and
sticking up for each other, because just look at the world.
Who's there for the poor American slob when he's in crusade
mode? Who's going to stand against the wall with us?

(Okay. We were drinking rum.)

Julio's. A joint. Bar and restaurant, mostly Cuban sand-wiches toasted flat by Julio's wife, Irma. A dark booth for both of us in the dark back just beyond the juke playing El Gran Combo, and that joyfully uniquely PUERTO RICAN mu-sic made me want to piss-fuck all over any Miami *cochino* who dared talk about salsa like it was invented by Gloria Estefan

and Myers missing the whole point about Celia Cruz NOT being the QUEEN OF SALSA because Myers was on his war kick. No time for music for art for writing, he had to ask me again just who was going to stand with us in the next war? And I had to blink a lot.

"Who is this we're fighting again?" Because I hadn't heard that part. Myers screwed up his face like he'd heard a bad note. This was impossible as El Gran Combo was still on the *vellonera*.

"I don't know," he said. "Pick a country." He emptied his shot glass. "Preferably one with a very large oil reserve."

"Are you serious?"

"Hubbert's Peak. The world's oil reserves will be ex-hausted by the year 2008. The U.S. reserve is already exhausted."

"So don't drive," I said.

"That's the thing the president should do when he ex-plains to the dumb American peephole about why the war. He should say, *HEY, you fat Americans in your fat gas-guzzling environmentally unfriendly 4x4s. You want to keep driving your cars? Cars need oil. So decide now if you want to spend your future walking to work, or whether you want this administration to go get you some oil.*"

"*Your* administration," I said, clinking glasses, "wouldn't last a month."

"That's the point exactly. Americans don't go to war because of reasons. They need to get pushed, to get angry, to feel they have no choice. Some bad things have to happen first."

The first pair. Rum and coke.

"Pearl Harbor," I said.

"The Lusitania. The Gulf of Tonkin."

Clinking glasses. "The Bay of Pigs," I said, like a toast.

"It could have been," he said, as we took the first sip. The carbonation floated that warm rum bite subtle. "It would've been, if only that son of a bitch Kennedy hadn't gotten cold feet."

"Remember the Maine."

"The wrestling fans got it wrong. Americans don't say, *Bring it on*. Americans say, *You started it. We finish it.*"

The Puerto Rican food was only part of it. There's that tall, broad golden man with the beer tummy who everyone calls *Pan Doblao* who has his colored buggy out by the stoop of his building on Tinton Avenue. Serves up freshly fried *bacalaítos*. Big, leaf-thin, crisp, and greasy like you get them on the island. I fed Myers *pasteles* and fat *rellenos de papa* from a *cuchifritería* near St. Mary's Park, and two *empanadas* from a Dominican place on Prospect. This was my master plot—to alter his DNA, lull the taste buds into that calm, lackadaisical whimsy state. Then came the real attack: Julio's, and those continual doses of rum. This was subtle at first, an after-bite to the Coke, then straight and gentle on ice, the warm of the brown against the stroke of ice-white. Puerto Rican rum hits slow, slithers up on the senses. It sometimes takes the stomach on dippy loop-the-loops as it starts to kick in. Then, the sweating, the feeling just after a good run. The loosening of the tie. At the right dose, Puerto Rican rum can be a far more effective truth serum than the scopolamine shit that Myers keeps talking about

first comes the happy
the slow dislocation of mind from senses
then comes the pensive
then comes the truth

though there is no telling how much mush and sentimental-ity can be jarred loose by such doses.

"Listen," Myers said, "let me hook your phone up to a ripper trace. The next time some bastard calls you a scum-bag, we can ride over to his house and beat the fuck out of him before he even hangs up."

(The slow dislocation of mind from senses.)

"Don't say no. We'll just ride over and kick his ass. No point going to Internal Affairs. What the hell for? You want to fill out forms for a year? Just take care of it yourself. I mean, you must be awful tired of this bullshit."

I could see him sitting right in front of me. I could see his mouth moving, but the words seemed to come from somewhere else, someplace inside me. Not even Lieutenant Jack had said those words. I stared at Myers. I was imagin-ing him.

"All those years you put into the force. I saw your record. Everything tossed down the toilet, all because of one lousy moment, one lousy choice. I could say you made the right choice. I could say you made the wrong choice. It doesn't matter a spit."

I felt drowned. I was falling backwards into a cave. That fucking Puerto Rican rum was betraying me. I wasn't thinking about David or Spook or the fucking blonde. I felt erased.

"You're a cop. You're a good cop, out there every day taking risks for these two-bit shits, for that word people like to throw in your face—*community*. You work for the commu-nity. But tell me this, where was the community when you stuck your neck out? Did your community do anything for you when you took this murdering asshole off the streets?"

His face was changed, different. Maybe it was the rum,

the way his face colored with emotion, the way his voice got deep. I thought he was talking about me. I thought he was talking about himself.

"No," I said, but I was barely audible.

"And there you are, every day, plugging away, hoping things will change. Things will get better, but cops have an elephant's memory. They won't ever forgive you. You know that. I know that. You'll end up choking on your own vomit."

Clink. Glasses. A hard, burning swallow. The fucking Puerto Rican rum was betraying me . . .

"So maybe it happens. Right at the moment when you're at your weakest, or maybe at your angriest. Somebody comes along right when you want to kiss it all off, and makes you an offer."

There was no reason for me to say anything. I preferred to let someone else tell the story this time. I was no deer in headlights. I stared full back. I gripped my empty glass like I would pop it in my fist.

"We're talking a good offer, not some halfway deal. A way to kiss off the whole shit. You even get back at the system that screwed you. Do you really think this is something so hard to understand?"

I didn't want to drink any more rum, even though the next round arrived. The drinks sat unnoticed. I grabbed the waiter's arm before he could go—no more rounds. I requested a bottle. How one mistake leads to another mistake, leads to another. I had to stand up for an entire generation of *boricuas*. Wasn't going to be beat by my own game and let a white guy drink me under. That fucking Puerto Rican rum! Lava, fierce red and churning. I picked up my glass.

"So where are you going with this?"

I downed my drink with no clinking.

"I'm not going to sit here and play fed with you. There are bigger things at stake than the rise and fall of a cop. I already know things the feds don't."

"You trying to put me to sleep?"

He emptied his glass now with no clink, shutting his eyes a moment. The waiter brought the bottle, thin, tall. Myers waited until he left to speak.

"I know you tried to stop it," he said.

"Did she tell you that?"

The juke with its shifting reds and greens had gone from El Gran Combo to Willie Colón, that '70s stuff imprinted in Puerto Rican DNA like a genetic inheritance. Myers seemed to lose some energy. Something about him sagged. I knew it was her. The waiter had opened the bottle for us and poured the first round. I ordered *empanadas*. Greasy, bulky, to fill the stomach and keep us from keeling over.

"Listen. If you think you can trust her, you're crazy. I was working on her a long time. I worked on her hard. She has something about her, unbreakable. It's always like starting over with her, every time. A real plum pit. Do you know Katharine Hepburn?"

I was lighting a cigarette. I don't know where I swiped the pack, but I pointed it at him, knowing he would want to brother right along.

"Katharine Hepburn, sure," I said. He took a cigarette. I lit him.

"*Bringing Up Baby*, did you see that? I mean, you can't argue with a mind like that. There's a thing a lot of people don't know about Katharine Hepburn: She had a photographic memory. Detail oriented. Every word, every scene. This girl has that. She's maddening. A gabfest that says nothing. She gives you that quiet smile. That Mona Lisa thing, she has that."

I couldn't believe this guy, all these doors opening on his face. Now he looked like a drunken, broken-hearted lover who gets dumped at the altar. I felt an odd mixture of pity and disgust.

"I hate that Mona Lisa shit," I said.

Clink. Glasses. Hot fire. Cigarettes.

"Did you ever see *Dishonored*, this Marlene Dietrich picture? She plays a master spy who does her job really well until one day she meets an enemy agent and falls in love with him."

"Is that why you think she did it?"

I made sure to refill that glass. He knocked the shit back fast and seemed to regain some energy.

"I thought that I lucked out. That David Rosario just happened to need an assistant. I had two ladies lined up to go get that position. I thought I lucked out, that it was her. I thought she was my best." I didn't have to move. He was filling the glasses again. "She was feeding me information, right up to the moment when David Rosario told her about these fake IDs . . ."

It was Felipe Rodriguez on the juke box now, the man Puerto Ricans call *La Voz*. It was definitely the right thing to go with Puerto Rican rum. It added to the narcotic effect. The rhythm of the congas slowed the heartbeat. Speeded it up. Slowed it down.

"That's when she cut out, started getting dodgy. I know she wasn't in love. She said that just to spite me. It's not about love. It's about rebellion, dismay. That's what this piece is about."

"Disgust," I said.

"She told me about you."

"I know."

"I didn't tap your phone, Sanchez. But I have you on tape. Calling David Rosario. Calling Anthony Rosario."

"Did she tell you I was in it?"

Myers grinned slow.

"You mean whether you were a member of the ten million club?"

I didn't like the grin. I didn't like sitting with him drinking. It made him laugh to say that. I didn't like that he was laughing.

"She's out to fuck you, Myers." I downed my drink. "She wants to destroy you. I wonder what you did to her."

"Maybe she thinks I stole her identity." He seemed to be pondering the question the way one ponders baseball stats. "She mentioned something once about wanting to become a real person."

"After she fled from David Rosario's apartment, she went to a man named Roman. I think you know a little about him from my files."

"But you told me he had nothing to do with it."

"That's right."

The *empanadas* sat uneaten on the table.

"She didn't go to him for help. She went there to drop off something." His eyes went glassy and vague. "She said it was from David but I don't believe her. It was a tape. From David's answering machine." Another shot, another burst of flames. "You know what's on that tape, don't you?"

"Sure."

"I mean, I figure you do. If you bugged his phone like you keep saying, then you have it on tape somewhere, which makes me really wonder what the feds would think of that, after all."

"Are we going to start talking now about federal investigative panels?"

"I was listening to this tape over and over. I don't think it exactly proves murder, but it does show knowledge of intent. It should be enough to bring up some questions about how you were privy to certain information, and how you used that information."

"I could say the same thing to you. We've both played before investigative panels. I think I have a better batting average than you. I'm sure you checked my stats. What would you say?" He poured us both drinks. "I think you've already been through that, haven't you?"

Did I have to answer that? The person who brings the charges has the burden of proof, has to bear the stares the impatience, to jump the hurdles of a system built to be impenetrable and intimidating. Cop vs. cop? There was no such concept allowable. "You are either with us or against us." I had looked him up all right. So far he had survived two inquiries that resulted from operations so convoluted and crisscrossed with agencies and jurisdictions that it was never clear who would be held responsible. In the last case, his name was struck, records too confidential, his identity protected by higher hands. The only clear thing was that he was involved, that he had gone before a panel and testified behind closed doors. I didn't remotely intimidate him. He already knew my story, knew I would be reluctant to go through all that again. The captain would be less than eager to listen to me after I started telling him Myers has dirt up to his eyeballs, that this operation stinks to high heaven, and that I want to open an investigation. He'd fight me and refuse to drag the department through the mud again, least of all because it's me. There was no way he would stand by me in any case. It would be a supreme waste of time to even start that kind of trouble. It was just that elevator going down. The squealing of a stuck pig. A gold shield on the captain's desk.

"I've talked to your captain," Myers said, filling those glasses one more time. "You know what you can expect from him. You'll be putting your neck out, and for what? What did this lousy setup ever do for you? Is that really what you think I came here to talk to you about?"

The juke fell silent. Red lights, green lights.

"I still believe you're tied to it, Sanchez. I know it. Just give me the girl. You know it's got nothing to do with you anymore. This is bigger than your life as a cop. Give me the girl and you can go back to it."

"Back to what?"

"Back to your life. As a cop."

"You mean back to my UNlife. As an UNcop."

His eyes seemed to be glowing.

"Cover me," he said.

"And what about David Rosario? What about Anthony Rosario? What about them?"

My question floated in the *nada* of voices, forks, and spoons. A clatter of plates, the clink of glasses.

"They can take you with them," he said.

All at once, the juke came to. Something by El Gran Combo to keep the senses edgy. The *empanadas* were sitting on small plates like lonely yellow eggs. The bottle was three-quarters empty. The shot glasses glistened wetly. Rum might fog things up for a bit, but what comes after the happy, after the slow dislocation of mind from senses—after the pensive, after the truth—is clarity, the loud waterfall sound that comes when you place a clean glass beside a dirty one.

I'd killed two people in the ten years I'd been a cop. I don't think about them very much. In both cases, the men were armed with guns. In both cases, those guns came swinging at me with full intent to do me harm. In both cases, I dropped them. Open and shut, me or him. To kill someone not pulling a gun on you, that was a different proposition. To perceive harm, harm coming or harm about to come, meant accepting a doctrine of preemptive strike, of acting on a perceived threat. This would be no open and shut, no clear case of a gun swinging my way. I just wanted to go somewhere and puke. If only he would leave me alone . . . if only she could . . . In the end they deserved each other, these Americans . . . we the people . . . you're either with US or against US . . .

"I went to see Roman today," I said, starting slowly. "It seemed to me from the path she took after she jumped off that bus that she was going to see him. It might not have made much sense to anyone else that she would go to him, but I had a feeling. It turned out Roman was going to contact me. Roman and I had been in touch for a while. I had gotten him to testify in my Dirty Harry case, and . . . she brought him the tape. She had met him because of the cards . . . Roman makes cards."

"He made these for David?" Myers was flipping the cards, examining them.

"These are spares. David Rosario used cards under this fake name to open a safe-deposit box account."

"Why would he give these to you?"

My head was throbbing. I wanted to close my eyes, forever. "I'm supposed to give them to you."

It was Daniel Santos on the juke now, rambunctious pounding. The voices around us seemed to grow, people forms becoming shadows down by the bar where they collected in swaying clusters.

"I'm supposed to lead you away from Roman."

"And why's that?" Myers had the cards flat on the table. He filled both our glasses.

"Because what you're looking for isn't in a bank. It's at this big old theater on Third Avenue. It's hidden there. The whole bank thing is a setup."

"A setup?"

"That's right, Myers." My stare was straight and hard. I had on my stiff poker face and he would never get past it. "We're supposed to do a bank search. Stake out some branches and hope to find her. She'll get away, and you'll think she took the money with her." I was lighting another cigarette. "But the money will be sitting right here in the South Bronx, safe and sound. Roman didn't come out and say it, but he pretty much offered me the money to lead you away from there."

"And what about the girl? Why would she drop you a tape? What did she want from you?"

I took a good deep puff, then swallowed down that shot. "She wants me to drop you."

Myers laughed. "Great," he said.

"She's going home. She didn't care about the money, Myers. She only wanted to fuck you over. I don't know what the hell you did to her."

"She's a woman, isn't she?"

"What does that mean?"

"It means it doesn't have to make sense. Listen, I really don't think I believe you for a minute."

"You don't believe her either. But it seems she loved David Rosario. She didn't plan to take the money from him. She left it with his people. She delivered it, hid it, and is making her way home. Wherever that is. Do you know where she comes from?"

His eyes went blank for a moment, two dark coals.

"She's from Boston," he said, reaching over to grab the cigarettes. He shook one loose.

"You were talking about choices," I said, feeling like the entire room was starting to swim hazy. "She wanted to leave you that choice. You can chase after her, or you can go get the money." I dropped the cigarette in the ashtray like I was disgusted, like I was through. "I don't think you'll get both."

"What about you?" There was something on his face I couldn't identify, which twisted and disfigured those pretty all-American features. "You're telling me you decide at the last minute to do the right thing, and screw yourself out of a quick break with the past, along with some big cash?"

I closed my eyes I rubbed my temples I fought off the sick.

"I made a mistake," I said, not sure if I was talking about now or then. "All I want is for you to go away. Take your feds and your Arabs and all your national security bullshit and just go away. Just leave the South Bronx out of it."

The music was a loud pounding and I didn't even know what it was, some rhythmic plodding monster with too much cowbell, too much timbales.

"I'll cover you," he said. "You've got a deal. Can we get the fuck out of here now? This music is driving me crazy."

20.

Monday morning.

Drizzle gray. Sidewalks stained a dark wet. Streets usual with cars, peds. Cops cruise lazy. Riot gates rattle upwards. Boxes of cheap sneakers outside a discount store. An electronics store booming bass tracks.

The row of fluorescents make musical clinking sounds as they wake. Escalators grr to step. The coffee machine sputters as it delivers. Elevators hum steady on test runs and blink lighted numbers. A certain stockboy lingers around the cuties at the cosmetics counter. Bankable realities, predictable even in sleep. There was no thread, no link. Alex could come and go at any time. Nothing would be altered. He would not be missed. It was the daily rut of life that hinted at permanence.

Monk told him it wasn't a bad thing, to remember. He gave him a copy of Kurt Vonnegut's book, *The Sirens of Titan*. It told the story of the army of Mars. It was made up of people kidnapped from earth. The people had been implanted with devices that caused them intense pain should they disobey by trying to remember who they were or where they really came from—from earth, the very place they were being trained to invade and destroy. Monk said it was almost the story of Puerto Rico. It was the first real good laugh that Alex shared with anyone all weekend. It was always true: When dessicated images rushed in, out of sequence, Monk was the best person to clear up the fog. He could hammer out the narrative, form bridges between moments. How funny that this time it seemed Monk who needed a bridge, who hung on *his* words, whose eyes showed wonder and amazement. Alex suspected that Monk did not believe what he had seen, a form of madness that served as inspiration. Alex confirmed reality, and in that same way Monk returned the favor. After he left Monk's, though, something else sank in. It was the return to the inner click of the clock. The return SNAP like typewriter carriage to the monotony of everyday ritual. It hit him worse today, the climbing solo into the tiny red Honda Civic, the driving solo to work, the sense of weary surrender to the obligations of another Monday Tuesday Wednesday Thursday Friday workday.

Henderson's department store was a block thick, 149th Street to Westchester Avenue. Five floors, twenty-one departments. Leading the way in the grand redevelopment of the South Bronx hub. Incorporated several independent businesses on the ground floor, including a restaurant, a photo shop, and a shoe store that ran along the Third Avenue side. In its long window, shoes struck poses. This was where Alex found Benny after he pulled up the riot gates.

Benny's problem lately was shoes. He had developed a severe fixation with them. He cut pictures from magazines and newspapers. He was banned from Miki's parties, because at her house shoes are removed and lined up in the entryway, two by two. Benny swiped shoes, swapping sometimes for whatever he had on. He asked Alex for catalogs, for lists of the best shoe stores in town. Looked up foot fetish clubs and websites. And he started making regular appearances at the shoe store.

"Not again," Alex said.

Benny was standing in front of the long window. Clutching a coffee and waiting for the curtain to go up on his favorite *vitrina*.

"Hey, I'm fine, thanks for asking," he said. "You don't have to act like I need therapy or something. I only came to visit. Maybe check out those new men's casuals that came in last week."

Benny followed him inside. The store was not open yet. Mac was still vacuuming carpets. Adrian and Douglas were unpacking the last shipment in the stockroom. They knew Benny. They all said hi. Benny looked awful nervous standing around all those tiers of shoes. The delicate way the high heels were tilted, posed ladylike to accentuate those curves—the strapless sandals, furry mules, studded suede. His face was shiny with sweat.

"I don't think you should be in here looking at shoes, man."

"It's not the shoes, Alex. Fixations always have their roots in something else. It's always like that. A man who collects stamps has a licking fetish. I just came to see you. Say hi. I know it must have been a long weekend. What with the anniversary and all."

"Anniversary?"

"Yeah, this weekend. You can't tell me you forgot. Damn, I feel like one of those spots on THE HISTORY CHANNEL. *This Week in History.* Something special happened this weekend. Can you remember what it was?"

"This Week in History." Alex covered his face with his hands for a moment. "The first woman to fly across the Atlantic. 1928. Amelia Earhart flew as a passenger in a plane that took twenty-four hours forty-nine minutes to cross the Atlantic."

"That's not what I meant."

"The plane was a Fokker FVII-b," Alex said.

"The lengths some people go to. I meant something personal. Something that happened to YOU personally three months ago this weekend."

Alex shook his head, walking toward the stockroom. "I don't remember."

"You don't remember. You think I believe that?"

Benny was the kind of person who you walk away from, who follows. Belinda was the same. She liked to mark anniversaries. There was that one month anniversary, that two month anniversary, that third month. Alex always forgot. Now she was gone and there were no more anniversaries to forget. There was no point now in paying storage costs. He had planned to waste away the weekend in a mad, delirious blur. It might have been just that, if he had maybe followed Monica upstairs. Maybe then, no flowered dress hanging from his shower curtain rod.

"Considering all that," Benny continued, "I thought it would be a very long weekend. The stiff need for extra medication. So I really only meant to ask you about the drinking." A whole wall of ladies' pumps, climbing steep to stiletto, gave him pause. "So how's the drinking?"

"No," Alex said.

"Is that what you've been doing, piling useless facts in there to cram out the unwanted? Amelia Earhart, Jesus Christ. Look, I brought you a coffee. Help sober you up. You know I don't drink coffee. I don't do stimulants of any kind. You know that."

Benny tried to hand him the coffee but Alex wouldn't take it. He had pulled out feather duster number seventy-eight quill, and was stroking the curvy strapless sandals with it.

"Oh yeah," Benny said, stepping back to watch. "Do that."

Alex stopped stroking. He grabbed the coffee, uncapped it, took a sip. Mac had just finished vacuuming. Adrian put the finishing touches on a sign for the window.

"Okay, here." Alex handed Benny the feather duster number seventy-eight quill. "Just look busy."

Benny snatched that shit and began right away dusting, at first too furiously so the high heels fell over from his overeager. Alex had to calm him slow him remind him that the shoes weren't going anywhere. They were his captives, his willing playthings. He could take his time and treat them like ladies. And so Benny calmed down, gradually working himself up again so that by the time he got to the *chancletas* he was sheeny with sweat.

"Six months, three months, does it really matter? You probably meet a new woman every day. Every new one takes a coat of paint off the old one. Does it work like that? It's a cycle, a mechanism. It's always related to something else. Maybe guilt? You'd be surprised how often guilt comes up at all these encounter sessions, I've heard it a million times. It's all about habits, man. That's what I've learned. A cigarette, a drink, a cup of coffee—it becomes a habit. Habits are hard to break, unless you replace one habit with another. Andrew Weil says that. It's the same with dieting."

He gave Alex a poke with the feather duster number seventy-eight quill.

"You have to burst the old bubble. You have to create a new habit, man."

Benny escorted him outside as if he knew it was time for the cigarette to go with the coffee.

"Don't fool yourself." Benny handed him the feather duster number seventy-eight quill. "By perpetrating these cycles of repetition, you keep the past alive. You're not getting over anything. On the contrary, you're making it a bigger part of your everyday life."

Benny handed him a card.

"Sexaholics Anonymous?"

"That's right, bro. Could really help you. I have a FEAR OF CROWDS group session coming up. I gotta get on the subway."

Benny gave him a pat on the shoulder, then headed up the block toward the train. He gave Alex a glance back, an admonitory finger-wagging.

Alex sipped the coffee. Lit a cigarette. Thought about her and felt a nervous twitch in his guts. He was thinking his life had always been meaningless. This memory-no-memory thing was just a symptom. A man wouldn't waste time trying to remember things that don't matter. He hadn't been trying to remember. His thing was forgetting. This time he felt differently about that. He had never had to think about this process before. It was unconscious, a result, whether drinking or not, whether some button he unconsciously pressed or not. This time, he was thinking about it.

Alex was thinking that he wanted to remember. He wanted to see her clearly, coming and going. He wanted to remember every moment that went down, whether bed whether fire escape window whether she was whispering in his ear. "I was never here." He had never been around anyone who tried to make him forget. That was new.

He was staring across the street now, at the grandiose Banco Popular. The permission letter that she had in her things had this address on it. It was one of those little synchronicities that left him a little more pensive.

"I think you'll see her again," Monk had said. Why? Why did he get that feeling?

"I think you're wrong," Alex had replied, as Monk walked him downstairs. They'd stopped by Hector's newsstand on the corner, the place where Monk punctually picked up his daily copy of EL DIARIO. "I have enough meaningless experiences. Maybe it's why I prefer to forget."

Monk had seemed to accept that as he nodded to Hector and grabbed his copy of the newspaper. "But maybe the thing isn't so much about how meaningless things are," he said, "as how much meaning you are willing to give them."

Now out on the street he started to think about the meaning or not-meaning of wasting his time working in the shoe store today. He had no desire to go back in there and try to have a normal day. He had never felt such a strong impulse to just walk away from it. When Adrian came out looking for him, he felt like smacking the guy.

"What is it? What? Can't you do anything yourself? Can't a guy have a cigarette in peace?"

Adrian grinned. "You're crabby," he said.

The coffee left a black stain on the sidewalk.

21.

The subway headlights made her squint. It was an action poem gone bad. The floaty slow rocking. A black tunnel through the belly. PJ Harvey asked, do you remember the first kiss? Red light, green light. She sat her ass right where it said PLEASE GIVE THIS SEAT TO THE ELDERLY OR HANDICAPPED, across from SAY GOODBYE TO BAD SKIN! Train sharp-dipped into curve with screechy howl. Lights flickered, cars bouncing slow glide into station. The rush of air WHOOSH as doors opened and bodies pressed in or made firm. The 59th Street N/R stop at Lexington has to be one of the worst designed train stations in all of North America. The platforms are narrow and obscured throughout by construction. People crowd the only two stairwells, so on both sides push-shove-jostle while waiting for first sign of train blowing in. Always packed because both uptown and downtown trains arrive on the same platform. Trains slam wind from opposite sides and rush hour's always on one way or the other. And yet, when the train climbs out from tunnel to above

one of the best views of Manhattan available on the N train as it curve twists along bridge to sky. Crossing East River to Queens PAUSING long enough for all tourist cameras to go SNAP at that crowded island, afloat asea with its two shiny towers

the thick steel masts of a great ship

(as she had always seen it on a card in a picture book through a dream)

Queens, the book said—the most populous and diverse borough in all of New York. (Aren't they all?) Blocks are long. Tons of newsstands, bakeries, and laundromats. Lots of Greeks who drive their cars as if the devil is chasing them. (More accidents on Queens Boulevard per capita than any stretch of road in the entire state.) Ava's knowledge of Astoria came from Trudy. Her boyfriends were generally from everywhere scattered, so she got to know places like Belmont like Bay Ridge like Brighton Beach, and this Astoria—how Ava remembered just off the N stop at Broadway, how their walk together took them past banks banks banks. At least five branches in a row of long blocks. Her home branch was on 86th Street, but there was no way she was going there. Could be people waiting for her. Same for her apartment, same for work. Alan would be looking for signs. He'd have his electronic ears wide open. The moment a transaction went through, he would know. He would trace her. Ping! She had seen him use bank transactions, credit card purchases, looped video sequences from mall security cameras. It was why she came up with this little side trip to Astoria. If he was going to spot her, she would make sure he got a bead on her in a place far from where she planned to go. Alan could also very easily put a block on her account. Not only could she not remove money, even from an ATM, but if she was stupid enough to try and cash a check at another branch of her bank, they might stall her and notify the police. She didn't think Alan would do this, at least not yet. Was she just hoping, was she being stupid? At the most, she could hope to beat him to it. The last thing Alan would want to do is give her some warning that he was on to her. He preferred to tail someone secretly and pop up on them, out of the blue. She would be entering the bank. She would be standing on line. She would look to the side and she would see him, standing beside a sign advertising free toaster ovens for anyone opening a new savings account. This was the stuff of screams. She would stick to the ATMs.

The first bank she hit was just one block down from Broadway. She kept telling herself to keep cool, keep calm. She could hit five banks in twenty minutes and walk off with about two thousand dollars, imagining him sitting in front of a map with his twinkling lights and his connect-the-dots. He was circling to TRIANGULATE her position, he would be sending out units, notifying police squads, while tracking her movements until he would lose her. Until she did something else to give him a new track, because it might be better to lead him toward something than away from—where had she heard that before?—and then she was dipping her card to get inside the ATM room of a bank still closed since it was not yet 9

just barely opening time as she inserted her card, thinking there was no way he could have done it, there was no way. (She typed in her pin code.) The screen seemed to freeze for a moment. There was a strange, ominous flash. The screen went blue.

WE ARE UNABLE TO PROCESS YOUR REQUEST.
ACCESS TO THIS CARD HAS BEEN DENIED.
PLEASE CONTACT A BANK REPRESENTATIVE.

The rest was blur. The rest was a mad rage a red light a green light and how she wanted to smash things. There was a block on her account! How? How had Alan worked so fast? There was no way he could have done that this very morning. He couldn't have done it over the weekend—the murder went down on Saturday. There was no way he could have known prior to that, or suspected she would run. Yet the block was there, already set up in the machine.

Now her card had been confiscated. She couldn't even try another machine. That's what made her the angriest, the thought that Alan had already laid a block on her by Friday, one full day before the setup, the handover, the action sequence. Alan had cut her off. Before any betrayal, he had betrayed her first. There was no other explanation.

She took out her cell phone as she hurried back up Broadway to the N train. She thought of just calling him, of telling him what she thought of his little trick. She thought about it long and hard as she walked those long and hard blocks.

When she got to the train station, she decided she would not call him. Not from Queens. The block being activated like that would already tell him she had been there. She had to be somewhere else, stepping off the N train at Queensboro Plaza. Crossing the platform to catch a Manhattan-bound 7 train. Alan could be scanning Astoria streets just as she disappeared into the belly of five million people

to Grand Central. Windows cathedral size and filled with sun. Stopping to check the big board with its flickering letters that sound like mosquito wings. Arrivals, departures. To wander the platforms of Metro-North. The smell of carbon and train exhaust. A strange, thick heat. Crumpled copies of the *New York Times*. Peeking into slumbering trains that stood empty, open-mouthed. The 9:40 to New Haven, Connecticut. Some place far north, almost hinting at a flight back to Boston

(there could be five million people coursing through the New York City subway system every day. At least)

while she walked through the empty train. It let out small breaths, like someone napping on a couch. Soon a dinging of bells, voices on the PA.

An engine sound. She picked a seat in a car she hoped would remain empty all the way home.

She pulled the cell phone out. Held it like Kryptonite. There was no air. It felt like the inside of a closet. She had the strange longing for a vodka, coffee, and a cigarette. That small kitchen. Him breathing out smoke.

"Changó, Changó."

She turned the phone on.

"Mink Presario Ravel Melendez."

The voice came through the small speaker by the phone. By the phone where the desk was. By the desk where the picture windows were. Boxes crates blank canvases paint supplies bursting from ripped cartons. A wooden floor. A pair of easels under a big chunk of skylight. (To work two at a time, that was the thing.) In moments of UNfocus, the picture windows were the go. To see street through them was to float above it. Head to toe it was Prospect Avenue and a view of the South Bronx pouring in was as captivating as any R. Crumb street scene any time any dare. It was a pure inspiration hit.

The skylight. Not dingy dirty frosted glass seen at the top of some stairwells. This was beautiful sunlit glass full of sky and old rain that collected along the edges. The deep green of thin vines hanging down, green lush dangling from skylight so nature one would expect birds, the flapping of wings. Instead, the squishy sound of wet brush. Into glob of paint on palette, that mixing board—he was a fucking deejay at his mixing board blending this tone into that. No instant color splash this time, but hours of pencil and charcoal to lead to this, having her first materialize in black-and-white. It was a big stretch, from sketchbook to canvas size, and he stretched them canvas big, about 200cm x 140cm. When the color attack came, it found him squeezing tubes searching through boxes looking for that weird metallic sunlight. Chrome glint, but no silver. A color he

would have to invent. To yellow some ochre. To materialize the face the body the curve the lower back almost like
that '50s pinup. Pulled out that big book on Vargas. Her
feet dangling from the edge of that sandy island. (Get it?
The island's floating OVER the ocean.)

"Mink Presario Ravel Melendez?"

His agent was Bruce Hornsby, a London art critic who
came to embrace all things mutliculti. Long after the term
grew cold in the United States, the Brits took it up. Mink
was doing well in London, but when faddy terminology
hits the skids, it generally takes everyone associated with
it along for the downride. Bruce had a good feel for Mink's
work, but lately whenever he called with a gig it was about
some fucking rootical tribal slave Yoruba Aztec jungle ghetto
CROSSING BORDERS show, and Mink didn't want that.
To him it was just cheap shoddy instant packaging by people who didn't know there was more to being Puerto Rican
than that. Mink wanted different packaging. Bruce knew
the song pretty well, and didn't call much. Besides, there
was nothing new to sell because Mink hadn't been painting. It was pretty much understood that whatever Mink
did now would probably not fit a faddy preconceived cultural market. It was a bit of a curse and a bit of a thrill, for
both of them.

"It's Bruce, Mink."

"Yeah, I know. How's it hanging and all that?"

(Mink mixing paints, lovingly slow stroking.)

"Good. You know I don't normally make it a habit to
call this early. I'm surprised you're up. I just sent you something by special courier. It's something from the Romero
brothers. I know they contacted you recently. Do you know
much about them?"

Mink dabbed red. The swirl of color upset him.

"Yeah. Entrepeneur spicks. Young. Music scene. Parties. Building some kind of skating rink."

"It's not just another skating rink. It's a whole new scene.

They're talking about turning the South Bronx into the next new hot spot for the well-to-do clubbing crowd."

Mink laughed. "We only spoke by phone. I thought they were inviting me to some opening. A big honor, they kept saying. I couldn't tell who was who, they kept talking at the same time. A big honor. I just laugh because, you know, this rink they want to build isn't far from my house. In some big old factory building down by the Bruckner Expressway."

"Mink." Bruce sounded prissy. "It's not just a skating rink. You're thinking Rockefeller Center. This is not that type . . . Are you listening?"

The different layers of red were parting, opening up. Hinting at space, depth. He dabbed in more swirls. Rose petals. Mixing it darker. A deeper hole, an emptier room.

"They're taking a big empty space and converting it into a multilevel, Euro-style dance palace. The first floor is going to be a roller rink. Not a frigging skating rink, a roller rink! Do you know the bloody difference? Jazzy birds in spandex shorts and inline skates will spin about while techno music pounds. A bar, a lounge. Video screens."

"I can't wait to see Madonna on skates," Mink said. Magenta, rippling the edges turbulent.

"The real dance floor is on the second floor. More lights, video screens, two big deejay booths. There's a frigging hole smack dab in the middle surrounded by a kind of mezzanine. You can be up there reclining on a rail, sipping your drink, while looking down on these gorgeous birds skating about below. The third floor has a lounge, a fucking executive VIP lounge with access to a rooftop Jacuzzi, sauna, and penthouse accommodations for those who stay late and don't want to brave the trip back to civilization!"

"Can you imagine the view from the roof?" Mink said, squeezing out another paint tube. "Who would come all the way up here for a view of the Bruckner Expressway overpass?"

Bruce sighed.

"Evidently, the Romero brothers found a lot of people who would. They're not like you or I, Mink. They're hip."

"Excuse me?"

"They're famous for running some of the best parties and raves around. People hire them to throw successful parties. Record companies, film studios, J. Lo. They know how popular the South Bronx has become in the cultural life of the bohemian underground, the white subculture. Just imagine London, a place where hip young people think of the South Bronx as the birthplace of hip-hop, graffiti art, fashion. KRS-One. Record scratching pioneers like Kool Herc, Disco-B, Grand Wizard Theodore. Didn't you see that piece last month in *Mojo*? It's not so unlikely that the bored rich famous might mount their trusty limos and head north, away from the crowded island run by a fascist dwarf who's been shutting down clubs, threatening museums, arresting people for carrying a beer can across the road! The QUALITY-OF-LIFE GESTAPO has been raiding every club that hasn't gone underground. Fuck, it's ALL underground! Didn't you see *Groove*, for chrissake?"

"I just don't see why you should be so excited about it," Mink said. A stroke of flesh color ripped across the canvas like a wound.

"Mink, they want you to cover the place from top to bottom with your art. Walls, ceilings, furniture. Your work would be intricately bound with the concept of the entire place. You're the whole presentation. It could be the commission of your life."

The words seeped through all beach all sand all surf. A door opened. He felt the breeze.

"You've been bitching so much about ending up on another LATINO-OF-THE-MONTH show. Well, here's one gig that doesn't fall into that mold. They've sent me the CD-Rom and now I've sent it to you. Give it a good look. Of course, they haven't really mentioned money, but I can't imagine on such a huge project as this, that they—"

Mink slammed his thick brush into the water can.

"Mink? Are you still there?"

Clatter clatter can cranking slam pounding that brush then tap tap tapping to drain it wetless.

"Mink! Caw, that sound . . . Christ, Mink. Are you painting?"

Rise and fall breath. Brush tap tap tap. She was NO blocks and cubes. That was funny. He laughed. Bruce laughed. They were both sharing it. Almost old times.

"I'll check out the CD-Rom," Mink said.

Those old Vargas books, those pinup poses splashed on bellies of B-17s. Her face, that face, there was a picture in his mind and the more he thought about it, the crazier the vibe felt. When he was sure he knew what he was looking for, he hit the speed dial on his phone.

"Monk is home or Monk is not home," the answering machine said in Monk's voice to a background of cascading crunchy power chords from a band called Feeder. *"Monk might not be here or Monk is listening to your message right now so make it brief and interesting."*

(beep)

"Monk. It's me, Mink. Hey, listen, do you remember that picture book about Eva Braun and Adolf Hitler we were thumbing through last week? I forgot what it was that took us there but I really want to look at some of those pictures again."

There was a click. Monk disengaged the machine with a peal of feedback.

"The book was *Eva and Adolf* by Glenn B. Infield," Monk said. "What took us there was you seeing a documentary about Eva Braun's home movies on THE HISTORY CHANNEL. I got it right here."

There was a feel of relief, a feel that things were now swinging into a regular rhythm. Uninterrupted unstoppable as always, whether painting whether not, whether writing whether not—there was Mink. There was Monk.

"You think you could bring it over, man? I mean, if you're not too busy . . ."

"Yeah, sure." No hesitation no pause no sense of discomfort, just the usual fusion with something new. "I picked up my copy of EL DIARIO. There's something in here I gotta show you."

"Come on down, bro."

The sense that things don't change. That buildings that streets may come and go, change colors change shape, but that things still stay the same. To Alex the problem wasn't the South Bronx, or the people. It was inside him somewhere and it made it impossible for him to be happy there. He felt stuck there. The air was gone. The clouds hung like gray drapes. He was thinking that a life is made up of events that happen, forming a chain that creates a narrative. It adds up to something, it becomes the story of a life. A direction is visible. Alex would have given anything to feel he was on a path, that his life was a sum of events leading to now. He remembered one night, sitting in Mink's apartment with Monk, talking out this blackout problem. Vodka flowing freely, plus Mink made killer cocktails that started subtle and turned deadly.

"Sometimes I think Puerto Rican history is one big blackout," Monk had said. "Some people have collective memory loss, a whole tribe. Other people train themselves, like the Americans are learning to do. It's picked up. A learned behavior. B.F. Skinner. Electromagnetic physics. The luminiferous ether."

"I think the problem is the narrative," Mink had said, getting a squint-eye from Monk. "The fucking narrative. The day-to-day. The sense of beginning and end that memory gives us. The trap of having to tell a story in its proper sequence. It's because of memory, Alex. You don't know how lucky you are to black shit out! I met her on a Sunday, I fucked her on Monday, on Tuesday she left me. But what if between every moment, there was a blank? A dark spot, a smudge on the tape? Something that obscured the narrator's voice?"

"A blackout," Alex said.

"Exactly." Mink snapped his fingers. Tore a scrap of newspaper from some nearby place. A chunk of charcoal. His hand worked fast. A slash, a few taps, some scribbles. "I would diagram it as

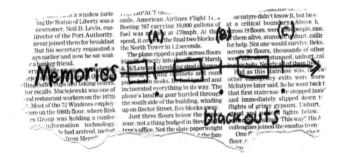

so that memories are a series of events that progress on a line, theoretically from A to B to C. The narrative moves the events along, gives them perspective and clarity. It's what we call the passage of time. But say we interrupt that narrative? If we cut into that line with a series of blackouts, events lose their connection. They become random, disconnected moments with no perspective, no predetermined flow."

Alex was thinking a lot right now about these disconnected events in his life that meant nothing. He did not want to accept that this Ava Reynolds episode was just another meaningless nothing event that led nowhere. He just couldn't get it out of his mind.

Robert trooped in late, more in the mood for a slow cigar and a long talk about the weekend's excesses, than work. Diana from the perfume counter came over and asked why he hadn't called her. Taína brought him a homemade *pudín*. He didn't really know her but she sat for twenty minutes, chattering away about how committed she was to the battle for *Vieques* before asking him what he was doing for dinner. There was that young girl checking out the flats who looked like Penelope Cruz and wouldn't leave. There were three women who made a habit of visiting him in the mornings, and this morning they all came at once. It had never happened before, and was vaguely stressful. Alex avoided it. Robert could be a real barnacle. He got rid of the guy by telling him Penelope Cruz was asking for him, then stepped outside for another cigarette break.

The clock moved slow. The streets teemed with life, a buzz of expectation. When his cell phone went off, he flipped it open, checked the screen, clicked the line.

"Monk," he said, almost breathless.

There was a sound, a clatter bang.

"Alex. Go to the newsstand and pick up a copy of EL DIARIO."

Alex didn't think to question. He crossed the street and cars honked. There, by the subway station entrance, was a newsstand. He plunked down some moolah and picked up the newspaper. Pinning his phone between cheek and shoulder, he walked like a hunchback.

"Got it," he said.

"Turn to page five," Monk said.

Alex flipped pages, almost dropping the phone. He tightened his grip, he arranged the page, he stared at the photograph in the story about a murder in the Bronx Saturday night.

"Shit," Alex said, feeling a deep chill.

"Okay, you got to tell me. Is it her?"

The picture showed her with that guy from the ID. The two of them snuggled together, smiling. He had his arm around her.

"Alex! Is it her?"

"Yes, it's her."

Just like that, the line went click.

22.

When I left Myers last night, it wasn't even raining. There was no air. The empty dark quiet was a shock. There was hardly a transition between night and day, almost blackout almost mirage almost a dream full of answers to be deciphered. I don't remember sleeping. It all flowed from wake to dream to wake, seamless like a montage. Milagros gave me a special bath of herbs that *Santeros* call a *despojo*. There was a lot for us to talk about. We were booked to fly to Mallorca in a week. Lieutenant Jack was not so happy I was heading off on vacation soon. Maybe he thought I would cancel the trip, like I would've in the old days when it was all pasion and fire. His round crinkled face was bursting with energy and it wasn't just the coffee or the cigarettes we smoked outside the window. It was his still-throbbing cop heart and the belief he had that he could solve the murders of David and Spook with that cop head of his, that cop heart. I couldn't tell him cop answers wouldn't work. I couldn't tell him about the answering machine tape, about a trail and where it led me. I knew if I told him, he would try to talk sense into me, talk me down from the ledge, talk me out of it. I just couldn't go there with him.

"Hey," he said, "what the hell is the matter with you? I've been blathering over here for about an hour already. It's like you're in a fuckin coma . . ."

"It's just this Myers shit."

"So what? What's that got to do with us?"

I sucked in that smoke. I closed my eyes. Cigarettes help the stall. A sick feeling came over me in waves.

"Jack, they're not going to let US find who did it," I said, knowing at once how crazy that sounded.

Jack ditched his cigarette. "Are you going to tell me what the hell is going on?"

There was an empty space. Between US, just words and time, which increased the distance minute by minute. I might as well have already been on that plane, crossing the Atlantic.

"I can't," I said. I could hardly look at him.

"You know I'm going to get to the bottom of this," he said.

"I'm banking on it."

He pulled three loose cigarettes from a pocket and handed them to me before he went back through the window and left me standing out there, fielding that call from Myers. The man always had timing.

"Yeah?"

"Sanchez. I've got her."

"What?"

"I've got a bead on her. We picked up her cell phone. She's on a fucking train!"

My cigarette, that flaming nib. Burned my fingers. Ditched down the grille.

"Myers, are you sure?"

"I've been waiting for her to turn on her fucking phone. I just knew if I waited long enough, it would happen! It looks like you were right about her. She's on a fucking train, heading north!"

"Myers! Listen to me." He was talking too fast, he was way worked up. "Why would she turn on her phone?"

"Just get your ass up to the helipad in Hunts Point! We've got our ripper trace and we're on our way over there with the bread truck! We'll meet you there."

I tried to tell him I thought it was a trick, that she was too smart to turn on her phone when she's making a run for it, but I was speaking to myself. Myers was too keyed up to listen. He was talking some gibberish about how the two of them went way back, about how he just knew that eventually those feelings she had denied would get the best of her. So of course, he was saying, of course she turned it on, on purpose. She knew he had been waiting. It was a language. There was no point in telling him I thought she had done it for a different reason, but what the hell? We all had a part to play, and I was playing mine. I had hoped to lead him away from her. I felt, once again, like I was the one being led.

I was in my car, driving. I had the sirens going. I had the pedal down all the way. This glinty silvery sun, off windshields off car chrome, off the flowy East River. The helipad was right by the water, far past Hunts Point. Myers was already there with his two boys, both carrying equipment. The four of us crowded into a police chopper. I had ridden in choppers before but this time the lift-off made my stomach revolt. There was a dizzy spin of sky and turf, the uncertain sway and lean forward as the pilot eased the stick down and we began moving over buildings all blur. Myers was yelling at one of his people who had a small box with a GPS screen and some blinking lights. I didn't want to be looking at that blinking light, that fine track that a train takes on its journey—unchanging and sure—there would be no sudden dips and shifts, no swerve to the left like some runaway car in a pursuit video. The train was a steady long snake. I was thinking how beautiful the South Bronx looked from so far up. The chunky thick tenements had a French toast color, the streets between all grays and blacks like the piping on a fine suit. It sure looked greener from up there, especially along the edges. Highways crisscrossed like arteries pumping fat corpuscles. There, on the tiny GPS screen, overlaid with a dispatcher's map, was Ava Reynolds, her red blip sitting on that long silver snake that moved under trees, under highways, and sometimes under streets. The Tremont Avenue stop was clearly visible from above. We circled, Myers expecting to catch sight of her stepping off, but her blip did not move, and was not moving. The train, so smoothly long, stopped at Fordham. At the Botanical Garden, it was lost under beautiful green shrubbery. Her blip did not step off.

"You were right," Myers said to me, looking almost grateful. "She's going home all right."

"She supposed to take you with her?"

"You get to know things about people after a while. I can't explain it to you. I can't talk logic. I can only say that I felt she would do this. It's the same way I feel that once I see her, find her, I will also find the money."

"I don't know, man." I was shaking my head. "This doesn't look right." At the same time I was wondering, well, what if it *is* right? Spook dead, David dead, the two of them reunited at some train station, and me standing there looking like the real sucker. I can't prosecute anybody, I can't arrest anybody. I can only stand there watching the two of them walk off into the sunset. And all I'd get for it would be the privilege of returning to my life, to the same tired turf.

The pilot's name was Jensen. He had a slow Brooklyn drawl and a good knowledge of the Bronx. With our train leaving the Williamsbridge station and Myers talking about landing, Jensen calmly informed us the closest helipad was Pelham. This put us at least three stations ahead.

I remember my legs feeling all springy rubber when I got off the chopper, that it seemed somehow I was still in motion. The lieutenant who met us there was named Mitchell. By the time we piled into a pair of squad cars with him and three other officers, the red blip was only a station away. I was amazed at how good Myers was at mobilizing the forces around him, and like a precision clockwork machine we were at the station just minutes before the train rolled in, already accompanied by a station manager and train dispatcher.

When the train rolled in, the Metro-North police had already sealed off all the exits. Once the train stopped, it wasn't going anywhere. The conductor kept the doors shut for us, until Myers and his boys effectively narrowed down that red blip to a specific train car. By that time, I wanted a cigarette so bad I almost ate one.

"It's this one!" Myers yelled, peering in through the windows. Not easy to see with all that reflection. Did I mention that he had been calling her cell phone? Over and over he had phoned, but she had not picked up. She had not said a word, had not bothered to acknowledge him. I had quit trying to tell him—I had quit. I hung back when the conductor finally opened the doors of the car, only that one. Myers stormed in with his boys, plus about six cops. I stayed by the doors, watching them all fan out across the narrow aisle, this way, that. There were only six passengers in a car that seats 112. Myers rang the number again. The guy holding the small GPS unit said, "It should be that seat there

because the blip is still there." The seat was empty, except for that cell phone jammed deep into the tight space between cushion and armrest

the ringer disabled, though the phone vibrated with his call.

23.

He had the newspaper folded in one hand, the cell phone in the other. Walking first to the corner, then back to the newsstand. Stood right by the subway entrance, swaying like he might just get blown down the stairs by the rush of people, the crowded to-and-fro.

He read the article twice through. Why shouldn't he believe she was running for her life? It went far to explain her erratic behavior, her having whacked him—her inability to say. It seemed she was avoiding words. There was no Monk now to help him do the math. The fucker had clicked off and Alex couldn't get him, getting instead the voice mail, as if Monk had already taken what he needed and was now pounding words out of his typewriter. Alex would have to make it up as he went along. There was no way he was walking back to the shoe store. Something had changed. He was not trying to blur events or speed through them, blot out or slide past them. It involved him. He was part of the story. Monk was right: It's not about how meaningless things are; it's what you do to give things meaning.

He thought now about that ID card with the dead guy's picture on it, that authorization letter she had on her. It was addressed to a bank just a few blocks away. He had no problem remembering that, no problem walking up that gentle slope leading to 149th Street. The masses of people: She could be any one of those shimmery blurs in the distance.

He crossed Melrose, checking both sides of the street to see if maybe he had gotten it wrong. Once he crossed Van Cortlandt, he saw the bank.

The yellow rose will turn to cinder
and New York City will fall in
before we are done so hold me,
my young dear, hold me.
—Anne Sexton, "Rapunzel"

No despair like the present. No despair like the now to make her walk fast, look behind, check traffic lights. The mass of masses bubbling all around her. It could be written on any face that looked at her, every casual glance that might do a double-take: "I know you." That cashier at the Hudson News when she was in Grand Central, black lady with shimmery Cleopatra hair, looking down on all comers with the same haughty arrogance royalty learned to project from birth, giving everyone short shrift as they stood in lines before her. A magazine, a newspaper, a stick of gum. She entered her prices fast, returned that change fast, hardly a glance, like she thought very little of people who wasted their money on such things. She liked to keep things moving, but the ones who came to her with a stack got a lingering stare as she typed in those prices. She got that raised eyebrow as the woman went through her papers, giving Ava the eye, the eye, three times the eye.

"You an actress?"

"Excuse me?"

"I said, are you an actress? A dancer? A model? You have six different newspapers. You waiting for a review?"

The question had too much bite. It was a school feeling, as if the teacher was glaring down on her.

"No," she said, "I'm waiting for my change."

Was every eye on her? The baseball cap could not hide her. Being in the subway scared her. Tunnel walls flowing by in the windows. A screech, a wail, a sharp curve—the lights blinked. At that early hour on the northbound 5 train hardly anyone so in her car she was totally alone and she didn't like it. Call it red light green light or maybe it was yellow, the train hit a slow curve and struggled to chug. In one of those blinking-light moments when the third rail is not in contact with the car, the lights went out and stayed out. A total black, a creak to stop. A steady hum, then the snap of those smoky emergency lights. Reminded her of some solitary late-night jazz club where the pretty girl has that last drink at the empty bar before going home. Going home? Where was she going that was home?

The newspapers did not help. Flipping through them fast, she saw. Most were just words, two of them had pictures. The waves came. Like retching, like shock. Folded into a corner seat. Seeing David's name in the papers made it official. Their two names together sealed the deal. The train jumped forward, slow like the nudge of a friend. *Hey. You okay?* The lights blinked on bright. Black tunnel walls moving past windows. A relief to climb out to sunlight, but people, so many people rushing. So many eyes looking, staring, turning. Glances rebounding back to her. Maybe today she would not stand out, but how, when she felt everyone staring at her? In a bad dream, her steps went slow motion as she hurried her walk up 149th Street. She was reading building numbers. Went the wrong way first, and crossed Third Avenue. Right near that big department store, that long window of shoes. She felt an Alex pulse, paused, got stuck there as if waiting. The South Bronx is truly a small town. But the numbers were wrong, the focus was off. She doubled back, she doubled away.

The place was just off Van Cortlandt. It was a sharp memory blast, the same way we know things in dreams, with David walking alongside her looking as grim and as humorless as she had ever seen him.

"You have to be fast," he said.

"I know," she said back, hating the interruption.

"Faster."

(Was it David or was it Alan, expecting results?)

The place was not large. To the left, a bank of tellers behind glass. To the right, a few desks, a stairway leading down. There was still that thick cushiony carpet, that smell of cheap colognes clashing. She went down the thickly padded staircase and walked right up to the lady behind the bars in the cage.

the soiled uniform of the Nazi
has been unravelled and reknit and resold.
—Anne Sexton, "Walking in Paris"

He was in the kitchen washing dishes when he heard the sound. Instinctively he knew someone was in the house. He picked up the serrated steak knife and crept into the living room. He had just passed the painting with the blonde lying on the island when the man crashed into him. Mink plunged the serrated knife into the man's gushy soft middle. It gave like a pillow.

The man fell back against the wall with an airless groan, teeth clenched, eyes rolling. "Ah shit," he said. "What have you done?"

The man was a cop, blood spreading across the light blue shirt. His head tossed, his hat fell off.

"What did you do?" he muttered, eyes glassing up like he was slipping into a trance. He grabbed Mink's hand, still on the warm, quivering knife.

Mink kept pushing and twisting the knife into his gut even though he could see it was a cop. The policeman sagged, sad gray eyes open and unfocused. He pushed Mink off, who was too stunned to do anything. He just watched, mystified, as the cop went over to the couch and sat down. The knife in his gut was moving.

"What did you do?" he mumbled, blank eyes staring empty.

There were other cops in the kitchen, their walkie-talkies chattering. It sounded like they were sitting at the table, playing cards. Mink was sitting on the floor, staring at the dead cop on the couch. Mink was thinking, *Come on, man. Get up. You're faking.* He kept waiting for the cop's face to break out from rigid stone, for the eyes to snap to focus and the joke to be over. But the cop was dead.

The door buzzer woke him up.

Mink hadn't meant to fall asleep. He had painted all night and into the morning, cranked so high that when he took a stop, sleep fell on him like a blanket. The first big painting, colorful, naked, was no blocks and cubes, nothing hidden under shapes or edges. It was real skin, real waves crashing to shore, a real blonde on a real island. He had only slumped against the couch while waiting for Monk, fell into wicked dream and realized he had killed it. Stumbling to the door to find Monk standing there.

"I killed him," Mink said. "I fucking murdered him in my sleep."

Monk blinked. "Who's that?"

"The fucking cop," Mink said, as Monk came in.

Mink added it up as he went, about how from time to time every artist has a cop inside, the keeper of authority and control. The one that says, hey, you can't go there. You can't do that. Don't go in that room.

"I stuck him right in the gut. The cop that kept me from painting. Some heavy metaphorical trip."

Monk wore a quizzical, tilted grin. "So I take it you've been painting," he said.

It could have been seeing Mink in that paint-spattered Ice Cube T-shirt, an old one from PREDATOR days that he had said was always his lucky work tee. Monk had never seen him in it.

"I take it you've been writing," Mink said.

It could have been seeing Monk in that tattered PJ Harvey T-shirt, an old one from her 50 FT QUEENIE days when she wore a leopard coat. It was sleeveless and seemed to have been nibbled by rats around the collar. It was his lucky work tee. Mink had never seen him in it.

The glow was on both of them. They seemed startled, maybe a little clumsy. They were not used to being around each other when working. It was a new thing, and it left them feeling a little uncertain about how to proceed. There was all of a sudden no need to kill time, to fight clocks, to have a reason to talk. They were suddenly both busy.

"I brought the book," Monk said.

Mink leafed through the pages, scores of pictures of Eva Braun. Once he saw her face again, bells of recognition rang. He knew now this was the face that had stuck in his memory since he first noticed it while watching TV with Monk. It had slept in him until he caught sight of the blonde in Alex's bed.

"This is the face," he said.

Words were not coming so easily. Something had changed. Mink realized there was no way he could talk about it. There was only a need to show him, to share this thing that had happened to him. He had fear about it, but he also had a great desire to show Monk what he had done, what had changed. He shut the book.

"Come see," he said.

Mink led him into the studio. The blond girl was lying on the island. The island was obviously Puerto Rico. The shape of it was clear. There was even a small bit of El Morro off the coast. She was stretched out, as if to soak up every last bit of sun and take up every last inch of island. She was, so far, naked, except for that red armband with a white circle in the middle which Mink chose to leave blank for now. Her skin tone, that sunny sheen, had the feel of the all-American girl Vargas was always putting on the bellies of B-17s. Mink's color attack had taken a new form, a chrome realism almost like sprayed-on Sorayama, a pastel glow like Rolf Armstrong, and yet the body had the sharp bite of a pinup by Peter Driben or Walt Otto, less the soft watercolor feel of these famous dream women. Monk's face changed when he saw her.

It's not finished," Mink said.

Monk was chewing on a thumb, eyes glued to the painting.

"I was going to tell you," he said, "that the night we fought, I saw this blond woman climbing up the fire escape, all the way up to Alex's apartment. I thought I imagined it. It was a kind of waking dream, the spark plug I needed to get started on my book. Then Alex came to me this morning and told me about this blond woman he woke up with." Monk came closer to the painting, as if he wanted to breathe in the oils.

"She climbed up the fire escape?"

"That's right," Monk said. "Her name is Ava Reynolds."

"Ava who? You mean you know her?"

"She climbed into Alex's bed."

"I saw her in Alex's bed."

"Did you see her in this morning's EL DIARIO?"

Monk pulled the newspaper from his backpack.

"Holy fuck, it's her, isn't it?"

Monk was staring at the painting.

"It's just the best thing you've ever done," he said.

24.

"Get the fuck off me," she said.

The two guys who grabbed her couldn't be feds. They were both big-shirted baggy-panted street clichés, regulation baseball caps set at the proper angles. One of them had a jacket on, could have been leather—and inside that pocket, a gun. He made sure she saw it.

"You just come and shut up," Leather Jacket said, again flashing the pistol. She jerked her arm away and tried to pull herself free of the other one, but he had a strong grip.

She had just left the bank. She had walked down the block and had just reached the corner when the two approached, one from either side.

"I said get off!"

The shove and pull got worse. People walking by now started to pull away, to stare. The two guys were trying to move her along fast, across Van Cortlandt. People started to gather.

"Hey, whassup with that?"

"Yo, get off her."

"What are you people doing?"

"Somebody call the cops."

Leather Jacket held up a wallet that flipped.

"I'm a cop, I'm a cop," he said, struggling with her while flashing some tin. They were dragging her toward Melrose. All sudden, a black 4x4 braked with screech. Its back hatches flipped open as the two steered her toward it. A very annoyed car let out a long honk.

"Come on!" One-Eye appeared at the hatch, seemingly unwilling to step out. "Hurry up!"

Now Ava really squirmed, struggling to get to the gun in her purse. Baseball Cap had the purse almost off her arm, gripping strap tight. Leather Jacket had the other arm.

"Ava! Stop fucking around and get in, we're trying to help!" One-Eye yelled.

"Fuck you!" she shouted back. She slipped and fell, struggling to pull the purse loose from Baseball Cap's grip.

"I'm calling the police," a woman said.

"Who the fuck are you?" a big guy with a Puerto Rican flag on his sweatshirt said, stepping right in Leather Jacket's way.

"Leave her alone," a young girl said, while picking up the Alex cap, which had flown off Ava's head.

Ava kicked Baseball Cap in the gut. It was a loud, resounding blow executed with such precision and style that the crowd went "*Whoah!*" It sent him tumbling backwards, pounding into a parked car whose alarm began to peal. She had the purse now, reached into it and drew the gun.

"*Oh shit,*" the crowd said, pulling back to scatter.

The car alarm twittered like psycho birds dueling. A woman screamed, people ran. One-Eye tumbled out of the 4x4 and tripped on the sidewalk. Leather Jacket was pulling his gun when Alex came out of the crowd. He punched Leather Jacket in the face in a forward motion, swift and sure. The sound was like the CRACK of a rifle shot. Leather Jacket fell hard, his gun clattering on the sidewalk. Now there were running bodies everywhere, screaming cars honking. One-Eye was scrambling up to his feet when Ava kicked him in the face. Another rifle CRACK. His head snapped backwards and his body rolled into the gutter.

"Jesus," Alex said, grabbing her by the arm because it looked like she was going to kick him again. "Come on," he said, pulling her down Melrose fast.

Siren sound, car alarm, what was that cracking sound? Could be shots, the peep squeal of a speeding cop car or two, traffic honking mad and the murmur of people seeming to open way for them as they ran down a street of small stores, of loitering types checking out skirts and tops on racks, boxes of sneakers, and those two small tenements that were mostly stoops and big windows up to only two or three floors.

"Jesus," he said, "will you put that shit away?"

He was talking about the gun that was still in her hand. She rushing along with him, trying to shove the gun in her purse. It was bumpy going, and that sharp turn made Alex almost take her arm off.

It was a small electronics shop. Huge speakers boomed bass all the way from front to back, more like a corridor than a room, mile-long counters on both sides stuffed with car stereos mixers receivers turntables car speakers while flashing lights and that intermittent strobe seemed to flow with that thumpy creeping Jay-Z.

Alex moved fast, negotiating tight turns around stacked boxes and booming speakers right to the back of the store. The people behind the counters seemed to know Alex, nodded to him. Alex waved, kept moving to the back, where past some boxes piled haphazard was a small staircase leading up to a steel door with a yellow plastic chain across it. A bearded man with shaggy hair was sitting there right at the end of the counter.

"Hey, man," he said to Alex.

"Is Preacher up there?"

"Yeah, but he—"

Alex didn't wait for it. He stepped over the plastic chain and pulled Ava along with him so she almost tripped on it, on stairs stumble quick, going up fast. Alex said something over his shoulder, pushed open the metal door. Cacophony noise voices all ceasing sudden as he stepped out with her and closed the door behind slam.

They were outside, in a cool rush of quiet air. It was an alley, just brick all around and sky above. Directly across from them was a steel staircase going up to another steel door. Alex pulled her up the stairs.

"Where are we?" she said.

He opened the next door. They were in the hallway of one of those small tenements. Stairwell to the left, long hallway on the right leading to vestibule. Beyond that, street. The walls were orange, floor tiles the honeycomb kind found in old bathrooms.

"I know this guy," Alex said, taking a moment to just breathe in the hallway silence. "His name is Preacher and he lives upstairs. Owns the building. Runs the store. Are you okay?"

She exhaled, checking through her purse. She stared at him with round, hopeless eyes.

"I lost your hat," she said.

"Come on," he said. "My car's parked near here."

They headed down the small stoop, right out on Third Avenue. They moved fast along the crowded street, crossed to the other side, walked down 158th where Alex's red Honda was parked. Once inside, they waited in the insulated silence of the doors' after-slam. There was not much on this street: the backside of some department store, the loading dock, a plastics factory. Behind them it seemed miles of neat, clean empty lots, sparkly chain-link sealing them off like farmland waiting to be seeded. It was a breathing space, a deep exhale. Alex started the car. A low blast, a low rumble. A steady hum.

"That one-eyed guy," he said. "I know him. What's he after you for? Is he involved in the murder?"

"No," she said, throwing him an inquisitive squint. "He was supposed to help me."

"I guess he changed his mind." The car whined as he backed all the way down the street. He made a sharp right, went straight two blocks, then sped along 156th Street.

"How do you know about the murder?"

The last sharp turn made her buckle her seat belt. She clutched the purse tight up against her chest.

"It's in the paper," he said. "Why didn't you tell me you were in trouble?"

"I didn't want to involve you."

"You could've told me," he insisted, as if insulted. Why was the car engine so loud? Was he really driving so fast? "I could've taken you to the cops. I don't normally think of involving cops, but you know . . . you're white. They'll help you."

"I can't go to the cops."

Red light.

Alex braked, tire screech, a shudder jolt. Turned to look at her real slow and careful. "And why can't you go to the cops?" (Getting a good look at her eyes, green and wide and staring right back.)

"They're the ones who are after me," she said.

Green light.

Alex pressed down the gas. Car surged forward, swerve-jerked as he made a right. Where was he going?

"Shit," he said, seeing a dark blob in the rearview mirror. "There's a black van behind us. Wasn't it a black van?"

"That's not it."

He made a left at this big Taj Mahal building and hit Kelly Street. A calm, treelined road with rows of quaint, old private houses. He slid into a spot by the curb and shut off the engine. She sank lower in her seat while Alex sat still, staring at his hands gripping the wheel.

There was absolutely nothing on the street, not even passersby. It was like driving into a postcard. A silvery sun streaked the rows of three-story Dutch houses. There was a soft swishing sound that seemed to slow everything down to a crawl. She looked back. A black man swept his stoop with calm, even strokes of a broom.

"Why did you do this?" she said, not looking at him.

"You're welcome," he said back.

"You don't know what you've gotten yourself into."

"Maybe now you can tell me."

"I'd rather clock you on the head."

"That doesn't work with me."

She was looking around, shifting in her seat. "Are we staying here?"

"I need a smoke," he said.

She undid her safety belt with a click. He thought she would go. She must have thought that too. But she didn't move. He felt calm, as if he knew her difficulty with words quite well by now. He did not force it. He waited. He pulled out his tobacco. She watched him. She shook her head slow.

"Why did you have to do this?" she whispered.

"You left your dress in my bathroom," he said.

He started to roll. The calm steady working of his fingers mesmerized her.

"Do you want me to roll you one?"

She went freeze for a moment, unable to use words. "I only want a few puffs," she finally said.

Now came that feeling of hesitation again, his, hers. She clutched her purse. He seemed about to say something, but nah. The calm steady working of his fingers. The voice she was hearing now was not Alan's. It wasn't Leni, Marlene, or Anne, but Sarita. Crystal clear through dream like a movie voice-over. "You'll be with someone," she said, "but don't fear him. He has strong guardians." An urge to stay. An urge to run, but to where?

"I've known a lot of people who were in trouble with cops," he said, licking his cigarette shut. "What makes them want to come after you?"

"It's not the cops. It's Alan." She found it hard to look directly at him for too long. She did it in small bursts. "He uses cops, but they don't know. They don't know what's behind it. Hardly anyone does."

"But you know?"

"Yes. Alan is what some people call a 'fixer.' People hire him to fix things when they go wrong. He was into some dirty business with David."

"The guy in the paper?"

"That's right. David's brother was a drug dealer. He stole something from some terrorists. David helped him hide it. The feds were on to the terrorists. They're mad it got stolen. They want to get it back."

Alex rolled the window down a little and lit the cigarette.

"That part wasn't in the paper," he said.

"The paper's not going to tell you that part."

The first fiery puff. (After that, it's downhill.) He passed it to her. A breathing in, a communal slowing of time which all cigarette smokers smoking together are familiar with. She puffed. The steady swish of that broom, sweeping away.

"I used to work for Alan." Her face looked different now, impenetrable and hard. "He sent me in to get the package from David."

"The paper said you were his office assistant."

"Yeah. Isn't that a bitch." Her eyes were glassy strange. She passed the cigarette back. "I was supposed to find the package and betray David."

Alex took in smoke slow. Sometimes you can get more information than you want to know about a person.

"Did you?"

The question froze everything. She covered her face a moment. (There was absolutely nothing on the street.) Alex saw how her green eyes tended to go brown in sunlight, how her blond in sunlight tended to go red. He had grown so tired of senseless weekends and events that created no chain, served no purpose. He had gone after answers this time, but now felt reluctant to hear more.

"I wish you would drive," she said, words muffled by fingers.

"I haven't decided about the cops yet," he said, contemplating cigarette tip.

"Your question wasn't specific," she snapped. "Did I what? Did I find the package or did I betray David? Which one do you want?"

"I want both."

"Yes," she said, fingers massaging her temples. "I found the package. But I betrayed Alan."

A strange burn hit his stomach. The tenseness was coming back. He checked the rearview mirror, adjusting it to get a better view of the street. She turned her face away. He nudged her with the cigarette, almost as if to remind her he was there, they had a deal, they were smoking together. She looked at him, her eyes red-rimmed. She took the cigarette.

"I promised David I wouldn't let them get it."

"But Ava, these people . . . there's feds involved."

"To me it's just Alan. I worked for him. You don't know the kind of person I am . . . I've been. I've been no person. I became somebody different with every job I do for him. I'm sick of not being a real person. This time with David . . . I really was Ava Reynolds. I felt like a real person. He made me feel so real."

Alex wondered. Her eyes so glitterful for someone, made him think of things he had forgotten, thought he had forgotten. Some things buried deep some place.

"I'm sorry," he said.

"Alan killed David and his brother because of me. I know it. I betrayed him. People died because of me."

Alex felt a deep dark heat. He closed his eyes. (She nudged him with the cigarette, almost as if to remind him she was there, they had a deal, they were smoking together.) He wished he could have admitted something like that. It was a realization that bit at him with piranha precision. Why now, these Belinda thoughts? She killed herself. He hadn't pressed any buttons or pulled any triggers. Benny told him, always told him she was sick, it wasn't his fault. But what if that one last betrayal was what did her in?

"She would be alive," he said, looking at Ava, "if she had been with someone else."

Ava stared at him. She didn't say anything.

Alex tossed the cigarette and started the car. He shifted, and it jumped forward, shivering slightly.

"I know a place we can go," he said.

25.

"Fear pushes you forward." Somebody said that. Was it Anne Sexton, pushing her way through dark rooms? Phantoms of some trouble, pursuing her? Voices? The mood could change in a snap. Could be bravery. Bravery is when you're too stupid to think twice, think it over, think again. All of a sudden you're emptying machine-gun clips and pulling grenade pins with your teeth. Maybe it was Audie Murphy who said that. Maybe it was a Sam Fuller film. A door, and you run through.

This door, two doors down from the Dominican restaurant. A thin narrow hall. Wooden stairs. The strong smell of glue, paper, machine oil. It felt far from the street on that metal landing with its lone lightbulb on a string. It was as if she had gone subterranean. There was a knot in her stomach. There was that gun in her purse. There was that Alex beside her, with his strong guardians and his way of saying nothing. Strange truths showed in his eyes. She was always checking in there. He was right not to want to go back to his apartment. It could be the first place One-Eye would come looking for them, though she told him it was unlikely he would mount a big search. One-Eye would probably be trying very hard not to be found. If Alan found him, he sure wouldn't have to use scopolamine to get him to talk. Alex thought of calling someone named Monk, but as Monk lived in the same building, he would call the next best thing, he said. A guy named Mink, who lived down the block. His door was painted with the most interesting rendition of the universe she had ever seen. It was lustrous black with silver stars and shimmery belts of planets. The Milky Way, the Big

Dipper, they were all there. The thing was, the planets the stars and all other things of substance were blocks and cubes. Not just flat squares with tight lines but three-dimensional objects of weight and depth. Real, unreal. Unseen before, but completely familiar. She stood there quite awhile after the door had opened, weaving her way past planets she knew, running her fingers over their stubby shapes, those vivid colors, those strange, glowy pulsations.

"Take your time," Mink said. "There's more inside."

Mink Presario Ravel Melendez; "Just call me Mink." Shook with both hands, like a statesman. A paint-spattered Ice Cube shirt. A way of looking into her eyes that made her feel he was standing closer than he actually was. He had the manner of a garrulous host at a gala opening, words all rush rush rush. Big, sweeping gestures, and a voice that filled the room. When Alex introduced them, Mink's face tilted when he heard the name.

"Your name is Ava?"

"Yes. Ava as in Gardner, not Gabor."

"Or Braun."

"Excuse me?"

"I've actually seen you before," he said.

"Really?"

"Yes. I went upstairs with Alex on Sunday morning. You were asleep. Alex wanted me to get a look at you because, well, frankly, sometimes Alex has problems with his memory and doesn't always recall where he picked up his last . . . He thought I might know you from somewhere." He turned to Alex. "You didn't tell her?"

"You kind of beat me to it."

"Well. You actually did pop up on the boy, he was really a little baffled—" Mink looked at Alex and cut his words short. The three of them stood there a moment, not saying anything. "We're used to him baffled," he added. "It's nothing new."

She had barely entered the place. The hallway was paint cans and piles of wood, canvases up against the wall. A box of tools. An empty fish tank, some bricks and colored rocks. Entryway to a kitchen as big as any found in a restaurant. Everything in there bright silvery steel, industrial strength refrigerator, gleaming Metro shelves. It was just a glimpse.

"So where's Monk?" Alex asked, into the weird quiet. "It's the second time I see you without a Monk attached."

"He was just here," Mink said. "He left after taking one look at the picture I just painted. Said he had a book to finish, and ran out."

"I couldn't get him on the phone."

"You can forget about that." Mink looked at Ava like he had just remembered she was standing there. "Did I tell you? He's writing a book about Alex. He's been wanting that for about a year now. Hadn't really been able to start it until this weekend. He needed a spark. Saturday night we should've been together someplace getting drunk. Instead we had a fight. He went home and was looking out his window around 4 in the morning, when he saw this blond woman in a minidress climbing up the fire escape."

"Really," Ava said, face showing no emotion.

"That's right," Mink said. "Some blonde climbing up to Alex. And maybe that was what he needed to start his book. I don't know if that's exactly what he's writing, but, you know . . . a spark. I've got some water on. Would you like any tea?"

He had walked them into the living room, a wide space that yawned out from the narrow entrance. Ava's mouth dropped. She did not know where to look first.

"Sure," she answered.

"You make yourself comfortable," he said to her, pulling on Alex's arm. "You come help."

The living room was lit from above by some shimmery

sun through a skylight. Not dingy frosted glass like you see at the top of some stairwells but beautiful bright glass full of sky and old rain that collected like tears along the cracks. She looked up, she spun around, she was Alice in fucking Wonderland.

"What the fuck?" Mink said, once he had Alex in the kitchen. "Is that woman safe to be around?"

"Yes."

"Right. Like Monk didn't tell me she hit you twice."

"She's been through a lot."

"You sure she's not going to go psycho on us or some shit?"

"I'm sure."

"Why doesn't she go to the cops?"

"Trust me. The cops can't help her."

"I'd believe that if she was a spick like us. She's a white girl, Alex. I never took you for the naïve type." Mink came closer and lowered his voice. "How do you know she didn't off that guy in the paper? How do you know she's not standing in my living room right now with a gun in her hand?"

Alex let those night images wash over him, of Ava moving in the moon dark. Of Ava lying beside him in bed. Of his fingers touching her wet face.

"I just know," he said, right as the tea kettle started to whistle.

It was warehouse size, it was loft without the tepid grandeur of Soho. It was Grand Central Station, the high ceilings all starry starry night, the smell of acrylic and wood. Stars zipped across walls, leaving trails like the kind she remembered seeing in children's books. A big leather couch. A group of theater seats swiped from somewhere, four in a row placed directly in front of the flat-screen TV.

Mink grabbed some mugs, popped teabags into them.

"When I first saw her face," he said, "I saw things there, even in sleep. It's a beautiful face. It has a smooth purity, like a black-and-white film sequence from a '30s film. It made me think briefly of Tamara de Lempicka, maybe of her *Sleeping Woman* painting or maybe *Young Girl with Gloves*, without, of course, that trademark tagliatelle hair. But there's something else, Alex. A hardness. A knowingness. She pulled strings. She's no curly haired innocent who just washed up on an island. She has a past, a heavy one."

"Everybody has a past," Alex said, picking up the tea kettle and pouring hot water into mugs. "Did you ever meet somebody and feel like you've already known them? Just from the get, have a sense of what they're capable of, and of what they're not?"

"No," Mink said, "I haven't."

"Me neither," Alex said.

There, bookcases full of art books exploding outwards across chairs, and end tables burdened with magazines and newspapers. A fat ashtray loaded with butts and roach clips. The paintings, up on the walls around her. She could spin around and around and still not take it all in. She sat down on the couch. Barely had she settled before she noticed, nudging against her with a papery crackle, a copy of today's EL DIARIO, a paper she hadn't seen, hadn't picked up, already folded to page five, all those Spanish words about her and that big picture of her and David. That sudden deep stomach spasm.

"Oh boy," she said, looking up. There were those green vines hanging down. Were those fake, or had she stepped into Mesopotamia?

"Actually, the Babylonians had the hanging gardens," Mink said. Green lush hanging from sky lit by nature so jungle she expected to hear birds, the flapping of wings.

Mink slipped a warm mug into her hand. She pushed the newspaper away but he saw, he knew. She was bracing for questions, she was looking at Alex, but he sat beside her on the couch clutching his mug, that calm face showing no sign of tension.

"I hope you like chamomile," Mink said to her.

"Yes, thank you." She took a slow sip. "I know these paintings from somewhere."

"Those on the far wall are some of my personal favorites: ALBIZU CAMPOS SKIMMING STONES WITH ALGER HISS; BULLET-RIDDLED BLOCKS AND CUBES NO. 6, and HECTOR LOVOE CAN FLY. They've made the rounds at shows and catalogs but I haven't sold them. My agent is furious, but I refuse to sell them, even though some are pretty well-known. That one there is called HE BELIEVES IN BOOTY. It was featured in a Björk video."

"What is this?" Alex said, tasting his tea.

"That's green tea. Helps fight off those free radicals. Why do they have to call them 'free radicals,' incidentally? Why not 'free conservatives'?"

"Conservatives are never free," Alex said, starting to roll a cigarette. "They always charge something."

"Have you been painting a long time?"

"Since 1993 or so, after dropping out of college. But I haven't really painted in about a year."

"I thought it was two years," Alex said.

"Will you stop nit-picking? The fact is, I just finished my first real painting in over a year. It's vastly different from anything I've ever done. I'm a little nervous about it, really."

Alex's phone rang. He whipped it out, checked the screen. "Hello," he said.

"I know where I saw you," she said, snapping her fingers. "It was freaking TIME magazine."

"I was in there, yeah."

"There was a picture of Kurt Cobain wearing a shirt you made, with these blocky cubes on it."

Mink was laughing. "Yeah, yeah, I have that picture

around here someplace. He autographed it for me."

Alex snapped the phone shut. They both looked at him. "It was my boss," he said. "I kind of walked off the job today."

"Shit, that's right," she said. "I got you in trouble again."

"No you didn't. I told him I had an emergency."

"I'm sorry, Alex. I didn't want to—"

"Forget it."

"No, I really feel bad."

"Just stop, okay?"

Mink watched them. Smiling to himself, he reached over to a nearby end table and pulled a framed picture out from under some magazines. He handed it to her.

"Ah shit," she said, her face softening.

It was the picture of Kurt Cobain, guitarist and lead singer of Nirvana. He had short blond hair and dark-rimmed glasses, his big blue eyes staring back earnestly. He was wearing the blocks and cubes T-shirt and had signed the picture.

"Boy, I miss him," she said. "I was nineteen when he died. So many of the people I admire have killed themselves."

"Oh yeah?"

Alex lit his cigarette.

"Yeah. Kurt Cobain, Marilyn Monroe, van Gogh. And a poet named Anne Sexton."

Alex's eyes seem to glaze over for a moment. He puffed on the cigarette. He was thinking about how suicide must be the meanest trick one person could pull on another, a painful stabbing, a forever jab. Maybe a way to get back, a way to get even. A way to leave a throbbing wound that never heals. He passed Ava the cigarette.

"You never stop blaming yourself," he said.

Ava puffed deep. Cigarette tip blazed orange angry. She didn't say anything. Mink noticed that just for a moment they both looked incredibly similar. Something in the eyes, the face. The way they passed that cigarette back and forth.

"Anne Sexton," Mink said slowly, as if trying to recall an image. "I've heard the name, but I don't know her."

The poem she recited was "Music Swims Back to Me." She rolled out the lines effortlessly, as if they came from the moment and not from the pages of some book, digested long ago. Mink's eyes went round and troubled. Alex took pensive puffs. It seemed a poem about being institutionalized. It seemed a poem about Ava herself.

After the words died down, there was a moment of silence, just for Anne.

"Wow," Alex said, passing the cigarette.

"How do you do that," Mink asked, "memorize a whole poem? I'm lucky I can memorize my phone number."

"I have a photographic memory. I know all of Anne, all of her."

"Can you just look at a page and know it?"

Ava grinned at Mink. "I can read a page, then give it back to you, word for word."

Something crossed Mink's face. It was puzzlement or suspicion or just the need to rise to a challenge. He fished around under the pile of magazines and pulled out a paperback. It was *American Psycho* by Bret Easton Ellis. Mink opened the book, picked a page, and handed it to her. "Let's see," he said.

Alex sighed, looking at Mink as if to ask, is it really the time for this? Ava took the book. Took a moment. Read the page. Then she shut the book and handed it back.

Mink laughed. "But shit, I lost the page!"

"It's page 278," she said.

There were four major air disasters this summer, the majority of them captured on videotape, almost as if these events had been planned, and repeated on television endlessly. The planes kept crashing in slow motion, followed by countless roaming shots of the wreckage and the same random views of the burned, bloody carnage, weeping rescue workers retrieving body parts. I started using Oscar de la Renta men's deodorant, which gave me a slight rash.

"Okay, I get it," Mink said, snapping the book shut after he had followed her line by line on the page. "I think I need a drink."

"Do you really want to start that?" Alex asked.

"Absolutely."

"I don't drink during work hours," Alex said.

The door buzzer sounded.

"I'll be right back," Mink said. "I'm expecting a courier."

The moment he left, Ava leaned forward and whispered, "What the hell are we doing? Should we even be here with this guy?"

"I'm telling you, we can trust him."

"Trust him how? We should get out of here, get moving."

"Well, what is it you need to do? You went to the bank, didn't you?"

Ava listened. There was someone at the door. Mink had opened it with a creaky steel clatter.

"Yes."

"Well?"

Ava seemed to hesitate between telling and not, between trusting and not. She could also be by herself. But this didn't seem the time for her to be telling stories, creating identities and making up facts for consumption. Alex knew her as Ava Reynolds. David did too. She swore she would be a person this time. There was no Anne voice this time to warn her about the treachery of a one-eye.

"I went to the bank and I picked up another key," she said.

"Another one?"

She waited. Voices from the hallway. The clatter crash of the door again.

"Yes. And a slip of paper with a number on it."

"A number. What kind of number? An address, a phone?"

"011493044377983," she said fast.

"What?"

"011493044377983."

"That's a lot of digits for a phone number."

"That's all there is, a number and a key. The number on the key is 53."

"That's not much help either," Alex said, just as Mink returned. He was ripping open a courier envelope and pulling out a CD-Rom.

"I was waiting for this. Could be my next commission. You wanna see?"

"Sure," Alex said.

"I'll need your bathroom first," Ava said.

"No problem. Down that corridor, right behind the wall of glass cinder blocks."

Alex watched her head down the hallway. Mink was pulling him toward the desk with the computer, but Alex wouldn't budge.

"Hold on," he said, and he followed after Ava. She stopped when she heard Alex coming from behind.

"What?" she said.

"You're not going to do that, are you?"

"Do what?"

"Disappear. Sneak out. Run. Are you going to do that?"

"No."

"Because if you are, just do it now. I told Mink not to be worried about you, that you were okay and that he didn't have to worry. No surprises no guns no conks on the head."

"And you're worried?"

"I'm worried you're going to pull a fast one, yes. That's all I know about you, you come and go. So I'm saying, if you're going to go, just do it now, in front of my face. No cheap tricks, no lies, no stories. Just go, if that's what you want." There was a strange burning in his chest.

She sighed. "But I didn't even bring my purse. I left it in the living room. With you." The way Alex was standing in front of her in that narrow corridor, she could not get past him even if she tried.

The painting across from Alex was a series of colorful boxes with keyholes in them. A pile of glittery keys stood at the far end of the canvas. It was called FIFTEEN PUERTO RICANS WHO PRAY FOR RAIN.

"Yeah, okay," Alex said.

The image of the two brothers on the computer screen seemed almost digital, as if they themselves were some electronic construct. Their faces were similar but their clothes looked different. Jose Romero had a large Fiorrucci flowered shirt with an orange tie, while Julio "Major" Romero was wearing a checkered shirt with a large black tie. ("We have to dress different, or our friends will kill us," said Jose in TIME OUT.) There were three Mink paintings behind them, paintings Mink remembered they had purchased three years ago. (That was a good year.)

"Estimado Mink," Jose said on the screen, "we both send big love and in this moment hope you are happy and close to loved ones. My brother and I are embarking on a phenomenal adventure that will change the landscape of the South Bronx forever."

"The South Bronx, to us, is the whole world," Julio continued. "It is music, it is fashion, culture, style, grace, passion. It is vision and violence. It is sublime and it is senseless. It is an inspiration and it lives in South Bronx people."

"To us," Jose said, "you are the South Bronx. Your work is all those things. It captures in a heartbeat everything we feel about the South Bronx that makes us salsa, makes us merengue, hip-hop, rock. Your work is freedom."

"We are starting a dance club in the South Bronx. By now you've heard about this. We have the space and are already almost done with it."

"There is just one thing missing," Jose went on, "and that is you. The touch of you, the touch of what we feel is the South Bronx. To us both, your work is the one crucial element that will make this place happen."

"I feel dizzy," Mink said.

"We feel we must tell you that hanging a painting or two of yours up on the wall will not do it. We want you to cover the entire inside of this magnificent structure with your colors, your dream."

"Your South Bronx," Jose added.

"Jesus Christ," Alex said. He was standing beside Ava, behind Mink, who was sitting at the desk staring at the computer screen like he was hallucinating.

"We've devised this CD-Rom specifically for you, to give you an idea of what we'd like to ask you to do." Now Julio looked at his brother, then continued: "We assure you that no copyrights have been infringed, neither have we put this CD-Rom or the work herein to any use other than as a special presentation, especially for you."

"That's right," Jose said, looking away, his eyes glittery wet. "Because we love you, man."

"We love you," Julio picked it up. "And so we hired some amazing graphic specialists to enable us to splatter your work all over this magnificent landscape. Your work IS the landscape, Mink. You can completely navigate the environment, explore the rooms, get a feel for what we were thinking."

"This graphic tool," Jose said, dabbing his face with a tissue, "enabled us to splatter your work all over these environments. Sort of like the work you did on our favorite Björk video? Only that was blue screen, honey. This is your work, truly made into walls, rooms. Atmospheres."

"The lounge on the third floor is your blocks and cubes piece, MU LATA TU LATA. The dance floor is your BACHATA BATATA, and the small lounge on the first floor is your bitter but somehow lyrical RIKERS BY NIGHT. We've used twenty-one of your paintings, some from your book, even on the surface of the roller rink."

"Of course," Jose rounded it up, "this CD-Rom is completely between us. If we have in any way offended or displeased you, just chuck it in the can and forget about it. Our respect for you and what you represent is such that we would not, could not, carry on with this project without you."

"We spent five thousand dollars making this CD-Rom for you, and even if you say no, it will still be the happiest five thousand we ever spent. I suppose we'll try to do the space without you if you should say no—"

"Not me," Jose interrupted. "I told you!"

"I heard you, stop!"

"Well, just don't lie! Don't play the suave businessman! It's life or death!"

"You be cool, just lemme finish it." Julio composed himself. "We'll call your agent again to talk about the money part, but it would be even better if we heard from you, Mink."

"We can only offer you $500,000," Jose said abruptly.

"Will you not talk money on the CD-Rom please?"

Mink pressed *stop*.

Alex put a hand on his shoulder. "Congratulations, man. Did you hear that?"

Mink turned, looking at both of them. His eyes were wet. "And that wasn't even the nicest part," he said. "I just don't know."

"But Mink," Alex said, "it's a huge commission. You got to at least look at it."

"It's a big space," Mink said, getting up from the computer like he was hypnotized. "It's a lot of work."

"It's a half a million dollars," Ava said.

He looked at her like she was a small child.

"They want blocks and cubes," he said, and left the room, heading down the slim corridor and out of sight.

"Well, there's one guy making money," Ava said.

"He doesn't want to do it," Alex said.

Ava sank into a cushy love seat nearby that was covered in throw pillows. "I don't either," she said.

"What does that mean?"

"It means I don't know where I'm going. I have nothing to go back to."

Alex sank beside her and said nothing.

"Alan is not going to give up, unless someone stops or derails him. That morning I socked you, I went to somebody about that. I just don't know if it worked. I don't think there's any way I'll ever know."

"And you came back," Alex said.

"Yes, I came back."

For that moment, sinking into pillows, her head fell against his arm, almost as if she could sleep there.

"Maybe you have to keep moving," he suggested.

She stared up at him. That strange burning in her chest was back. He was moving closer or he was moving away. A clock was ticking and she was thinking of Alan again. Alan on the rebound after her parting gift, the cellular in a train-seat trick. She smiled vaguely, thinking she had to tell Alex the story sometime. There were all kinds of stories she wanted to tell someone. Moving closer or moving away.

"Let's try that number," Alex said, pulling out his cell phone.

She gave him the number slowly so he could enter it right. Took a few tries before he pressed *send*. The phone got busy but there was no connection. He was trying it again when Mink came in.

"I mean, it's an honor and all that," Mink said, as if

continuing something he had already started, "but blocks and cubes? I mean, did it have to be those fucking blocks and cubes? And I'm thinking I should talk to Monk, but he's holed up and not picking up his phone, and besides, maybe it's a bad idea to ask him. He might take it badly, you know, a big commission for me, and him, well, just the idea . . . that I'm doing better than him, you know. I mean, you already know that he's the one with the ego."

"Yeah," Alex said.

"Who you calling? Monk?"

"Nah. This number." Alex handed him the phone. "We can't get it on my cell."

"011? That's an international call," he said. "Cell phones are weird about that sometimes. Let's use this one."

There was a phone right by the computer. He hit the speaker button and a dial tone sounded. He punched in the long series of numbers and waited. A series of clicks. The ring was not at all like the American bell ringing sound. It was more like a long toot. "*Toot.*" And then someone picked it up.

"Service Point, Bahnhof Zoologischer Garten," the woman's voice said.

"That's German," Mink said.

"German?" Alex was wide-eyed. "That can't be right."

"Hello," Ava said, stepping up to the phone. "Can you speak English? We are calling from America. United States. Hello?"

"Yes, please," the woman said haltingly, as if rearranging her brain. "How can I help to you?"

"What is this number," Ava asked, "this place you are?"

"This is train station Zoologischer Garten, Berlin," she said.

"A train station?"

"Yes."

"A train station in Berlin," Alex said. "Why would it be—?"

"Thank you very much," Ava said.

"*Bitte schon,*" the woman said.

Ava clicked off.

"That's Berlin, Germany," Mink said. "You know someone in Berlin?"

"Yes," she answered. "I have to go over there."

Mink looked at her again as if she were a small child. "Just like that?"

"Just like that. And right away," she added, glancing at Alex, who seemed startled. His face was ashy, something confused in his eyes. He looked at Mink and shook his head.

"She has to go to Berlin," he said.

Mink peered at both of them, one to the other. A vague smile played on his face.

"Are the police really after you?"

She hadn't expected the question, coming cold and sharp like that. Mink nailed her with a penetrating look that he saved for emergencies.

"Yes," she said.

"Okay," he said. "You give me a minute. I'll be right back."

He stepped out of the room, back down the corridor.

"Where the fuck is he going?" Ava asked, springing up from the desk.

"Take it easy. I told you you can trust him."

"No you didn't. How do I know he's not calling the cops?"

Alex laughed. It was an actual laugh, something she had never heard before. He was laughing at her fear, her terror, her panic as she reached for her purse to feel the security of a gun nearby, ready to correct mistakes.

"Mink would never call cops," Alex said, still laughing. "He's got twelve skunk plants up on the roof in the little greenhouse. You should relax."

"I can't relax." She was pacing. "I have to get to Berlin and I probably don't have enough money for a ticket. That bastard put a slash on my account. The ATM I tried to use this morning confiscated my debit card! . . . What's so fucking funny?"

"I'll lend you some money, calm down."

"No, I won't calm down."

"You should. Everything happens for a reason."

"Oh yeah? Is that your attitude, Mr. Blackout?"

Alex nodded slowly. His silence created an empty space, left her desperate for words, a fight, something. There was nothing. He was just looking at her, and she was looking at him, when Mink returned. He was holding a dingy plastic bag and an envelope.

"I was thinking," he said. "We can't just let her walk out of here, Alex. With that blond hair on her, she'll get spotted in a minute. Cops notice stuff like blond women walking down a South Bronx street."

"Especially white blond women," Alex added.

"So, check these out. I picked them up in Europe. I met this girl in Amsterdam named Sasha. She used to change her hair color about three times a week. Keeps people guessing, she would say. She told me to use the stuff for painting, and I did—*The Sasha Series*. I guess you could call it my experimental stage."

He uncapped one of the cans, shook it a little, and sprayed into his palm. A blob of black foam.

"Black mousse," she said, grabbing a can from the bag.

"Yeah, it's hair color. I must have ten cans of this stuff. You foam it up, then splugga into your hair."

Mink laughed again.

"Twenty minutes later, no blond. Just like that. All those nosy cops searching elsewhere."

Ava looked from Alex to Mink and back again. Her eyes brimmed hopeful. Some weird thought about not being blond. Some weird thought about losing her identity, if Ava Reynolds was supposed to be blond—some deep philosophical issue about what makes a person.

Mink must have read her thoughts. "It comes off eventually."

"Okay," she said. "Thank you." She rushed up to Mink and hugged him, planted a kiss on his cheek like a grateful little girl. Alex too. Got a long hug, though she lingered a bit more, pressed closer. His arms went around her waist and they were now face to face.

"I'll be right back," she said.

"You won't go out the bathroom window?"

"No."

"No cheap tricks, no lies, no stories?"

"No way," she said.

Were they going to kiss? Mink thought so, and when she scooted down the corridor with her cans of paint, he was staring awful wary at Alex, who looked like he had been kissed. He leaned against the desk and took out his tobacco.

"What are you getting yourself into?" Mink said. "Are you sure about this?"

"Yeah, she has to go to Berlin. The least I can do is drive her there."

Mink squinted. "Hello. Car?" He made motions, like he was behind the wheel. "Plane?" He shot a hand upwards like a 747. "You're taking her? See, I figured that. You don't know what this woman is carrying with her, Alex! You're not drunk now, you're in total command of your senses, right? What do you really know about her, that you should take so many chances?"

Alex thought a moment, holding his clump of tobacco. "But it's always like that. I'm only taking her to the airport."

"I knew that. That's why she should at least not be a blonde. I don't want you catching whatever she's going to get. Though seeing you now, I figure you've already caught it."

"Yeah, well. Are you going to show me what you painted?"

Mink's face tilted like he'd heard a musical note. "I'll show you both," he said.

In a letter to a fellow poet, Anne Sexton wrote about how she had been having blackouts. In Dr. Kenneth Rangle's book, *Blackouts: The Memory of Not Being There*, he cited twenty-nine case histories of people clinically treated for blackouts. People who lost whole chunks of life like loose change falling down a subway grating. People who learned to switch situations, react, make it up as they went along. It was a dance, an acting job. It was like modeling. To make it up as they went along from one slide to the next.

The pictures that came to her were fast speed. She saw it two ways: she, cringing, bullets, spatter. Like water splashing, hot grease. The other way was harder to make out through all the harsh lighting, those tilted camera effects and zooms. She would not fill in those blanks. Anne was there to fill spaces with words and pictures of her own. She might give you a handful of links. She would not, piece by piece, reassemble the chain. Dr. Kenneth Rangle pointed out that blackouts are sometimes self-inflicted. Created barriers, firewalls, a pop-up blocker.

She would have blacked it out if she could. Anne was her blackout. There were no blank spaces she did not fill. There was a semblance of circus music. Marilyn Monroe in fishnets atop an elephant. Seals clapping. Marlene Dietrich, the master of ceremonies. A pair of aerosol cans. She read instructions in English in Dutch in German in Spanish. What was it Alex said about the god of disguises?

This Mink. A real guardian all right. Could take over any chapter in any book, all lines were his. He was storm, he was calm. His hands never stopped moving.

She stared into the mirror at that blond face, she immersed in dark, in hot flaming water that dizzied her head, and barely twenty minutes later, no blond. Still curly, still those large eyes, now in a darker frame. She stared and stared.

When she came out, they stared and stared.

"Wow," Alex said.

"You don't like it?"

Immediately after she felt so stupid to have said it, so stupid to have let such a thing slip, and now she stood looking at him, hopeless.

Alex stepped closer, to touch. "It's pretty," he said.

"It's a different girl," Mink added. "*Bella, bella.*"

Her eyes had not left Alex's. "But you can still look at me?"

"Yes," he said. "I can still look at you."

"Now there's something I want *you* to look at," Mink said. "But first, here." He handed her the envelope he had brought out before. As she opened it, he passed her a sheet of paper. "Can you sign this?"

She glanced at it, glanced back. "What is it?"

"It's a release form saying it's okay I painted you. That goes together with the envelope."

Ava opened it. Inside was cash, and a receipt.

"Three thousand dollars? What did I do for this?"

Mink smiled. "Let me show you."

The studio was separated from the living room by a glass block wall made sturdier by bookcases. It shared the skylight and was raised in the center like a stage. Here were those big picture windows, from floor to ceiling. To see the street through them was to float above it. Canvases were stacked against the wall. A fish tank of colored rocks. Tin cans in rows, bristling with brushes brushes brushes.

The chairs, small end tables, stools, all looked like props. He shoved them offstage. Full center was the big picture. A smaller one on a second easel stood right off the stage, a little below, just crowned by light. It was a bare skeleton yet, with dabs and shadings of gray.

The painting of the blonde on the island looked done. He said it wasn't. He was still working on the right color, the final touches that he couldn't define yet. Alex was speechless when he saw it. Ava came close, almost to touch but not quite touch.

"That's me," she said.

"Could be," Mink said.

"It's not blocks and cubes," Alex said.

"She's got an armband." Ava sounded like she was in a trance. "It looks like a—"

"Yeah, this poor girl's got a past. A bad one. Maybe she ran away this time. Maybe she escaped."

"Maybe she came back," Alex said.

"It took me all this time to get here. Now I have these Romero brothers asking me to do blocks and cubes. Right when I've broken with them."

"Maybe you should do it one more time," Ava said. "A grand kiss-off. The way to send it away with a big bang. While this one," she smiled, looking like the hostess in a gallery, "you can show your agent."

"I like this girl," Mink said. "She's going far with a brain like that."

Alex stared at the painting with glassy eyes. "All the way to Berlin."

Ava moved to the big table and signed the release form.

"It's beautiful, Mink." She hugged him. "Thank you for everything."

"Sure," Mink replied. A hesitation hit everyone. "Will you be making a move?"

"Yeah," Alex said, looking at Ava.

"You coming back?"

The question caught Alex off guard. He stared at Ava. Her dark hair shaped her face in a new way, it was almost like meeting a different girl. There were still those large green eyes though, already too familiar to belong to anyone else, blond or brunette.

"Yeah, he's coming back, he's only driving me to the airport," she said.

The door buzzer sounded.

Ava looked at Alex. She slipped a hand into her purse.

Mink checked the video screen. "It's Monk," he said, buzzing him in. They could hear him clomping up the stairs fast. The walk to the door was a little awkward. Alex seemed to have withdrawn and become his old, wordless self, grimace grinning like a Steve McQueen still.

Ava kept her hand in her purse as they waited for Monk, reminding Alex that she wasn't quick to trust. "But she trusts me." He spoke the words under his breath as if the charm they carried mystified him.

"If there's anything about that boy," Mink said as he opened the door and caught it on a stopper, "it's his timing. He never misses anything and he usually comes in at exactly the right moment."

Monk looked thin in that worn PJ Harvey T-shirt, arms boyish bony. His eyes were fevered and luminous, glazed, yet with an intensity that seemed manic. Mink flicked a switch and turned on the light outside on the landing. Ava immediately saw that the universe of blocks and cubes on the door was only a fragment of the universe that Mink had painted on the surrounding walls and even part of the ceiling.

"Thanks for calling. I'm glad I caught you before you took off," Monk said.

"Me too," Alex said back, the two of them clasping hands.

"Ava, this is my good friend Monk."

Monk kissed her hand. "*Enchanté.*" There was an energy to him that radiated kinetic, stubble-faced and no cap on this time to crush down that bush of curlies.

"I've heard a lot about you," she said.

"Some of what you've heard could be true," Monk replied, pulling a book out of his backpack. "Alex told me you two were leaving and I busted my nut trying to think of what to give you, you know, to take with you, and of course I thought *book*. My book and Mink's pictures—"

"A copy of *Shadowtown*," Mink said. "I could've given her that!"

"It's mutually autographed," Monk said, showing the page where they both signed a long, long time ago. "It's got him, it's got me, a quick way for you to take both of us along."

He shoved the book into Alex's hands.

"But then I thought, man, that's so stupid. You guys on the run and everything and I'm giving you some dumb book to carry around. Not what you really need, so I kept beating my brain. I knew there was something I had of yours . . ."

"Of mine?" Alex asked.

"That's right." Monk fished around in the backpack. "You remember that time we went to Spain with Mink?"

"Yeah, of course."

"You crashed at my house for three days after we came back, remember? You left this. I've meant to give it to you for a while now, just kept forgetting."

He handed Alex his passport.

"You might need it, you know. ID and stuff. Cops always ask for shit like that."

There was a weird silence. Ava and Alex glanced at each other.

"No, no, not that you'll be running into any cops . . ."

"We have to get out of here," Alex said.

"Yeah, we have to go," Ava agreed.

"Sure, sure, here, take this." Monk passed Alex the backpack.

Alex shoved the book in there, along with the passport.

"Thanks for that." He looked at Ava, then Monk. "I'll see you later."

Alex gave Monk a hug. It was a tight, quick back-slapper. Ava hugged Mink and Alex smiled sheepishly at him.

As Ava and Alex started to descend the steel steps, Monk touched her arm, making her turn. "I just wanted to thank you," he said.

"Thank *me*?"

Ava saw the strangest look in his eyes. It was reverent, grateful, compassionate. It was the look of a satiated house guest.

"Thank me for what?"

"For a hundred and forty pages," he said.

The words made her laugh, the same way a little boy saying "eleven-teen" or "eleventy-seven" would, some nonsense line when she expected grandiloquence. It was a relief to laugh, and Monk laughed too.

Outside, the late afternoon felt slow, the sun blinding. They moved quickly so as not to be seen coming out of Mink's. Alex pulled Ava along by the hand, toward Fox Street. They saw Mink and Monk standing in the big windows, but they could not wave.

26.

he wanted to ram me, I could just sense it. His need to hit out, to get results to force the issue. He wanted to say it all along, just scream it: "You knew! You knew all along she was pulling that cheap trick." He couldn't get away with that, since I had urged him from the beginning not to follow. I had urged him on another path. The drink was rum, straight. No need for truth serum this time, more like bandages. There are plenty of shady spots and shadowy back tables. Places where the dudes at the bar never turn around to look. Cops can quietly go there and sulk.

"I told you she was good." Hoarse whisper. Hot rum shot to make a man wince. Finding that phone jammed into an empty seat took a piece right out of him. I had never seen a face so thoroughly slapped in my life, the moment that agent dug into the train seat and pulled out that vibrating phone. Lieutenant Mitchell was a sturdy bull of a man who couldn't have been thrilled to get sent on this wild goose chase by some young goof with a letter from the DD/I. Nonetheless, there was no sarcasm when he asked, "Any chance she jumped this train?" Another example of the deep-hearted decency cops display to other cops and yes, even feds, when things go wrong.

The station manager was talking to the dispatcher, who was speaking into his portable radio. They seemed to be waiting for some word from Myers. Fan out, search the weeds, patrol the small towns trackside? The motorman shot down the notion of a jumper. The safety features on these trains would insure that the crew would know about any open door. Had anyone spoken to the passengers?

"That seat's been empty since Grand Central."

It was Myers who put an end to the charade. "Lieutenant Mitchell, thank you for your trouble," he said with a hand-shake. "She wasn't on the train. Please thank your people for me."

An officer drove us back to the helipad at Pelham. There was hardly a word spoken. The chopper ride was the same, a solemn journey that felt like a bad tourist trip. The sun was high in the sky and filled the cab with heat. The world below slanted tilt like the view through a fish-eye.

"You didn't say I told you so," he said. The churning blue East River bent below us.

"No, I didn't," I said.

"It's only now that I'm hearing what you were saying."

I couldn't read what was going through his mind. I doubted it would get me off the hook. I was "point man," no matter what.

"She's forcing you to make a choice." The sound of the chopper blades spinning made me feel I was talking in a vacuum, and talking louder only made it worse. "For all you know, she's still in the Bronx, or Manhattan."

"How about for all *you* know?"

His stare was more than just a challenge. The case was falling apart. He'd need to bring home something, anything. A pound of flesh, some result that would convince whoever hired him it was worth the investment. He may have lost the girl, but finding the money would be one big payoff.

"I told you we should've hit Roman's." I said it like that was all he was going to get. "I would have never gone on this chopper ride, man."

"Pah. They told me you could find anybody."

"Boston's not my turf," I said. "Washington, neither."

The Bronx skyline shimmered on the water like a glassy mosaic. The captain had no problem working with the FBI. He handed the files over to me. I waited two cigarettes long while Myers argued with the DD/I, then his two team members jumped into their car and sped off. I drove Myers back to his car. We were almost there, but when he said that shit about needing a drink, I detoured to a dark rum place. I wasn't looking for any hidden truths this time. I was stalling. I was just trying to put it off. Somehow I didn't want to let Myers out of my sight. The thought of him disappearing, taking everything with him. I was damn sure now I needed that sense of resolution I had been putting off. Had nothing to do with her. If I let him vanish now, I would never be sure that he wouldn't pop up again someday.

The slow game was over. No more stakeouts informers insiders to build pathways to the top, no slow steady progress to "the man." The FBI raided the files. They claimed every name every location, sent rats scurrying with wide sweeps. Went with the big show. Caps and jackets. FBI, DEA, ATF, all like husky fans in football parkas. They stormed up stairs, they pounded down doors. The department decided not to be outdone and launched their own HIGH-PROFILE DRUG RAID NEWS AT TEN reporters mass arrests cameras ratings sweeps. They were the big noise I was the small noise. I was good cop bad cop, I was give-it-a-shot-for-one-more-day cop, lost in the rush of blue uniforms and flak jackets.

Where was Myers? His agents went one way, he went the other. There were two FBI agents posted at my office door. The yellout between the captain and I had nothing to do with any of it. It was something that was a long time coming. When words tapered off, we stared and saw past each other. Planting my shield on that desk would be a formality. The captain was staring at a dead man. "At least try to put on a good show," he said.

Where was Anderson? Jackson Avenue, raiding Wiggie's. A bad hallucinatory film. The ranks of them storming through smoky storefront glass

what about when they're coming for me

flooding the street blue? Me running into an old theater like Lee Harvey Oswald, sitting there staring flickering images waiting for the moment when they turn off the film, waiting for the moment to spring. One fed two feds when have I ever seen so many feds in one place?

A loud crash. Spray of glass. A rolling cloud of dirt. Anderson came at me through a crowd of flak-jacketed G-men. He wore the wide smile of a winner, a man in charge. The political front runner, the one who makes things go. He shook my hand, he escorted me through chaos glass and dirt to a place of words.

"What an amazing job you've done on these files," he said while I was cigarette cigarette, how had I forgotten all this time about having a smoke? I shuffled I shifted I searched my pockets. "Quite an interesting narrative. Interesting characters and situations. It's almost like reading Balzac, except this is all real." A boom and a crash. Fifteen agents stormed into Wiggie's garage after tearing down the riot gate. When that one perfect white cigarette rolled free to tumble from some pocket somewhere, I went down after it. Picked it up off the sidewalk. Needing a smoke had nothing to do with dignity. A quick flick. Light. Draw. The deep exhale. Anderson was still talking and, I'm sorry, what was the question? I didn't know what was on his mind or how he was planning to approach me. I could only see this mass of police machinery flooding this petty storefront. All that work to get to know what was happening behind the scenes now useless—connections, talkers, watchers, all fled to hole up somewhere else.

"I didn't have time to warn them," I said.

"You're a strange cop. Compiling your stories as if it's not this very ending they're supposed to have. This is the culmination of your years of police work. This is the final result, what it all leads to."

Twisted. The very fibers. No nation no flag could ever explain away. The feeling between. Wiggie dragged and pulled arms pinned behind they were trying to duck his head down to force him into the van when he looked across he looked past his eyes locked directly with mine. He took a spit that got him bapped in the face, forced down, shoved into. A scramble of arms and legs. Thump and screaming.

Myers gone missing. Why am I holding the bag? What's in the bag? This started with a murder investigation, a double murder, can I make that point? What was the most important thing here? All this noise, all this empty show.

"There's nothing here," I said, stepping up to bat. "You've got nothing on these people."

"They'll all have their day in court." Anderson frowned. "And you? Is it going to take a subpoena?"

Now came the dizzy slow, the hit the bang the almost blackout. I was suddenly lying in the tub. Hot foamy water, churning bubbles. A warm hum. She was lying with her arms behind her head, sheen of soap film making her breasts seem sprinkled with glitter. Her eyes: a calm dark radiance. She had packed her bags at the last minute and it was 4 a.m. and nobody cared. Started with the jangle jingle of that new ankle bracelet and newly lacquered toenails. Hibiscus oils and rose incense. There were flower petals on the bed.

"Are you sure we have to do it like this?"

The one time she asked. We weren't using condoms anymore. I could stay inside her all after. Straight through to the second time after these slow talking moments. These touching moments, these soft slow—"Yes," I said.

"And what if something goes wrong?"

"Nothing will go wrong." I could tell that just by looking in her eyes. "In a week I come and meet you for our vacation. Just like we planned."

Sun. Sand. Beach. Spanish. Houses sold to foreigners on very favorable terms. We weren't using condoms anymore. I could stay inside her all after.

"We're trying to have a kid," I said.

The clamor of agents and megaphones. The beep of a truck backing up. Another crash. I didn't want to look at the people being pulled out, I didn't want to see them. Watching Wiggie take a spit at me was enough. It was a cold strange feeling, a far deeper alone sense than any I'd ever had. Suddenly I wanted OUT, I wanted to tell Anderson everything because there had to be ONE PERSON one at least some place some fear, some big fear came and I think Anderson saw it on my face.

"If you can get a subpoena," I said, because I couldn't tell him shit. I wouldn't trust him, I couldn't. I would talk to him "after," not "before." He might talk me out of it. He might insist there is a way for the system to deal with system-bred errors like Myers. It was a faith the bastard was pushing, a belief system. A fraud.

"When I first noticed Myers's interest in you, I figured it was just another in a long list of aberrations, the trademarks of his psychotic mind at work."

The room was warm, the lights too bright. There was a pack of cigarettes on the table. There seemed to be no conditions attached to them, but I fought the urge to have one. I thought about Myers talking about scopolamine. They could put that shit in cigarettes.

Anderson sat across from me in the "after." He ripped open three packs of sugar and poured them into his coffee. He had brought me a cup but I hadn't touched that either.

"It turns out, Myers hooked onto you for a reason."

The cassette recorder was also sitting on the table. I could look right into it, see the tiny tape spools spinning slow and methodical.

"I'm not planning on making a statement," I said.

"Humor me. I'm lousy at taking notes."

"You told me you just wanted to talk."

"That's all," Anderson said. "And look. Whenever we want." He shut off the machine with a click. "See that?" He switched it on again. "Whenever we want."

I looked in his face and I saw Myers. *Good guys bad guys.* Nobody plays fair when everybody's looking to cut a deal. The wheel kept spinning. It lit up with colors as it turned, that glowing silver disc in the juke box. Anthony Santos: "CORAZÓN CULPABLE." Why this simple *bachata* song was dogging me I'll never know. From place to place I could hear its strains, its insistent chorus coming at me from open windows, from passing cars, up and down stairwells and even here in this nowhere bar: *"Yo sé lo que fué."* I had brief manic Vonnegut dreams. "Billy Pilgrim has come unstuck in time." I was with Anderson, I was with Myers. Two different moments on the same page.

The drink was rum, straight. Not so much bandage now as liquid courage.

"I can get the APB, I can get the coverage. Train stations, airports, bus terminals. So what? With the FBI in the picture, we get screwed the moment they find her."

"Myers. You're doing it again. She knows those tricks, man."

"So what? Am I giving up now? Whose side are you on?"

"You think that matters so much now? You ran off to chase a blip this morning and didn't listen to me. I've been totally straight with you, but you didn't listen!"

Those Myers eyes. A dark shiny radiance, indecision mixed with regret. All those bad decisions. How one mistake follows another mistake follows another.

"It's true," he said.

"You can chase after her. You may even catch her one day, but you won't get the money. Isn't that why you came to begin with? She's forcing you to make that choice."

He was looking up at me from the bottom of a well.

"One or the other, Myers. You can't have both."

He seemed to slowly grip himself. A dawning realization.

"You've got to make a choice," I said. Hadn't I just lit that cigarette? I stamped out the fire, I crushed out the light. "I can't lead you to the girl."

Myers tipped his head a moment, as if he had somehow discerned the high-pitched note of a transmitter. I was taking him back to Julio's, a hazy rum flashback. The rhythm of the congas slowed the heartbeat. I thought back to the moment I'd asked him about David and Anthony Rosario. His face had gone blank, no flicker of recognition. How shrunken small they had become. Collectible homies from a gumball machine.

"You made a deal with Myers?"

(Even Anderson skips past the Rosarios, no matter how much I try and bring them in.)

"I only told him I couldn't lead him to the girl," I said. "The rest of the math he did himself."

"And who gave him the idea you'd know where the money is?"

I thought of Ava Reynolds. I thought of the can of worms I would open if I mentioned her. Would Anderson know she was the one who led Myers to me? He sure was no poker face. He couldn't be playing the same hand as Myers.

"I gave him the idea," I said.

The rum had its effect.

"She was just a bait to lure you away from the money," I said. "The money is hidden in the bowels of the old Majestic Theater on Van Cortlandt. The captain wants a nice high-profile raid from the department side. We can give it to him. While the lieutenant and his boys are making the big splash, you and I can settle this."

There was nothing broken about Myers now. Maybe the rum had fired up his blood, lit up his mind. Maybe he was at his best at times like these, when things go wrong and he has to do the dodge ball. The dark glassy aspect to his eyes had nothing weak about it. He tossed back that shot and laughed.

"Yeah, right. As if it would even be there."

"It's there all right."

"Really. And it's going to sit there all snug and patient and wait until you and the entire New York City police force just walk in and get it?"

"That's right."

(Light another cigarette. Make a lot of smoke.)

"And this Roman guy, he's just going to sit tight and let you?"

"*Sit tight.*" I laughed. "That's exactly right. *Sit tight.* I like that." I laughed again, Myers cocking his head, not getting it. "Myers, there is only one person directly linked to the money right now, and that person is Roman. I told you I saw him yesterday."

"So?"

"So after he told me where the money was, I couldn't let him go. He might disappear with the money, or just disappear, and I might need him. The FBI won't need scopolamine to get him to talk."

Now Myers started laughing. Then he stopped. "Get the fuck." It was dawning on him now. "You didn't."

I shrugged, puffing on the cigarette. "I beat him, I cuffed him, I threw him in my car." Right in front of his boys, red-faced and confused. Were they supposed to do something? *You wanna do something? I'M A COP!* I'd screamed. "I took him someplace I know, someplace safe."

"You're trying to shit me, Sanchez."

"Tied him up, hand and foot. Gaffer's for his mouth. There's an old bed in an old shed. Isn't that a country song?"

"You should stop trying to shit me, man, because—"

I dropped the two Polaroids on the table. One was of Roman's face before I taped his mouth. The other was of him gagged and bound and lying in the bed. An old bed in an old shed. I tried to sing the tune but couldn't quite hit it. Myers stared at the pictures, eyes disbelieving, mouth twisted to mock. His head slowly shook no no no.

"Where do you have him?"

"Like I would tell you. Every person connected to the money in this case has been murdered. You're the last person I would tell."

"Fuck you, Sanchez. You ain't got shit."

"Actually, I do got shit. I got ten million. I guess that's the last thing left that can save your case. I mean, short of you eliminating every trace this ever happened—but the FBI is on it now. It might be better for you to turn up with the money. Give you some collateral. You can set yourself up again. Choice choice choice, it seems every time we end up talking about this choice you have to make. You can choose not to believe me. I can choose to go to the FBI."

Myers eyes glass. Spacey. "Why don't you?"

Slow grin. "I'm Puerto Rican," I said. "I don't like the FBI."

Myers smile vague. I could tell he was working all the variables. He could probably hand *me* over to the FBI, show I was involved, give them my information about where the money was. But that meant the FBI would get it. He could put a bullet in my head anyway, collapse the case, wipe the traces and vanish—but no money, no guarantee of getting it if anything should happen to me. Outside of Roman, I was the last direct link to the money. And I had denied him Roman.

"The classic Daffy Duck conundrum: Should I shoot him now, or wait until I get home?" His eyes went blank, empty. "I should just shoot you now, should I shoot you now? A place like this, people won't even turn around. A simple dispute between cops . . . Look, okay, okay." Myers seemed like a person having a three-way argument, interrupting himself to interrupt himself. "Fine, fine, look—okay, I'll do this, I'll do it your way, but on this one condition. If for some reason the money isn't there—"

"It'll be there."

"—if it isn't there, then I want Roman. You give me Roman, understand?"

He had leaped across the table he had grabbed me by the shirt. Spilled glasses clink and the stink of rum dripping off the edge. Then it all sagged from him, energy spent. He sat like a sack. He righted glasses he wiped at spills he ordered another pair of drinks. Like nothing ever happened. I almost didn't experience it in real time.

"I better not drink anymore," he said, loosening his tie. "I'll probably be talking to the FBI later."

"About me?"

"No. How long before the raid on the theater?"

"It'll take me at least a day to mount the operation. I can get it going tonight and maybe tomorrow we—"

"You think we can wait? What if somebody else . . . ?"

"There is no somebody else, I told you. Nobody else in Roman's posse knows about the money. It's safe, nice and tight. We just have to go in and get it. Listen, Myers, if you tell the FBI about me—"

"My case status is still confidential. I've been ordered to secure my information and not hand it over . . . The agency and the FBI are going to have to fight it out. You handing over this money will go a long way in getting you off the hook. You understand what I'm saying to you?"

We shared a final cigarette outside in a frisky wind that seemed to smoke the cigarettes for us. In the middle of a sentence he seemed to simply vanish, slinked around the bend, wasn't even there anymore. I felt empty strange when he left, pursued and on edge. "I've dismantled my team," he'd said, as if this really was the final scene coming, a half-laugh linked with cough. "They'll never find that bread truck."

He had lied—we would find the bread truck the very next day. Made the radio rounds from a fire department call. "There's a big bread truck on fire, Edison and Burnside, abandoned . . . Some kids must have set it on fire." It was an empty truck. What I knew about Myers was that bread truck or not FBI or not he would always have that information, that bit of me that he would hold onto for the rest of his life. Maybe now I was part of his team. Maybe he would never leave me alone. I knew too much. That Ava Reynolds wasn't on the train proved to me she was going to go through with it. She was taking that ten-million-dollar club all the way to the finish line. That meant I had to as well. It was another obligation to David.

I picked up the radio and called the precinct. "Jack, I need you."

A whole day. Myers and I didn't talk. I didn't talk to An-derson. I didn't talk to my wife. She was already flying. A se-ries of planes. Only one call at 4 a.m. from Lisbon Airport.

"I love you," she said. "Are you sure you're going through with this?"

It was that soft voice from my conscience again, what was left of it.

"Yes," I said.

"Are you sure you can't just get on a plane and get out of there?"

"Yes, I'm sure."

The big empty bed. Her words in my head like a dream. A long feverish day of plans and maps and phone calls to the D.A. Jack and I like the old days, big raid, adrenalin rush, but with a difference I felt when I caught a glimpse of the cap-tain—it was my last time. *Last time*, what does that mean?

At night I left a message for Myers. "It's on." I went to bed with my gun by the pillow, waiting for maybe the crash of the shattered front door, the scurry of feet rushing in. Cop feet, Myers feet? Good guys bad guys. Didn't register. Didn't sleep. I only knew I wanted Milagros again, I just wanted a chance to see her again, to lie beside her on that sandy white beach. It was as simple and as basic as my desires got.

The warrant was a piece of cake. Choice of: pirate CD

op. Weapons stockpile. Stolen goods warehouse. A drug processing center. "Police acted on a tip." Where was Roman? There were only three people in the funeral parlor when we swarmed in. The two squads dismounted fast from buggies, with a detachment to cover the street all the way around the corner to secure possible escape routes. It was tall Jenkins who entered with me, Jack, and Myers. The few people in the funeral parlor offered no resistance. I didn't waste time on them, rushing past to the basement and the corridor leading into the theater. *"¡Corre, que ahí viene la jara!"*

"Myers and I go straight," I told Jack, "and we'll meet you on top."

What was it with Jack peering at us from a distance, giving Myers that strange look? "Okay," he said.

"Does he know," Myers asked as Jack disappeared around the bend, "what we're looking for?"

"Hell no. Come on."

I pushed on down the long corridor. Of course Myers was behind me. I didn't like it, but what was I supposed to do? I felt he wouldn't plug me as long as the money was still the goal and I was the one taking him there. Going down the corridor I figured the Jenkins group would be coming across the roomful of weapons by now. Jack and Peters would hit the stairs which bypassed the main floor directly above us to the top floor where the fenced goods were stored. It was big up there, full of CD-ripping rigs and Roman's office where the forging equipment was. I wondered who would come blasting out on the talkie first as I led Myers along those stone walls. The ceiling got lower. A little darker in this space, a warm black alcove before the shaft of light that streamed down from the large windows on the side of the elevator shaft, going up. I paused. Myers paused. Breathing space. In all this time, he hadn't said a word. Not much even when he'd arrived in the morning, straight to business.

"What if it isn't there?" he said.

"That's more your problem than mine." We were hunched

and moving toward the light. He put his hand on my back. I turned and noticed his eyes, vague and round.

"We've got weapons here, chief," Jenkins said into the talkie.

"Where are you, buddy?"

It was Jack, groping for me by talkie.

"We're coming to the elevator shaft," I said. The big yellow pipe, jutting out of brick, disappearing into floor. You had to either crawl over or crawl under. It wasn't easy and you couldn't do it quick. I had to go first, pipe cold and gritty. I could expect—the perfect moment for that bullet in the head. He could pop me and claim . . . claim what? That I was in on it all along. (He had the tapes.) I must have made a move on him in the dark. Myers was lucky he drew in time . . .

"Enough guns here for a battalion," Jenkins said into the talkie. "Man oh man."

I felt squeezed between cold wall and cold pipe. I passed through, came out in the elevator shaft.

I was thinking that Peters and his cops would go across the top floor pretty fast to clear it before really checking it through. They might not get to the stairs that led down to the floor right above us. I pressed my talkie button.

"Jack, where are you?"

"We just hit a room full of car parts, believe it or not."

"Let me know when you hit the stairs, chief."

"Copy that."

Myers had taken the opportunity while I was on the talkie to tackle the pipe. He was trying to move fast. He seemed stranded between wall and pipe. Wriggling small, buglike. Rats scurrying from a drain pipe. Roaches panicking when the light comes on.

I hate bugs. I've always hated them. Always pull that *chancleta* out to wham SPLAT that shit fast, no thinking, just pulled out that pistol. The blow crumpled him folded, crumpled him heap. Moaning, or maybe it was cursing. I had to hit him again he was moving so much.

I went through the corridor on the opposite side of the elevator shaft, where the steel door was. I shut it, then hopped up a series of steel steps jutting from the stone. What was that noise? Cop voices, shuffling, boxes. A loud crash. "Hey! Watch that shit, will ya?" Talkie chatter.

"Hey, buddy, we're at the stairs now," Jack said.

I was fiddling with the box that stood a few feet from the elevator shaft. I could see Myers. He could see me. He was moving again, touching his head. I was messing with wires. I was cursing my luck. I was hearing cop chatter talkie chatter my wife Milagros chatter and a blonde with big green eyes that were still following me. Things blurred around me, I had to blink fast. A sudden tunnel vision. A liquidy blur like when the fish tank sweats. (A ride at the front of the 6 train, that front window and how I fought to get the view on tippy-toes.) I was looking down at Myers. One moment he was all blur. The next, he was clear.

"Hey! What the fuck are you doing?"

It was a Myers scream. At first I thought the voice was in my head. It couldn't have been Myers. He was looking up at me from the inside of a well. There was blood on his face. I must have hit him pretty hard.

"Jesus, what are you doing?"

"The elevator's broken," I said. I fiddled with the box some more. There was a loud clatter boom. The platform far above jerked. Started to move. Fell, with a hydraulic whining grinding crash

the squealing of a stuck pig

27.

The drive to the airport was effortless. There was no feeling with them together in the confines of a small car that they needed to talk, or make talk. They didn't have to be cordial or fight to avoid long silences. In fact, they loved silences. When questions would come, he found she would answer them. Not with evasions or long tales or even coy pauses. She would just say as she thought it.

"Why do you think a train station?" he asked, the first question after a particularly long silence.

"A train station in Berlin?"

"Yeah. How come?"

"David told me he had a cousin who was stationed in Germany. I don't know where in Germany. Maybe he helped arrange it. I have a key with a number on it."

"Fifty-three," he said.

"Right." She seemed pleased he remembered. "I suspect the key is for a storage locker. You know, like they have in train stations."

The road was smooth. The New York City traffic flowed. The sun came out strong and bright. He would look at her and smile. She would look at him and catch him smiling and she would smile too. They would both look away.

"What?" she asked.

"Your hair," he said.

"Is it funny?"

"No."

"But you're laughing."

"No. I'm smiling."

She let that sit for a moment. A restful silence was broken. They were both hungry and took a moment to stop at a gas station, to eat their salami sandwiches with lettuce and tomato and share a cigarette together.

"You're lucky," she said as they got back into the car. "You have good friends."

"You mean Mink?"

"Yes. Especially Mink."

"I am lucky," he said, jerking the car into drive. "Don't you have friends?"

"No," she said. "I was never in one place long enough."

"Sometimes it happens that you can take your friends with you."

"It's never happened to me." She was finishing the cigarette, and put it to his lips for the last puff. "The only people I had around were people I worked with. I didn't really feel like they were my friends. It wasn't that kind of job."

"I've always had friends," he said.

The toll booth they passed was fun because she leaned far forward so that she could be seen by the attendant, as if to push fate. She was a black-hair now. Her face was not yet on a *Wanted* poster hanging in every post office. It seemed that no one really noticed her. It made them both laugh.

He tossed her the tobacco and asked her to roll them one. She rolled a beautiful tube of a smoke that wasn't too tight and yet wasn't too loose. It wasn't thin and small or bulby and pregnant. She lit it for them and took the first puffs. When she passed it, he was duly impressed.

"Where did you learn to roll like that?"

The cigarette even tasted better.

"I used to roll a lot of joints," she said.

Alex started to think about what would happen when they got to the airport. Was he supposed to just drop her off? Is that what she expected, or would he park the car and make sure she got on a flight? They hadn't called ahead or booked anything. Ava was uptight about making reservations or leaving any kind of trail. There was the possibility that there could be people watching out for her at the airport, or that her name could be on some sort of list. They could prevent her from buying a ticket or getting on a plane. They could hold her there until Alan.

"That's why I was thinking," Alex said, "that I should probably not just drop you off. I could park the car and go into the terminal with you. Just in case, you know."

"You don't have to do that," she said, but she took his hand and squeezed. Her eyes seemed to be saying, *Please do that.*

"It's no trouble," he said, squeezing her hand right back.

Alex started to think about what would happen after he returned home. Could it be that this one-eye guy would come after him? He could probably sleep over at Benny's for a while, until maybe things blew over. But then it happened again when he started to think about himself: Somehow, she crept into the picture. He started to think about what might happen to her in Germany.

"But do you know anyone in Berlin?"

"No."

"And you're just going to go there with this key, to pick up some package?"

"Yes."

"How do you know this isn't some trap? That you won't get killed the moment you pick it up or something?"

"I don't know that. But I have no choice."

"Why not?"

"Because I could stay here and get killed."

Her answers did not remotely sound irritated or bitter. She was almost talking dreams to a child, or telling a story, or giving directions.

"It could be that I get there and I end up picking up a package that has an address on it. I take the package to the address and hand it to someone, and then maybe this is over."

"You think so?"

"It could be."

"But you don't know."

"No, I don't." She exhaled a thin stream of smoke and passed the cigarette. "Maybe David wanted to keep this in his family. Maybe he *didn't* want it all in the family. I don't even know what he wanted," she said tiredly. She gave him a long stare that he could feel, laser sharp. "Maybe you could come," she said.

Alex felt a strange burning in his stomach. He was thinking about that empty apartment, his job at Henderson's, and the danger he might be in if he went back to life as usual.

"I just mean," she went on, still holding his hand, "that you could fly with me to Berlin."

He was thinking about blackouts, drunken weekends, and how today he hadn't even thought about having a drink. This was the first time he could remember wanting to be awake, wanting to catch every moment and not miss a thing. In a way, he felt he had been asleep for a long time. Her hand was still in his. He found it hard to look at her. She finding it hard to look at him. Her glances to the side, out the window, away. Looking. Throwing glances.

"I don't know," he said. Squeezing her hand, feeling the tremble.

The tails of those parked airliners appearing along the highway.

"I bought two tickets," she said.

He had wanted to go up to the counter with her but she had refused. There were cameras up there and she didn't want Alan to possibly spy him with her on some snatch of tape, so he waited for her to come back. They had stopped at an ATM. His card worked. He had withdrawn money and handed her his wallet. "Just in case you need extra cash," he said.

He got a coffee and browsed through some magazines, figuring that sometime soon he would turn around and she would be gone, as quickly as she had appeared, some phantom, some product of a blackout dissolve, that dark spot between frames that happens too fast for the human eye to register.

It wasn't like that. She came back to him, running, excited, like a young niece sent on an errand just accomplished.

"I bought two," she explained, "because I thought of asking you if maybe you could accompany me to my gate and you know how it is here at JFK where only ticketed passengers can go in, and besides, I prefer an empty seat on a long flight . . . Anyway, here." She handed him his ticket and his wallet. "I got your name right, didn't I?"

"Yes." He felt like something was choking him, making talk difficult.

"We'll settle all the money stuff later, okay?"

Her eyes were glittery wet, and what was happening to him? Why did things come all at once?

"Now come," she said, "twenty minutes to boarding . . ." Pulling him by the hand. Why do people in airports think having no luggage is suspicious? (So is paying with cash, Ava said, but she's a fast talker when the role requires it.) Is a woman not supposed to change her hair color just because of a passport? The blank-faced agent who checked hers didn't even nod smile or wink. No hand luggage, just her purse, sans the gun. This had already been disposed of in a gas station trash can on the way. No beeping items, no sense of just passing through—Alex hated goodbyes. Airport scenes gave him stomachaches, and here, being

held by the hand, walking the crowded concourse, the perfume shops, the newspaper stands, the stink of fast food
frying—her dark hair—he would look at her and smile. She
would look at him and catch him smiling and she would
smile. (She looked away.)

"What?" she asked.

"Your hair," he said. "I can't get used to it."

"The blond will come back. Is it funny?"

"No."

"But you're laughing."

"I'm smiling," he said. The crowd all strange around
them, blurred dark blobby unreal. The call of the flight the
whirr click of the ticket machine like a stapler, and the
voice of the woman handing back those ticket stubs. "Have
a nice flight," over and over like a recording. He looking at
her fighting off that mad rush of feeling and questioning.
What was there to fight off?

"It makes me happy to look at you," he said. Cupping
her face with his hands, those small trembling lips, those
sparkle bright eyes.

"So don't stop," she said.

The kiss was salty. Was lips was soft sea and swimmy
waves and eyes closed and hands clasped and bodies
pressed and that flowery smell, flowery smell of her new
hair. A few more kisses, by mouth, by cheek.

"Thanks for saving my life," she said.

And then she had to turn, to walk from him, to go
straight to the ticket lady and the whirr click STAMP of
the ticket machine and her stub appearing on the other
side: "Have a nice flight."

The smile and wave she gave him just before rounding
the bend down that corridor to the plane was not a pity-me
sadness. It was a blessing, as if all her feelings had been
compressed into her eyes and her fingers. It was the best
thank you she could have ever spoken. It was better than

a painting or a photograph. It was a memory no blackout could ever erase. The three words she mouthed he heard across the distance as if she had been still beside him and had whispered them into his ear.

"Yeah," he said, "me too."

Once upon a time
I was the only child forbidden to climb
over the garden wall.
—Anne Sexton, "Eighteen Days Without You"

A little time to kill before going back. The two of them doing roof. Some drinks, some pipe hits, some sense that something marvelous had happened. Something came. Something went. Their country was not at war, or: It felt like the last night before the start of a big campaign. The air was spiced with something burnt. Something came.

"I didn't even get to tell her," Monk said. "About her black hair."

Mink was wet-eyed and red-faced. "You think Alex is coming back?" He handed Monk a lemon slice and poured tequila into the glass.

Monk put some salt on his hand. Licked it up. Downed the glass, then bit into the lemon. He squinted at Mink. "Again," he whispered.

Mink set up a round by pulling out another glass and filling both. "It's the first time," he said. "The first time we've been working at the same time that we . . . that we've been working at the same time. We got all kinds of habits together, but this . . . this is a new habit."

"New habits break old ones," Monk said, thinking he'd heard that somewhere before. They clinked glasses.

(Salt. Drink. Lemon.)

The sky was growing lighter. The seagulls had started to buzz the rooftop by then.

The seagulls were just like them—creatures of habit. They were probably the same seagulls that swooped by every morning on their way to hangouts along the East River. They knew that roof because many times Mink and Monk would be sitting up there when they came by. Monk had a drum of junk up there for them. Banana peels, bread, pizza, salami-and-cheese sandwiches. Mink would tip the drum over so they could come and browse. Monk would select choice bits and toss crap up to them. They hovered with their quivering tremendous wingspans, their wide unblinking eyes, their snapping beaks as they caught crap in mid-flight. Some would land and stand as if posing on the parapet, watching the festivities like spectators. All sudden, after twenty minutes or so of show, it was as if someone offstage had blown a whistle. All the seagulls would take off in a pack, like surfers eager to catch a wave. There was another metal drum. Mink and Monk would light a fire in it, and no cops would come.

"I didn't even get to tell her," Monk said. "I saw her going up the fire escape."

The vibe turned boomy bass and drum dub. King Tubby's or one of those old Clocktower Records. They played the CD-Rom, manipulated their way through seven different atmospheres, all floaty Mink blocks and cubes. "We can only offer you $500,000." The South Bronx finally pays off. Monk laughed so hard *baba* came out of his mouth.

"There's no way that's real," he said.

"That's what I thought."

"But you should do it anyway."

The last two cigarettes of the pack. Shook one out for Monk. Lit them both.

"I don't speak blocks and cubes anymore. Besides, I

don't think I want the South Bronx to became a mecca for the ultra-hip."

Monk was staring at him. It was a faraway stare, glassy and from a great distance. Mink got the distinct feeling that Monk saw right through him, saw straight through artifice and wordplay and smoke screens and all those pretty things words do to throw people off. Something wistful on his face. Some people never fall for three-card monte. "If only things could stay the same." All snug and small town, insular and well-preserved. The air was spiced with something burnt. Something came, something went.

Tequila sunrise. A long, uneventful silence.

Mink said, "I wonder if Alex is coming back."

At that moment, a great flapping, an agitated shriek. A great big spotted seagull, that last late straggler, swooped over the junk drum, nervously chattering. Hovering and dipping, he scooped up that old pizza crust and flew off fast, making great strides to cut through sky and catch up to the fleet.

28.

the dream was about his father.

he was on the island, that small tin roof house on a hill. slope going straight up. (he used to think, straight up to heaven. walk up to the stars.) palm tree leaves thickly moving from strong wind. water poured down from green, turbulent skies. inside: *"raindrops blasting hell on a tin roof."* his father, gruffly bearded, creaked the rocking chair. the pipe he sucked on made a hollow sound. he looked just like he did when alex visited him last year, but that house, and that sound of his mother *machucando* in the kitchen, was all from childhood. alex it seemed had his twenty-five-year-old head shoved back into his six-year-old body. sitting there in front of his father's rocking chair. playing with a green dumptruck.

"live and learn," his father said to him. "women are only good for one thing," he said. "life."

alex woke up before her. heard the steady rise and fall of her breath. he thought about his father's words, and how he had never found out if his father had meant "life" like living, or "life" like a "lifetime sentence." his father never stayed with any woman too long. alex had five brothers and they were all from different mothers. his father was still healthy, vigorous, and still out making more brothers. funny how alex was six in the dream. six was the year his mother died, six was the last of anything he remembered about her. he felt he should have tried to hold onto the dream, to stay. she had been in the kitchen, *machucando*.

maybe if he had gone looking for her and found her, she might have told him something. puerto ricans believe the dead visit you in dreams. they tell you things, or sometimes give warnings. many times, though, they just want company and can stay as long as you don't start blubbering or reminding them they're dead. once you do that, they leave. you wake up.

her stirring. soft murmur. his arm was her pillow.

alex wasn't thinking of his father. was thinking about himself as a little boy in puerto rico. walking the beaches near home, collecting shells. he used to take whatever he liked. bright colors, sharp shapes, shiny smooth ones. he would spend all day with them, stuffed in his pockets like marbles. pulling them out to admire them, showing them off to friends who collected crab shells, starfish, and glittery stones. then, as the sun went down, he would toss them back into the sea as far as he could throw. how nothing had changed with him! mink had told him just after belinda: "plenty of fish in the sea, especially if you keep throwing them back." the old knee-jerk trick. "this is around the time I wake the girl and say, hey, it's time you go. I got stuff to do . . ." no girl stayed longer than one night. not after belinda. maybe it was still his father's genes. five brothers and they were all from different mothers.

whimpering sounds. like a puppy when it dreams. a shiver, a toss. she gripped his arm. the way a cat scratches.
    "david," she said, her eyes fluttering. "no, david, run."
    he touched her face. soft, slow waking. she looked scared. then she saw it was him.
    "hey," he said.
    (his arm was her pillow.)

"you should have seen her face," he would tell monk one

day, "when I walked onto that plane." she had her eyes closed when he sat down, her head resting on a pillow placed against the small round window. her grin, nonetheless. her hand brushing against his hand. and those words that came dreaming.

"what took you so long?"

a pocketful of seashells he would keep this time